INTO
THE HIGH
BRANCHES

Book two of the Deep Woods Adventure

INTO THE HIGH BRANCHES

by P. M. Malone

Illustrated by Terry Lewison

*Raspberry Hill, Ltd.

INTO THE HIGH BRANCHES
Copyright 1992 by P. M. Malone
All rights reserved

A Raspberry Hill, Ltd. publication
P.O. Box 791
Willmar, MN 56201

ISBN: 0-9631957-1-9

Library of Congress Catalog Card Number
92-61736

1st printing: August, 1992
2nd printing: December, 1992
Printed in the United States of America

FOR MY FATHER, HARRY FRANCIS MALONE,
OCTOBER, 1911 - DECEMBER, 1955

The woods is quiet without your voice.
But the trail is clear;
I follow your footsteps yet.

INTO THE HIGH BRANCHES

LIST OF CHAPTERS

INTRODUCTION : INTO THE HIGH BRANCHES

Hello! How nice of you to come by. We've been resting here, on this broad old oak stump, sort of catching our breath. We've already had quite an adventure, you know. We've seen and heard a number of interesting — I might even say amazing — events out here in the deep woods. Pretty much centered around a young gray squirrel. Perhaps you'd like some idea of what's happened so far. It might serve more than one purpose. Familiarity with old paths sometimes smooths new ones.

Near winter's end we became friends with a young squirrel named Ephran. Curious little chap, Ephran. The first we saw of him was when he wandered away from his family, who were sleeping soundly in their nest. He came back to find two humans (Many Colored Ones), attacking his tree with a chain saw. Understandably, I think, he panicked, ran away, and got lost. Didn't even wait to see if his family survived the big tumble.

Well, poor little fellow searched unsuccessfully for mom, dad, sister and brother, right up to a place called Corncrib Farm, at the very end of the woods. Got into one scrape after another, with everything from cats and owls to a fox and a hawk. After getting a bit of encouragement from a cottontail rabbit called Mayberry, he was taken under paw by Rennigan, a wise old fox squirrel. Ephran was young and inexperienced. He badly needed a good teacher. Rennigan was that all right. When Ephran left the nest of his teacher, he built his own place near a wonderfully quiet and peaceful place called The Pond. Made all sorts of interesting and unlikely friends there, including a red squirrel, a pair of mallard ducks and, of all things, a skunk.

It made us feel good all over when Ephran rescued two helpless ducklings from a hawk and met his future mate, the lovely Kaahli. We thought that might be sort of the end of the story. But we were wrong. No sooner did things seem happy and settled than Ephran and Kaahli set out on another search; this time for both her family and for his. Let me tell you, that search turned out to be plenty exciting...danger in the form of everything from a hungry mink to a hail storm!

They eventually found Kaahli's family all right, but her father and brother were trapped in a cage. If you can believe, those two clever squirrels managed to open the cage and set the prisoners free! Then they discovered Ephran's family as well, nesting near Corncrib Farm...right where Ephran had his original run-in with the cat.

The whole family spent a wonderfully happy summer together, but when Ephran and Kaahli set out for their Pond they nearly perished in a forest fire. If you don't know how they survived that, I think you should peek into the story of our adventure, which I've set down in a book called OUT OF THE NEST. Some adventures must be told in their entirety.

When Ephran and Kaahli finally made it back to their own nest and the twinkling Pond, they found sadness. Their friends, the ducks, had been hunted by humans with loud and deadly things called thundersticks. The very special father mallard, Cloudchaser by name, had been badly wounded and sailed off toward Lomarsh, an evil place from which the animals believe all bad things come and no good thing returns. Then, one day as the snow of a new winter began to fall, the hunters returned and shot Ephran from a tree as he drew their attention away from Kaahli and his red squirrel friend. None of us could believe it when a big green-headed mallard showed up and flew off with Ephran on his back! That duck looked exactly like Cloudchaser. The whole business defies imagination. Maybe it was imagination. Maybe Ephran never fell. Then again, maybe he did. And maybe he never got up. It was snowing, you know. Hard to see precisely what happened from the distance we watched.

Needless to say, we're all more than just a bit curious to know what happened to Ephran. In a moment we're going to set out down this woodland path and try to find some answers. We'd be delighted to have you come along. So, if you feel up to it, let's get started. We'll never know what we're up against if we don't get our paws moving.

OLD FRIENDS...AND OTHERS TOO
(Whom we've met before, around The Pond)

Ephran (Ee - fran): A young and curious male gray squirrel who lives with his family in the deep north woods.

Mianta (Me - an - tah): Ephran's "first" sister. (A female littermate)

Phetra (Fet - rah): Ephran's "first" brother. (A male littermate)

Odalee (Oh - dah - lee): Ephran's mother.

Jafthuh (Jaff - the): Ephran's father.

Maltrick (Mall - trick): A wily red fox.

Mayberry: A male cottontail rabbit.

Truestar: A female cottontail. Mayberry's mate.

Blackie: A female black and white farm cat.

Rennigan (Ren - a - gun): An old bachelor buck fox squirrel.

Cloudchaser: A large drake mallard duck.

Marshflower: A female mallard. Cloudchaser's mate.

Klestra: An excitable little red squirrel. Ephran's friend.

Smagtu (Smag - too): A shy skunk.

Kaahli (Kay - lee): A beautiful female gray squirrel.

Laslum (Lahs - lum): Kaahli's first brother.

Aden (Ay - den): Kaahli and Laslum's father.

Roselimb: A female gray squirrel. Phetra's mate.

Fred: A yellow hound dog.

Frafan (Fray - fan): Ephran's "second" brother. From Odalee's next litter.

Janna, Tinga, and Ilta: Ephran's second sisters.

NEW ACQUAINTANCES

Kartag, Mulken, and Darkeye: Forestwatchers (Crows)

Fastrip: Small buck cottontail rabbit, Warden of Great Woods Warren.

Sorghum: Tiny female cottontail, Fastrip's mate.

Highopper, Longrass, and Sweetbud: Young cottontails, offspring of Mayberry and Truestar.

Redthorn: Large and hostile male rabbit.

Milkweed: Redthorn's mate, sister to Truestar.

Darkbush and Fairchance: Other rabbits, inhabitants of Great Woods Warren

Ruckaru: A rooster pheasant with very precise speech.

Farnsworth: A bashful young raccoon.

Flutterby, Payslee, and Peppercorn: Pigeons. Sisters who live in the big barn on the Farm of Cages.

Queesor: A young male gray squirrel who lives in the park.

Wytail: A large gray squirrel; bully of the park.

Steadfast: The oldest and most experienced gray squirrel in the park.

Brightleaf: A rabbit from Bubbling Brook Warren.

Not knowing, Not knowing.
   Quiet pain in a darkened room,
Lack of sight in shrouded gloom,
   Silent fear of a cold tomb.
Not knowing.

Ruminations of Waldemeer
Verse xiv

CHAPTER I

MESSENGERS FROM GREAT HILL

J t was snowing...the third time Frafan had seen snow fall from the sky. The air was cold enough, but the forest floor was still too warm for delicate flakes to survive there. The time for the snow to stay where it fell, covering yellow and red leaves, and to grow deeper and deeper, was not far away.

Frafan was a gray squirrel, and not a very big one at that. His tail was a rather scrawny affair, his legs were skinny, and his ears were too big for his head. But his mind was quick and he had big, bright eyes that watched with interest as thick grey-black clouds rolled toward his perch in the red maple tree. Cold and clammy air blew against the side of his face. Currents from that direction, from where he knew lay The Pond and Great Hill, usually meant water from the sky — water in one form or another.

Ephran had taught him that moving air would pick things up. Skywater, snowflakes, falling leaves, smoke...anything that was not attached to something else could be moved. Things in the forest didn't change position in such a haphazard fashion as most of the animals believed. And whether the air was cold or warm often depended on which direction it came from...

"You must be thinking about something important again," said Blackie. The plump black and white cat smiled up at him from her usual resting spot in thick grass near the lilac bushes.

"I'm sorry, Blackie," Frafan grinned back. "I didn't mean to ignore you. You're right, I was thinking. I'm not certain what I was thinking was so important though."

The aging female cat and the young gray squirrel were close friends. A most unusual friendship it was — between hunter and hunted. They'd met on a very hot warm season afternoon, quite by accident, near the lilac bushes. Shortly after that initial encounter they discovered an amazing thing: they enjoyed one another's company! At first Frafan kept his visits with the cat a secret. Eventually his unexplained absences became too frequent and his family discovered where and with whom their inquisitive son and brother was visiting. They did their best to understand that Frafan valued Blackie as both friend and teacher. It was not easy. Especially for father.

The cat's nest was in the elderly Many Colored Ones' white den at the edge of the woods on Corncrib Farm. She had learned a great deal about the forest that surrounded her, as well as about those creatures upon whom she'd come to depend for food and shelter. Since she quit hunting she'd often been bored — until she met Frafan. He was simply too full of questions and new ideas to let anyone get bored.

"How do you like the snow?" she asked.

"Oh, it's beautiful! Very soft and quiet. Sort of peaceful. The only thing I don't like is that when snow comes I'm supposed to spend most of my time in the nest...with my eyes shut." Frafan wrinkled his nose.

"You curious little rascal," laughed Blackie, "you don't like to close your eyes...or your ears, do you?"

"Seems a terrible waste of time," he sighed.

"Quite necessary, however," said Blackie soberly. "There will be plenty of time to carry on with all the things you want to learn when the snow changes to water."

"Will there?" Frafan stared through the falling snow in the direction of The Pond.

Not that Frafan was dissatisfied here, near the farm with the corncrib, in the den of Jafthuh and Odalee, his father and mother. Gracious, no! And he was perfectly happy to share the cozy nest with his three sisters: Janna, Ilta, and Tinga. It was just that there was so much to do...and to see...and to learn. And he knew a great number of those things simply had to lie far away, beyond the treetops he could see from his nest.

One older first sister, Mianta, and her mate, Laslum, had a den nearby. An older brother, Phetra, and his mate, Roselimb, weren't much further away. They were all great fun to be with but they were more interested in food and in playing games than they were in answering questions or exploring.

The other older brother, Ephran, was the one he really wished had a nest near Corncrib Farm. Ephran understood him better than anyone else. Ephran was interested in everything that happened in the woods. Ephran was very brave and clever. Unfortunately, Ephran's den was a long way from here.

"Ephran is back home near Great Hill, you know," he said.

"Yes. You told me that some time ago, after your other brother returned from The Pond," said the cat.

"I wonder if Ephran and Kaahli have found a new tree yet."

Blackie did not answer. Frafan was talking to himself again. He did that fairly often.

Ephran and his mate, Kaahli, had spent part of the warm season here with the squirrel family. It had been a wonderful time for Frafan. Ephran knew so many things about the deep woods: how to get where you wanted to go by using the sun and wind, how to find hiding places where most gray squirrels would never think to look, how to stay quiet and interpret the garbled speech of crows, how to tell if the sky might become angry. Many, many things.

For his part, Frafan had been able to teach his older brother a few

"Frafan! Come down, into the lower branches."

curious facts about The Many Colored Ones, those strange and unpredictable creatures who spent so much time in their white den at the edge of the woods...

"I wonder what these scalawags want."

Blackie's voice interrupted Frafan's thoughts once again. Frafan looked up to see two large black birds flapping toward him.

"Crows!" said Frafan. "Watchers of the forest."

"Fancy title for scavengers, if you ask me. Not much in the way of decent birds around this late in the season," observed Blackie.

The crows flew silently through the snowflakes. They must have a destination in mind, Frafan thought. When they flew aimlessly, exploring or looking for excitement, they shouted constantly to one another, making a racket that could be heard a great distance. Most young squirrels would have been frightened of them. Their eating habits were atrocious.

"Frafan! Come down, into the lower branches," said Blackie. She had risen to her paws and stood at the base of the tree.

"Why?"

"Because I don't trust them."

Blackie looked as though she was ready to climb the tree. She hadn't climbed in a long while.

"Don't worry, Blackie. I'm certain they mean no harm to either of us."

The birds settled on a bare branch in the tree next to Frafan's. One of them looked directly at him.

"Eeyah! Treeklimer; you a'den Jafthuh 'n Odalee?"

He didn't answer immediately. What an astonishing question — right out of the clouds! No small talk here. No "Good day" or "Cold, isn't it?" or anything like that. Besides, how did the crows come to know father's and mother's names?

"Y...Yes. I am Frafan, from the nest of Jafthuh and Odalee," he finally answered.

The crows looked at one another. "Wherep 'arents?" asked the slightly larger of the pair.

"What business is that of yours?" interjected Blackie.

The birds were unperturbed. One said, "Brin knews — knews f'ramly Jafthuh 'n Odalee."

They seemed very somber and concerned. That, all by itself, was unusual...almost as unusual as the fact that they were speaking to other forest creatures in the first place. When crows did speak, it was rarely to utter a civil or friendly word. It was common knowledge crows were mischievous gossips — loudmouthed, carefree, and given to joking and making sport of others. These crows said they were bearers of news. And they were acting so strangely that Blackie said no more. Frafan felt

4

a shiver run all the way down his long skinny tail.

"I'll lead you to the den," Frafan said. "Follow me." He tried to smile reassuringly at Blackie. "I'll be back."

The old cat nodded and lowered the one paw she'd placed on the trunk of the tree.

Frafan's home was not far away. He ran and jumped carefully through the snowflakes and the treetops. The crows watched silently until he reached the den. Only when he stopped and looked back did they lift from their branch and fly toward him.

"Father! Mother!" Frafan called into the dark nest.

Odalee appeared at once. "Sshhh! Goodness, Frafan, your father is napping. What do you...?"

Her mouth dropped as dark wings hovered over her head. The crows came to rest on a branch just above Frafan and his mother.

"Get father," he said. "These watchers of the forest say they bring news."

Odalee looked into the eyes of her youngest son and, without another word, slipped quietly back into the den. At that moment Frafan caught sight of two gray squirrels approaching through a cluster of nearby basswood trees. He recognized his older sister, Mianta, and her mate Laslum, just as a groggy Jafthuh climbed out of the hole.

"What's going on here?" father asked sleepily.

Mianta arrived in time to hear her father's words. "My thought exactly," she said, eyeing the crows with obvious distaste.

Frafan turned to the uninvited guests. "What is your news? This is the family of Jafthuh and Odalee. Part of it, anyway."

The crows sat for a moment, as though trying to decide if this was indeed the company for whom their message was intended. Finally one croaked, "Eeyah! I Kartag. Dis Mulken." The bird nodded toward its companion. "We cum Gree Till. Red longtail saycum. Klestra, frien d'Ephran saycum."

"Are you trying to tell us that a red squirrel sent you here?" asked father. The amazed look on his face matched mother's and Mianta's.

The crow named Kartag nodded slowly.

"Klestra...that is the name Ephran spoke, isn't it?" breathed mother. She was too worried to stay surprised, or to be annoyed. This whole odd business smelled of trouble.

"Yes," said Frafan, "Klestra, the red squirrel. The one who knows of hiding places in the earth."

"Why does Klestra send you?" she asked.

Kartag did not hesitate. "Tell tha' Tephran dis'speared."

The gasp was unanimous. Father stared at the crows with large eyes. He waited for one of them to continue, to explain. When they didn't, he said, "Disappeared? What do you mean, 'Ephran disappeared'? Disappeared where? You're making fun again."

"Yes," Mianta said loudly, "you crows are always teasing and tormenting others. Is this another of your sick jokes?"

Mulken looked at Mianta with a pale yellow eye that expressed nothing. Kartag simply gazed off into the distance. Mother's body was tense. Her face said most clearly that she did not think the crows were joking.

"Tell us...," she said, "tell us what happened to my son."

The one called Mulken said, "Female, ween owe little. Not dere when 'appen. All know is'sMany Colored One s'cum to Pond..."

"Many Colored Ones!" interrupted Laslum. "Phetra told us They had been there, and that They attacked the ducks who made their home near the water. They must have returned."

"Dey cum back," confirmed Kartag, "wit t'understik. Hunt Kaahli, mayt'Ephran. Klestra say Ephran run n'oer top, draw dem 'way. Run noff inna hibe 'ranches. Ephran not cumback."

"Not come back?..." Odalee repeated vacantly. Jafthuh turned and slipped into the den. Just as his tail vanished, three sets of wide eyes appeared in the hole — those of Janna, Ilta, and Tinga — Frafan's sisters. Their father had slid past them with an expression they had not seen before, and they were afraid.

Laslum hugged Mianta, whose body shook with silent sobs. Frafan watched the crows. They were telling the truth. Their eyes were sad, and avoided those of his family as they studied the cheerless sky.

"When did this happen?" he managed to ask, surprising himself a great deal by speaking calmly and clearly.

"Nosee since firs'snow," replied Kartag.

The first snow had fallen, turned back to water, and sunk into the ground. Many days and nights had passed since then. Ephran had been missing for some time.

"Has anyone searched?" asked Frafan.

"All not dugin dirt or fly warmp'laces look," said Mulken.

"Weef fly o'er Gree Till 'n Lomarsh," said Kartag, "weelock 'long Rock Eek Reek. W'ask frens 'n cusins whensee dem. Ask dey see dis grey longtail, dis Ephran, in hibe ranches..."

"He gone," said Mulken.

Gone. Final words...like the end of any possible hope.

"Did The Many Colored Ones take him?" Mianta choked.

"Not know," said Kartag, brushing a black wing under his eyes, "we not....not dere t'watch."

"How is Kaahli coping with this?" Odalee managed through tight lips.

"Ephran mate, she gontoo."

"...Gone too?" mother repeated again.

More and more bizarre! Ephran and Kaahli both missing? How? Why? If the crows weren't so serious, if they weren't acting so totally out of character, one would have thought the whole thing was indeed a terrible trick.

These thoughts passed through Frafan's mind as he watched the black birds. He wished he could detect some sign that they were making a joke, sick though it might be. But they just sat there, looking for all the world like they wished they could take their message back and leave these distraught treeclimbers in peace.

"I must go to The Pond."

The words were out of Frafan's mouth before he'd taken time to think, and they reached Jafthuh's ears as he reappeared at the den's entrance. The older squirrel faced his youngest son with reddened eyes.

"The cold season is here, young one," Jafthuh said. "This is no time for traveling. It's time to curl tightly in the nest — and to close your eyes."

"I know that, father," said Frafan, "but Ephran and his mate are missing. And his red squirrel friend sent word to us. I think he must expect us to come and help him look for Ephran and Kaahli...or something."

"If he expects that, he expects too much," said father. "A red squirrel idea. Far too risky to be running through unfamiliar trees now. Snow will soon fall heavy and thick. The air can turn bitterly cold. Sometimes the flakes move so fast that an animal can't see — or breathe."

"We're young. We can find our way. We'll find out what's happened to Ephran and Kaahli," chirped Janna.

Everyone was taken aback. Mianta stopped crying and stared at her second sister with open amazement. The other two faces crowded into the den entrance with Janna tried to turn and look into her eyes, to see if she was serious, but they were too tightly packed in the small hole to do so. They could not see the resolute look on her face.

Frafan, upset as he was at the crow's message, almost smiled despite himself. Was this little squirrel, so certain about finding her way through the trees to the faraway Pond, the same one who cried in fear when they were out of sight of the den? Was she who would challenge the bitter cold season the same one who cringed at the sound of distant thunder? Was this gentle female, who would brave hunters in the open woods, the one who whimpered and curled tightly next to mother when an owl hooted in the darkness outside the nest?

"You would go to Great Hill with Frafan?" asked mother, her wet eyes still wide with surprise.

"I would," said Janna.

7

"Do you realize how very foolish such a journey would be?" asked Jafthuh.

"Why do you say that, father?" asked Ilta.

"Because it serves no purpose. It would put you in danger for no good reason."

They were all silent then, waiting for him to speak again. He was, after all, the one among them who had traveled this woods the most. He had run through the branches for more warm seasons than any of them. It was he who had led them here, to this good place, the place of his youth, when the family tree at the base of Great Hill fell to the monsters with rows of shiny teeth. He knew the treetops far along Bubbling Brook and down Rocky Creek, nearly to Lomarsh.

"Where do you think Ephran and Kaahli would go if they wanted to escape danger at The Pond?" he asked no one in particular.

Silence.

"You all know as well as I do. They'd come here, of course. They'd come to their family. They know the way. You could leave for The Pond by one route and they could arrive here the next day using another. Then what would we do? Chase after you? Put someone else in danger?"

Still no one else spoke.

Jafthuh continued, "If they've been taken by The Many Colored Ones, there is nothing any of us can do. Your trip would be wasted either way. I wish I could feel otherwise."

They sat for a time then, in the chilly air, each with his or her own uncertain and melancholy thoughts, indifferent to the beauty around them, the soft white flakes falling slowly and soundlessly to the forest floor.

Laslum, related by mateship rather than birth, thought he might break the silence. "Jafthuh," he said, "what you say, though wise, may be proven false by courage. Ephran himself showed us, and most especially me, that to be captured by The Many Colored Ones is not necessarily a hopeless situation. Remember, he and Kaahli rescued me and my father from a cage."

"Father," said Frafan, "if Ephran and Kaahli had been able to come here the day of the first snow, they would have been here many days ago. And from what Ephran told me I'm certain he considered his red squirrel friend very intelligent. I don't know why Klestra would send these crows if he didn't expect some sort of answer. Perhaps he has more information. Perhaps there are other possibilities besides escape or capture."

He turned to the crows, still sitting quietly on their branch. "Does Klestra want someone to come to The Pond?" he asked.

The one called Kartag answered, "Klestra'd not say comp 'ond.

No saye danger 'f come. Only saye wha t'you heard."

With that, and without another look back, the crows lifted from the branch. With slow, deliberate beats of large black wings they rose into the hazy sky, caught a high current of cold air, and vanished into the falling snow.

CHAPTER II

DESPERATE DECISION

Fphran was told, more than once, not to wander far from the nest during the cold season," Jafthuh said, addressing no one in particular, "but he was curious. Just like Frafan...couldn't lie still when there was a big woods out there, waiting to be explored."

The old gray squirrel hesitated as he stared at the granite colored sky where the crows had disappeared.

"I couldn't make myself angry. I knew that sooner or later he'd have to find things out for himself — without mother or me tagging along. And he learned well. He learned more than I might have dreamed. He learned more than I could teach. It wasn't his fault The Many Colored Ones came."

Tears finally spilled from Odalee's eyes. Jafthuh's chin trembled and, if there were more memories, they remained voiceless.

"We have to find out where he's gone," said Frafan. "I don't believe that any of us would sleep the whole cold season if we didn't try to learn what happened at The Pond."

"Frafan is right, father," said Mianta. "You told me a long while ago the cold season is sometimes slow in arriving, even after the first snow covers the earth. The trip to Great Hill is not so long. I remember Ephran telling us, if one keeps moving along, only two or three days might pass while a squirrel runs between this place and that. Someone should be able to get to The Pond before the great snows come. If they come."

"It seems everyone but me thinks we must look for answers right now," said father, "and I still say the whole idea smells of danger and holds little promise of accomplishing anything worthwhile. Animals in the forest fall to the earth all the time — and never run again. But how can I argue with so many of you? And what do I say when I know you are right about sleep — that my eyes will not rest easy? What do you think, mother?"

"The crows say Ephran disappeared," said Odalee. "They did not say The Many Colored Ones took him. They only said our son led the hunters away from Kaahli and now both the hunted have disappeared. I must know..." Her voice trailed off.

"Who will go then," asked Laslum.

They all began speaking at once, trying to get one another's attention, arguing why they should be the ones chosen to travel to The Pond.

"Shush! Shush!" said mother, "listen to your father."

Jafthuh took a deep breath. His young knew it was affection that caused him to worry for their safety. And they understood it was only his great love for Ephran that forgave their foolhardiness and overcame his better judgment.

"If some must go, it must be few. Too many squirrels traveling through bare branches would be certain to attract the attention of hunters. Mother and I are getting old. Such a trip would be hard for us. Mianta will be having little ones when the warm season returns. I think she and her mate should stay here. They will need each other — and their newborn will need them." He turned to his youngest son, nodded slowly, and said, "Frafan and Janna. I would choose Frafan and Janna to go. And they should stop on their way and seek Phetra's help. He has traveled the path to The Pond."

Tinga and Ilta protested immediately.

"Why shouldn't we go as well?" asked Ilta. "Last warm season, when Ephran and his mate came here, they arrived with Kaahli's father and Laslum. That was four squirrels, all traveling together, and they got here safe and sound."

"Ah, but you tell the story of our success without realizing it," said Laslum. "It was the warm season, as you said. The trees were thick with leaves to hide our movements from hunters' eyes. And my father was with us then. He is much wiser in the way of the woods than we were. The trip here was not uneventful, you know. We needed the experience of Aden, and of an old friend of Ephran's named Rennigan, to reach this place safely."

"Besides," added mother, "we may have need of you here. I hate to think it, but what if Frafan and Janna went and did not return? What if they became lost? What if something happened to make them change their plans? What if we had to send someone after them? What if the chance arose to find Ephran and Kaahli along some other...some unplanned path?"

"Yes," said father, "perhaps the crows will bring us more news and perhaps they won't. The big black birds make no promises. Do you understand what we're saying, young ones?"

"I don't like it," said Ilta. "But I understand your words."

Tinga still pouted but said, "I want to go but, if I must, I will wait here. It won't be easy though."

"Your turn will come," Odalee said softly.

Mianta changed the subject. "One other thing...," she said, "We spoke earlier of Aden, father of Kaahli and Laslum. Shouldn't he be told this disturbing news? His nest is not far."

"His nest may not be far, but we don't know exactly where, only that it's close to The Spring," said Jafthuh. "What do you think, Laslum? He's your father."

Laslum sighed and said, "I believe it best not to worry him. There is nothing he could do. He may be asleep by now and I think we should wait until something more certain is known."

"This is all very curious and upsetting," muttered Jafthuh. "But then, why should I expect otherwise?"

Everyone curled up in their dens early that evening, but sleep did not come quickly. Many eyes stayed open well into the dark hours. There were plans to make. There was worrying to do.

The bright hours arrived slowly, gray light creeping between thick trees near the Many Colored Ones' den. The sun itself did not show its glowing face, and when Frafan looked into the sky he could not tell where it was hiding. The clouds must be very thick.

Jafthuh nibbled on a kernel of corn. He too peered at the overcast, as though trying to discover something there. "I don't like it," he said. "The air doesn't move and it feels wet."

At that moment Janna and Mianta arrived at the oak tree. Janna's eyes sparkled with excitement. Mianta was so enthusiastic that one would have thought that she was about to leave on the adventure herself.

She overheard Jafthuh's mumbled comments about the weather and said, "Oh father, you fret too much! So what if the air doesn't move? You finally believed Ephran when he told us that air moving from where the sun rises should make us think of angry skies. Besides, clouds have covered the sun so much lately that we're almost certainly due for some decent days and nights."

He could not bring himself to argue with her, even if it didn't feel right. Maybe what she said was true. Maybe he was becoming an old grouch, trying to find trouble at every turn, inventing it where it didn't exist.

Conversation over the first meal of the day was sporadic. Frafan was lost in thought, but that was not an uncommon state of affairs. However, this morning his thoughts were considerably different from most mornings.

Usually he thought of things he'd learned the previous day, trying to commit them to memory so he could use them if the opportunity arose. Or he would tell himself what he might do that day: where he might go, who he might visit, what he might see. His thoughts, he knew, would probably not be of great interest to the rest of the family. Sometimes he wondered if any of it would ever be of any use. Today he realized everything he'd learned — from father and mother, from Laslum, from Blackie, from Ephran, even from The Many Colored Ones — any or all of it may now be important. He hoped, when the time came, he would remember what needed to be remembered.

He'd eaten even less than usual when he jumped up, dropped the hickory nut he'd been toying with, and said to his father and mother, "I must say good-bye to Blackie."

Little brother was off to bid farewell to a cat. Strangers would have been struck speechless. As it was, no one in the family thought twice of it.

Frafan scampered through familiar trees to the weathered farm den, but Blackie was nowhere to be seen. The little squirrel ran down the trunk of a young maple and to the back entrance of the big den — directly to a small scuffed and soiled wooden flap, cut into the bottom of the big entrance used by The Many Colored Ones. He'd seen Blackie come and go, many times, through her own private entry.

He scratched on the wood and chattered, "Blackie!"

Frafan moved aside as the flap swung open. Alert black ears came out first, then soft yellow eyes, finally long black and gray whiskers.

"Frafan," Blackie said as the remainder of her pudgy body squeezed through the door, "disobeying your parents rules again, I see."

"They know I'm here, that I've come to say good-bye," said Frafan.

"Ah, you're leaving then. I suspected something like this. What did the crows tell you?"

"That Ephran and his mate have disappeared. That they've not been seen since their part of the woods was visited by hunters — Hunters of Many Colors."

"And you believe the crows?" asked Blackie.

"I don't think they were lying."

"And now you are leaving for The Pond?"

"Yes."

"Surely you aren't going alone?"

"My sister Janna will go with me. We plan to find my other brother, Phetra, along the way, and get directions from him."

"Well, I wish I could go. But I am too old." She sighed deeply and said, "I can only hope you aren't too young."

"I think that some of what you taught me will help make up for my lack of experience. Still, I imagine the air will get very cold and I suppose I'll be hungry a good part of the time. But my entire family is unsettled. We must try to find out what happened to Ephran and Kaahli," said Frafan.

"Yes, I suppose you must," said Blackie. "Remember to keep your eyes open. Use better judgment than you used just now. Look at yourself — down here on the cold earth — and right next to a den of Many Colored Ones at that! I know you came to say farewell to me — and I am pleased about that. But I tell you to never do it again. You had no idea what or who might have come through that wooden flap. Sometimes friends are not what they seem. Nor, quite obviously, are enemies."

"See what I mean!" laughed Frafan. "You're lecturing again! How can I possibly be unsuccessful in this search when I have such a persistent teacher?" Then his expression grew serious. "Good-bye, Blackie. I promise to be careful. And I will be back, to tell you all about it, in no time at all."

"I will look forward to it. My eyes will be glad to see you daydreaming on your favorite branch," said the cat.

Frafan and Janna left the big oak soon after the family finished eating. The farewells were somber. This was not the jolly start of an exciting and wonderful experiment — a quest undertaken with light hearts and promise of full bellies. It was the beginning of a mission, a most perilous search that would lead them who knew where. It was a journey they all knew could very well end in sadness. It held every possibility of leading the seekers into dangerous situations, some that might be foreseen and prepared for, some that could not be expected.

They followed the path toward Little Lake, the one Ephran and Kaahli had taken the day they left for The Pond. How very long ago it all seemed now! That day had been hot and dry, and though he'd been sad to see them go, Frafan had felt a sense of excitement and happiness for them; they were going home. "What in the name of Sweet Plump Acorns could have happened at The Pond?" he mumbled to himself.

The air was still and the forest quiet as Frafan and Janna leaped from bare branch to bare branch. The air stayed quiet but, Frafan had to admit to himself, somehow threatening. He put his worry about the weather out of mind. There were too many other things to occupy his thoughts.

The familiar farmsite faded behind them. Frafan took the lead but he stopped frequently to keep his bearing and to watch for landmarks. Janna kept very close to him. She tried not to show what she felt like doing. What she felt like doing was running back to her parents' nest.

She was about to ask him where they were, how much further to Phetra's den, when Little Lake appeared ahead. The water looked slate grey through the leafless branches and its hue and tone gave the impression of a dreary heaviness. Heavier and drearier, in any case, than it looked during the warm season. She thought she could almost feel the cold vapor rising from it, even this far away.

"We should be nearing Phetra and Roselimb's home," said Frafan, checking the sky once more, trying to find a bright spot in the dense cloud cover.

"On which side of the lake is their nest?" asked Janna.

"It should be on this side," he answered, "the side facing the place from where the cold air comes."

They worked their way through the trees, watching in every direction for a worn hole in a tree...or a nest of leaves.

"Frafan...Look!"

Janna had jumped to a small aspen. The grass beneath was thick and still mostly green. A cluster of fir trees they had just passed was dense and robust. But just ahead the forest had been transformed into a nightmare scene.

Large trees were more than just bare of leaves. They were black. Devoid of even the little twigs that healthy trees should have. A long spruce was identifiable only because of its shape. It was a skeleton — all its dark green needles had vanished. The earth was barren, save an occasional tuft of grass, long and healthy, heedless of the devastation all around.

They gazed for a long while. Janna finally whispered, "Frafan, what happened here?"

"I'm not sure," he said slowly. "But it looks very much like what's left, what they carry out of their den, after The Many Colored Ones make fire..."

"Frafan! Janna!" The greeting came from behind them.

"Phetra!" Janna shouted.

Phetra's mate, Roselimb, looked on with a smile as Frafan and Janna hugged and nuzzled their older brother. Then they hugged her.

"So...you finally came to visit us!" said Phetra. "Not that it makes a great deal of difference, I suppose, but you picked a rather strange time to do it."

"Oh, Phetra," said Janna, "we didn't choose the time."

"What do you mean, 'you didn't choose the time?'" asked Roselimb.

"She means," said Frafan, "that we didn't really come to visit. We bring news. And we're on our way to The Pond..."

"You're going to The Pond? That's crazy! It's much too late to undertake a journey like that. The cold season is here. Does father know of this? Or did you just take off without asking advice?" Phetra was plainly upset.

"Let them finish speaking, my dear," Roselimb interjected.

"We are going to The Pond to look for Ephran and Kaahli..." began Janna.

"Well, quite obviously that's the place to look for them, since that's where their nest is. That doesn't answer my questions. Don't you understand what might happen if big snow comes?..."

"Phetra, would you please be quiet for just a moment!" Roselimb gave her mate a stern look.

"Ephran and Kaahli have disappeared."

Frafan managed to slip in the shocking announcement before his

16

brother could start scolding again. The silence that followed gave Frafan and Janna the chance to tell of the crows' visit and about the limited message they brought.

"...And since you are the only ones in our family who have been to Ephran's home, we wanted your advice as to the fastest and safest route," said Janna, finishing their story.

"This is most alarming news. Now I see why you feel travel is necessary," said Phetra. He cast a questioning glance at Roselimb. She nodded back.

"It appears that we both feel the same way. We'll do better than give directions," he said. "We're going with you."

CHAPTER III

SNOWSTORM

Before setting out for The Pond, Roselimb insisted they rest and build their strength by eating some of the nuts she'd stored in and around the nest. The tree she and Phetra nested in was a rather seedy-looking affair but the hollowed-out den inside its thick trunk was spacious and airy. The floor was soft and pliable, and Roselimb had selected wonderfully sweet-smelling leaves and stems to weave into it. The four squirrels lay together inside, choosing lunch from a generous pile of hickory nuts, acorns, and walnuts.

"You say the crows brought you a message," Phetra said to Frafan. "How do you know they're telling the truth?"

Frafan looked up from the hickory nut he'd been working on. "Why would they lie?" he asked, surprised once again that honesty among the big black birds was such a questionable entity.

"Do you know what crows eat?"

"Of course I do," answered Frafan. "Come now, you can't be thinking..."

"I am thinking," said Phetra. "I'm thinking it might work to the benefit of a crow's appetite if a group of squirrels started off on a long trip just as the cold season rushed down on them."

"Oh, Phetra! You've never trusted crows," said Janna.

"That's true. I never have. Though I've witnessed some pretty unusual behavior from one or two of them near Ephran's Pond, I doubt that I ever will trust them. Anyway, all sorts of bizarre things happen around The Pond. As you have already heard."

"Well," said Frafan, "I have more than one reason to think that these crows were telling the truth. For one thing, you had to be there to sense their sincerity. I believe they feel Ephran is a special squirrel. Also, if they were so interested in our carcasses as a meal, I would think they'd have said we were needed at The Pond — instead of leaving the decision of whether or not to go entirely up to us. At the very least they would have followed us from father and mother's nest. And I haven't seen a crow since we left home."

"I don't think it matters whether we trust crows entirely or not," said Roselimb. "We have no way to judge them in this situation. It appears that we'll have to find out for ourselves."

"What about all of us traveling together?" asked Janna. "Father was very concerned about more than two of us leaving the nest at one time."

Frafan shrugged. "It increases part of the risk, no doubt," he said. "But I think traveling with the two of you, who have been there before, more than makes up for it."

Phetra said, "I agree. So, if we're all ready, let's be on our way."

"Phetra and Roselimb...before we leave, I'd like to know what caused the woods just beyond Little Lake to look so...so black and...and sad," said Janna.

"Ah," said Roselimb, "you are talking about that part of the woods that was caught in the path of fire."

"Just as I thought," Frafan mumbled to himself. "Those trees and grass look like what The Many Colored Ones throw out after the cold days — when smoke comes from the hollow branch in the top of their den."

"Remember when Roselimb and I returned from The Pond?" asked Phetra. "When we welcomed Ephran and Kaahli back to their home they told us of the fire they survived only because a fox invited them into its den in the cool earth. Well, that same fire destroyed part of the woods and, along with trees and bushes, our old nest."

"I'm sure we told you that story," added Roselimb.

"I remember now," said Janna, "I remember the day you came back to the den of Jafthuh and Odalee after being gone so long. All the stories you told about Ephran and The Pond were so incredible that I'd forgotten the one about the fire."

"Most of Ephran's adventures make for peculiar stories," said Phetra. "He seems to have a talent for finding himself in the right place at the right time — or maybe the wrong place at the wrong time, depending on your point of view."

Frafan murmured, "I only hope he's ended up in the right place this time."

The four treeclimbers set out then, at a brisk pace, planning to get as close to Rocky Creek as they could before stopping for the night. They skirted the scorched part of the forest, and soon turned entirely away from the blackened landscape, toward the place from which the warm air would some day return.

Although the mood was solemn, travel through the bare branches was easy, the fresh air invigorating, and the sense of freedom and adventure that always seemed to accompany the start of a journey put spirit in their leaps. Soon they were chattering and laughing. Having Phetra and Roselimb along did make the whole business seem considerably less dangerous. Phetra remembered a small group of hickory trees near a larger cluster of spruce and, since Janna and Roselimb were getting hungry, he attempted to lead the expedition toward the food source. He did not try to use the sun or the movement of air for help, as Ephran did, but instead looked for landmarks.

Ephran had told Frafan that landmarks were very nice things to have around when one is looking for something. Problem is, he said, even if a landmark looks familiar, one has to make a decision as to whether it is a significant landmark or if it just stuck in one's mind because it is somehow different or interesting. Then, if one feels quite certain that this landmark is a real guidepost, one has to be able to remember why it is memorable, and how it's supposed to help in finding the thing one wants to find.

This, unfortunately, was Phetra's problem. He was son to Jafthuh and Odalee as well as brother to Ephran, so he naturally took an interest in unusual or curious happenings and objects. He was also adept at remembering them. But he had great difficulty connecting these sights or sounds with a specific destination. So it was that he missed the spruce trees by a considerable distance. Luckily, Janna spotted the dense thicket of greenery a long way across a clearing. By this time they were all hungry and they turned out of their way to find nuts.

Phetra's memory concerning the hickory trees themselves was accurate. Soon they were all busy looking beneath the blanket of leaves on the forest floor. It became something of a contest and each new discovery was greeted by a happy shout and good-natured teasing. They ate on the earth. Not the most ideal dining place perhaps, but the most convenient. And certainly less dangerous than it might be at other times or in other places. The ground was flat here, underbrush was sparse, and what few bushes grew nearby were bare. They would have to be sound asleep to be surprised by a hunter.

"The air begins to move."

Roselimb made the casual observation as she cracked a nut with her teeth.

Frafan had been paying no heed to the air. Earlier in the day he'd interrupted his breakfast to say good-bye to Blackie. And at Phetra's nest he'd been too busy thinking and talking to eat much. So it wasn't surprising that now he was very hungry. His attention had been focused on a grumbling belly. Now he turned his face to the sky. Fleetingly he remembered Ephran saying something about not letting growling bellies interfere with alert eyes and ears. When he'd said those words Kaahli had nodded vigorously at Frafan, as though she understood all too well what he meant.

"How long would it take us to get back to your den?" he asked, putting a half-eaten nut on the leaf next to him.

"Back to the den?" Roselimb echoed, a startled expression on her face.

"Never mind," said Frafan, "I was thinking aloud. I know we've come too far to get back in time."

Janna, who'd gotten to the point of feeling downright bold about this little trek in the woods with two stouthearted brothers and a wonderfully brave and older female, was alarmed.

"Frafan," she asked, "What in the quiet old woods are you

21

concerned about? Why should we even think of going back?"

"Because the sky becomes troubled," said Frafan. "See how the air moves from where the sun rises and dark clouds come from where it sets?"

"Ha! Another of Ephran's theories," said Phetra, who had been startled at Frafan's question, but didn't care to admit it. "One theory contradicts another. I thought Ephran always said that moving air pushes things along in the direction it moves. If that's true, why do clouds go one way while the air moves another?"

"Because the clouds are up there with their moving air and we're down here with ours. The air doesn't have to move in the same direction, at the same time, in the woods and in the sky," said Frafan, who at last looked at Phetra. "In any case, this is not the best time for lessons about clouds and air. I suggest we look for a hollow tree."

"Hold on a minute there, youngster!" said Phetra. "Before we go running off in all directions, you'd better explain yourself."

"Believe me, Phetra, there is no time," said Frafan.

Roselimb rose to her paws, tension in her muscles. "There is something wrong, Phetra. I feel it too. We can talk later. Let us seek shelter."

Phetra decided not to argue, though he would have liked to. This second brother of his was acting weird again, and upsetting the females. He was going to have to discuss these brash theories of Ephran's with Frafan. Those two had spent too much time together last warm season when he hadn't been around to add some practicality to things. However, just in case there might be some truth in this moving air business...

"Let's find a tree then," he said and they set off in different directions.

Every tree, or group of trees of any size, was carefully inspected from all sides. A hole big enough for four squirrels must be found. The hunt intensified as the wind did likewise and, in an instant, the air was filled with tiny pellets — pellets of half solid water! It was still too warm for real snow, but it was getting colder by the minute.

Roselimb found it increasingly difficult to keep moving forward, into the whistling air. She had to squint to see anything. Just as she was about to give up looking in that particular direction she caught a glimpse of massive linden trees. They stood in a cluster, as they often do, and through partly closed eyes she could see a large hole halfway up one's large trunk.

Meanwhile, Janna had quit looking. She'd found many young trees without holes and plenty of prickly spruce. Nothing, however, that offered any real security. She came to the edge of a clearing and realized that while she'd been concentrating on finding shelter, snow had begun falling thick and heavy. She could see only a short way and decided that she better join the others. Maybe they'd had better luck.

"Frafan!" she shouted.

No answer.

"Phetra! Roselimb!" she called, as loudly as she could.

The gusty air took her voice, tore it into small pieces, mixing it with the blowing snow and scattering it among the trees and bushes. All she heard in return was the wind moaning through bare and creaking branches. She'd never felt so completely alone. Overwhelming fear filled her chest so suddenly that she didn't notice how very cold her paws had become.

"All she heard in return was the wind blowing through bare and creaking branches."

CHAPTER IV

LOST

A s soon as she realized she'd found shelter, a hole that would accommodate all of them, Roselimb turned and looked for her companions. As luck would have it, Frafan had spied the same cluster of trees from a different angle, and before Roselimb could call his name he appeared on the branch next to her. Phetra was on his brother's heels and, in the excitement of the moment, no one thought to ask him why he followed so closely.

"Good for you, Roselimb," Frafan cried into the swirling air, "You found us a warm den."

"Did I find it or did you?" she shouted, smiling.

"Doesn't matter, does it?"

They scampered through the dark hole, Roselimb first, and found themselves in a very large hollow den. The hole had had other occupants but, by the looks of it, some time ago. The tree's inner core was rotted all the way to the ground. A cold draft rose from below, through cracks in the fragile wooden floor and through crisp leaves and twigs that made up what was left of a nest. Frafan pushed loose leaves into the crack while Roselimb and Phetra scraped soft decaying wood from the walls to pad their refuge.

They were all very busy for a while. Frafan's mind had been filled with dread when the storm started and, in the frenzy of finding shelter and making it comfortable, he hadn't paid attention to who was and who was not scurrying about in the semi-darkness. Now it occurred to him, jarring him as suddenly and violently as a branch breaking beneath him.

"Janna!" he cried. "Where is Janna?"

Phetra, wiping melting snow from his face with one paw, looked at Frafan vacantly. Roselimb shook cold water from her fur, her eyes registering bewilderment in the faint light.

"I thought she was with you," she said, "behind Phetra."

"And I was certain she had stayed near you," answered Frafan. "I thought she was already inside when we met you on the branch outside." He started toward the hole. "I have to find her...,"

"No!" said Phetra, and he shifted his body, placing himself between the hole and Frafan.

"Let me pass! I'm responsible for her!" cried Frafan.

"Who told you that? Who said you were responsible?" Phetra stood solidly in his brother's path.

"Well...well," he stammered, "no one had to tell me. Mother and father expect that I'll watch out for her."

"Are you sure that the opposite might not be true? Isn't it just as

25

likely that they expected her to watch out for you?" asked Phetra.

"But she frightens easily," objected Frafan. "She won't know what to do if one of us isn't there to tell her."

"Is that so? She was brave enough to come along, wasn't she? I don't think you give her — or father and mother — enough credit. You were the smallest of the litter, remember, and, if you don't mind my saying so, the most likely to find trouble."

"But someone has to look," Frafan pleaded.

"You know, it wasn't long ago that a group of his friends had to convince Ephran that a search he was planning was a bad idea. A good friend of his, a duck called Cloudchaser, was hurt by thundersticks. The drake fell into a nasty wet place called Lomarsh and Ephran was determined to go and find him. It took some hard words from the drake's mate to convince our brother that he could not help his friend, even if he did find him. All he would do is put himself at risk. I'm afraid we've got the same sort of situation here."

"We must find her!" Frafan was near panic.

"Take it easy, Frafan," Phetra said in a calm voice. "I know exactly how you feel but I can't let you go out there. None of us dare go. Janna is clever. She'll find a safe place. She'll be just fine."

The air outside howled madly through the trees. What Phetra said made sense — at least the part about searching in an unfamiliar place in the midst of a blizzard. But his brother's logic gave Frafan no comfort. It was the same advice father had given about setting out on a search as the cold season tried to push the warm season out of the woods. Only then the danger had seemed remote and unlikely. Now it was very much right here, roaring like a caged beast around the hole in the linden. His mind accepted the advice but his heart ached in his chest. She was out there somewhere and he was not one bit convinced that she'd be "just fine".

"Let me at least take a look at what she's up against," he said.

Phetra looked into his brother's eyes, decided that he did not intend to run off into the storm, and moved aside.

What Frafan saw through the hole was not reassuring. The cluster of spruce was no longer visible. Actually, the entire forest had disappeared in a moaning, swirling cloud of snow. It was getting dark — darker even than the violent storm. And still the savage air and snow flailed the defenseless woods.

It grew colder and colder, and they curled together to share their warmth. But none of them slept, not really. Frafan's eyes might slide shut now and again, from sheer exhaustion, but they would pop open every few moments. And there would always be another pair of open eyes, shining dimly in the darkness.

After what seemed a very long while it became a wee bit lighter in the hollow linden. It was hard to tell if the sun was really somewhere up above the thick clouds or if it still hid behind the edge of the woods. Air continued to whistle through bare branches, but the sound was less shrill than it had been. Frafan thought perhaps the wild and raging air was weakening.

They were all hungry, and exhausted from lack of sleep, but that was of no importance. Janna was lost. Though they might wish otherwise, they knew that a terrified Janna, far from a home she'd not left before, would almost certainly have looked for her brothers rather than try to find her own shelter. Though none of them said it aloud, they were all thinking the same thing: A young and inexperienced squirrel would have little chance in that horrible storm.

The moving air finally became a whisper, and it stopped snowing. The squirrels climbed out into the cold air and beheld a changed forest. Earth, brown grass, bushes, and small trees were buried. A thick, undulating blanket of white covered everything. Here and there snow had twisted around a large tree trunk or a thick cluster of spruce, and formed a drift — a long, cold, white wave with a delicate curl at its edge.

Shafts of yellow, pale pillars of light, seemed to rise from the virgin whiteness, soaring through breaks in the fluffy gray clouds moving rapidly away, opening like a curtain on an infinitely vast and brittle blue sky.

"Where shall we look first?" asked Roselimb. She gazed off into the distance.

Frafan did not speak. Phetra was older and had more experience. He'd been in this part of the forest before. He'd had to step in and take charge when Frafan became confused and wanted to look for his sister in the midst of a blinding snowstorm. Frafan thought maybe he should feel some embarrassment about that, but he didn't. Deep inside he still felt — dangerous or not, foolish or not — he should have tried to find her right away. He was very much afraid that looking now was looking too late.

Though Frafan waited a long while, Phetra said nothing. When Frafan felt a chill working its way up his front legs he announced, "The angry sky is gone. It won't be back soon again. I think we should search right here. Janna wouldn't have been able to travel far in any direction. She certainly wouldn't have been able to tell the way to Great Hill, not in that storm."

"I agree," said Phetra, "and I have to apologize and tell you that I will not argue again about your ability to read the signs in the air and the sky."

"Thank you, Phetra," Frafan said quietly.

"Can we stay together?" asked Roselimb with a shiver.

"It will waste time," answered Frafan, "but if that's what you want to do, that's what we'll do. We'll have the best chance of finding her if we move in ever-widening circles away from this tree. Like ripples in the water when a leaf falls in."

Phetra looked relieved, and he and Roselimb nodded in agreement.

There were really very few places to look. The kind of shelter they had used, a large hole in a tree, was the most suitable retreat for a squirrel caught in bad weather. Such refuges were not plentiful in this part of the woods. That much became obvious as soon as the storm arrived. They had been very lucky to find the partly-rotted linden. The only other havens that might permit survival would be the innermost limbs of a thick and bushy spruce tree...or a tightly constructed leaf-and-stick nest of a large bird or another squirrel.

Besides trying to find Janna, they faced another problem, one which became increasingly important with each passing moment. Roselimb gave voice to their common concern when she said, "Food is going to be very difficult to find."

With the air having turned so cold their bodies demanded more food than usual...food to help keep them warm and the juices flowing. The fallen snow was thick, heavy, and nearly unbroken. No bare spots, where one might search for nuts, were visible from where they sat. The hickory grove, where they'd been eating when the storm started, might as well have been at the other end of the woods. Frafan thought ruefully that father's misgivings about squirrels traveling through the forest during the cold season seemed well founded indeed.

The hunt for Janna lost focus and became, at least partially, a ragged and disorganized search for food. The sighting of a distant patch of brown in the white forest would send them scurrying for possible nuts or seeds beneath withered leaves. They were invariably disappointed. Sometimes the drab patch was nothing more than a large slab of tree bark, blown from the trunk of a rotting elm by the blustery air. Sometimes it was the stark branches of a clump of sleeping bushes. Sometimes it was only a shadow, playing a trick on their eyes, fading into heart-slowing frustration as they drew near.

Finally they realized they had run full circle and were back near the lindens that had offered shelter. Exhausted, cold, and forlorn, they sat and rested on the limbs of an ironwood tree, thinking their own thoughts.

Phetra eventually spoke. "We have seeds and nuts stored in our den near Little Lake," he said. "I think we can make it back there if we start out right now."

"But...what of Janna?" said Roselimb. "We can't just leave Janna!"

"I don't think we have a lot of choice," Phetra said wearily. "We are in a serious predicament. Even if we find her I'm not sure we'd be able to help her. It has been a long time for her to be out in the snow and cold. We're in trouble ourselves. This bitter air is about to turn us into hard furry rocks. Unless we starve first."

Tears of fatigue, confusion, and despair welled up in Roselimb's eyes. She turned to Frafan and said, "You're very quiet, Frafan. What do you think?"

Frafan lifted his head. "I don't know what to think. What Phetra says is probably true. The wisest course would be to return to your den. There's no sense in all of us staying here."

"What do you mean, 'all of us'?" asked Roselimb. "You can't be thinking of staying here alone!"

"That's exactly what I'm thinking, Roselimb. I'm not leaving."

"Frafan!" Phetra rose on his hind legs. "You must come! The great and brave search for Ephran and Kaahli is over. It was a grand idea and sounded like high adventure, but I sadly fear that it has already cost one of us breath. It could easily cost three more."

"My dear brother," said Frafan, "even if I wanted to go, which I don't, I doubt I could run so far as your den. As you said yourself, I'm not very sturdy. I don't have a lot of strength, and what I had at the outset is nearly gone."

"I'll carry you!" cried Phetra.

"That would be even more foolish than looking for Janna at the height of the storm. You are already hungry and near exhaustion. Small as I am, I would be a heavy load. Neither of us would make it back to your den."

"I'm willing to try," said Phetra, voice shaking.

"And I will help," offered Roselimb. "We'll take turns."

"Thank you both," said Frafan, "but I couldn't leave even if I thought I had a chance of getting there."

Water rolled freely down the cheeks of both the older squirrels.

"Be on your way now," Frafan said sternly. "I promise I'll see you again before the next batch of hickory nuts ripen on the branches."

They sat a while. Phetra's mind was in more turmoil than the sky had been during the storm. His undersized brother could not go much longer without food. Nor could his mate. Frafan was right, there was no way he and Roselimb could carry him so far. It might be possible during the warm season, with many stops for rest and food. Now, in their weakened condition...

A breath of painfully bitter air, born in the farthest reaches of the cold season's womb, caused Roselimb to shiver — and Phetra to make his decision.

"Come, Roselimb," he said quietly. And he looked into his

younger brother's eyes for a long moment before he turned and followed her through the branches.

Frafan watched as Phetra and Roselimb made their way through the trees toward Little Lake. They looked back twice, and both times he waved merrily, as though this whole affair was the happy ending of a big party and they were just parting ways after a joyous family reunion in the middle of the warm season. When they finally became tiny grey dots on the branches, and then disappeared over a rise in the earth, Frafan felt absolutely empty. Not just hunger-empty. It was like everything inside his fur had been drained out. He was terrified!

His legs ached from the cold, and a spasm, part chill and part fear, shook him. His stomach had stopped growling but it felt emptier than it had earlier. What bothered him the most was his mouth. It was numb and dry. He peeped through half-closed eyes at the snow beneath him, sun glittering merrily from countless tiny crystals. It sparkled like the water on Little Lake. And why shouldn't it?

"It is water, isn't it?" he said to himself.

He crawled down the trunk of the tree. His head felt light, like it might float away. For the first time he could remember, every move he made required thought. He was sure he'd fall if he moved too fast. Carefully working his way down the trunk, tail up, his face finally reached the smooth white surface. He opened his mouth and took a big bite.

This was really not acceptable. If mother were here she would say, "Frafan! What in the big blue sky are you doing now?"

The snow was stunningly cold on his dry tongue, but it warmed quickly and left him with a puddle of water in his mouth. He very nearly spat it out. No squirrel he'd ever heard of drank water. But he forced himself to swallow. The liquid was soothing and cool. He took another mouthful. And another. Although he was still very hungry, he was refreshed. At least there was something in his belly! His spirits lifted.

Frafan looked around and tried to assess his situation. No matter the odds, he wanted desperately to see Janna. She carried much more fat beneath her thick fur than he did. She would be able to go for a long while without food. If she'd found any sort of decent protection at all...

It would do little good, of course, to find her in the condition he was in — half frozen and half starved — unless he knew in advance where there was something to eat. Finding food, then, would still have to be the first priority.

He began examining all likely (and even some rather unlikely) places that might conceal dried seeds, a nut, or even soft leaves or stems. He peered closely into hollows where big branches met the trunk of their tree, he scratched and dug in those few tiny places where the snow was not far over his head, he even painstakingly worked his way through the

Into the High Branches

They looked back twice,
and both times he waved merrily...

wispy limbs of a chokecherry cluster to comb through an abandoned and snowfilled bird's nest.

He found nothing.

Getting weaker by the moment, he took another mouthful of snow and slowly climbed into the low branches of a little elm tree. There he found a comfortable place where two branches grew close together. He sighed peacefully, blowing out a tiny cloud of breath, and he gazed off toward where the remote and frigid sun was nearing bare treetops.

"This is really just my second 'Alone Time,'" he smiled to himself with the memory. He'd had another, after Ephran and Kaahli left for The Pond, but that supposed test of his maturity had been no test at all. Long before father took him off by himself Frafan had been an explorer. His curiosity had led him far from the nest many times, and Ephran's lessons always led him back home again. It came as no surprise that the place father chose for his trial was well known to him. Actually, the place turned out to be one of his favorite hideouts: a little valley, thick with trees, not too far from the den of Jafthuh and Odalee, well-concealed but delightfully familiar. He'd even buried some nuts at the base of the very tree that Jafthuh left him in! He'd thought at the time that he ought to say something to his father, because it felt like he was cheating.

He had said nothing, however, and he spent two days in idle comfort, food in abundance, knowing exactly where home was any time he wanted to go there.

Now he knew where home and food was alright, but it was too far away to reach. There would be no cheating this time. This would be a real test. Probably (he tried not to think of it), the final test.

The little tree he sat in would be a good place to close his eyes and rest for a while. He was weary and it seemed harder to take air in with every breath. The air didn't feel quite so cold though. Maybe it was warming up. About time! He could relax then. In the morning he would look for food. Now he would sleep...

"Frafan!"

In his dream he thought it was mother calling. What kind of trouble was he in this time? He couldn't think of what he might have done to make her angry. He'd tried to do his best. It wasn't his fault that he couldn't find...whatever it was he was supposed to find. He wanted to answer mother, but it was very hard to open his mouth, or his eyes.

"Frafan! Please..."

Something or someone seemed to be trying to push him off his perch. He opened one eye partway — to size up his adversary. His eyelids were nearly sealed with crystals of frozen water. Frafan's view of whoever had their nose buried in the fur of his neck was blurred.

Then the face came up.

"Janna!" he croaked, "I've found you!"

She started to laugh through her tears. "Yes, you crazy little brother. You found me." She turned away from him and shouted, "Did you hear that? He says *he* found *me!*"

Then she laughed harder. And cried harder too.

Who in this cold old woods was she talking to? Frafan struggled to open his other eye but it was stuck shut. Foggy vision revealed nothing in the nearby trees. He glanced at the ground. Sitting on fluffy tails, in the snow at the base of his tree, were two rabbits. They were looking up at him. One, he noted, had a crooked ear.

Janna helped him down the trunk of the tree, babbling and crooning to him the whole while. He thought he should tell her that they could not run on the snow. They would sink into it. They would have to stay in the trees. But he was simply too tired to say anything. And when he reached the earth at the base of the elm he found there was snow there alright, but it had been flattened and compacted, by someone or something, so that he and Janna could stand on it without sinking at all.

He peered through half-open eyes at the rabbits. They were looking right back at him.

"Mayberry. You're Mayberry, aren't you?" he asked — in a voice that didn't sound like his.

"Yes," said the rabbit with the deformed ear, "I am Mayberry."

Frafan turned to his sister. "Janna," he mumbled, "How did you manage...? Where did you...?"

"Later," she said, "we'll talk later."

"Come with us," said Mayberry, "we must get you to a warm place. I think your stomach needs filling too."

"It's not far," Janna reassured him.

Stumbling with cold and weakness, unable to summon even enough strength to ask more questions, Frafan allowed himself to be led along a hardpacked path through the snow. The trail they followed was well-concealed. It wound through clusters of tall brown grass, bowed and pressed to the earth by heavy snow, through dark stems of barren thorn bushes, and around a gigantic rotted oak stump. It occurred to him they should not be traveling on the ground, but he was very nearly beyond worry or fright.

The rabbits led on, and Janna walked beside her brother, nuzzling him and murmuring words of encouragement. They soon approached what appeared to be a very large, lumpy, and angular pile of snow. Frafan thought he might have noticed it earlier, while he was searching for Janna. The path led directly to a gaping black hole at the very bottom of the strange snowdrift. The rabbits disappeared into the hole. Frafan balked.

"It's all right, it's all right," Janna said, and pushed him firmly ahead.

Totally defeated by confusion and the numbing cold, he shuffled into blackness, eyes tightly closed, waiting for gigantic stonehard teeth to sink into his neck. Or for a powerful blow to crush his spine. Who could tell what terrifying monsters might attack a squirrel who dared enter a hole on or in the earth? And, at this point, who cared?

Instead of chilling teeth or claws he felt warmth — it engulfed him — soft luxurious warmth. With it was the friendly smell of cottontail rabbits, many cottontail rabbits. Mixed with that smell was yet another wondrous odor; the unmistakable sweet smell of preserved vegetation; grasses, buds, and seeds. He nearly fainted with relief, but struggled to stay awake. There were so very many questions!

Mayberry and the other rabbit had stopped in a large and roughly circular cavern. They stood against a far wall and turned to face their visitors. Vague and diffused light came from somewhere (through the snow above them?) and Frafan could barely make out a number of rabbits along the side of the chamber. He felt Janna sit down next to him.

"Your eyes will get used to the dim light," she whispered to him.

"Frafan, I bid you welcome to Great Woods Warren," said Mayberry. "and to this special part of the warren that we call Gather Place. I know you have many things to wonder about and to ask, but you must eat while we talk. It appears that hunger and the storm have nearly finished you."

One of the rabbits near Frafan nudged him with its nose and pointed to seeds and dried buds, neatly piled on a large oak leaf, and so close to him that he'd nearly sat on it. He didn't have to be asked twice.

Janna coaxed him to go slowly and he tried to eat with some semblance of dignity — they were all watching him — but it was impossible. He was so very hungry, and it tasted so very good!

As frozen water, turned back to liquid by the wonderful heat, dripped from his ears and nose, he stuffed his mouth with sweet buds and crisp, nut-like seeds. He could feel warmth returning to his body and clarity to his mind.

"I know squirrels don't drink water," said Mayberry, "but what you eat is very dry. If you feel you need something wet..."

"Yes, I know," said Frafan, "I will take a mouthful of snow."

A smile spread across Mayberry's face.

"There is no doubt in my mind. You are brother to Ephran."

CHAPTER V

GREAT WOODS WARREN

T hough he felt he could eat more, Frafan knew he better not stuff himself or he'd be sick. Another oak leaf was pushed toward him. This one held a small heap of half melted snow. He took a large mouthful. It was wonderful. Something worth learning had come from a bad experience. He sighed deeply, changed the position of his legs, and sat back on his tail.

"Frafan," said Mayberry, "I would like you to meet my mate, Truestar, and some of my young ones who are, I am happy and proud to say, quite numerous. This lad here," and he nodded to the rabbit who had been with him outside, "is my son Highhopper. Next to him is his brother Longgrass. Sweetbud over there..." A pretty young female smiled at Frafan. "...is my daughter. Some of their older brothers and sisters have left this warren to find mates. Some nest in Bubbling Brook Warren, near Great Hill. The other cottontails you see here are kin to Truestar or myself, or else mates of kin. After a while you will learn their names. I doubt you would remember them if I told you now."

A number of the rabbits smiled and bowed and said "Hello" and "Nice to have you" and "Glad you're here instead of out there" and things like that. What wondrous creatures these cottontail were, thought Frafan, that in time of trouble they should welcome him and his sister as one of their own. Frafan smiled back at them. He was deeply touched.

"I hope I get to know some names," he said, "but we must be going soon. You see, we are searching."

"Janna told us why you travel at the beginning of the cold season," said Mayberry. "We will talk much more of this. But we will have time later, after you feel more comfortable. The air outside, I fear, will remain very cold for some time. And the snow will stay deep. There will be no food for you in the woods."

During the ensuing chatter, one of the larger male rabbits, back against the far wall, caught Frafan's attention. The dim light made it difficult to be sure, but it seemed every time he looked in that direction this particular cottontail was looking back. And the look was not a curious or friendly look. It was more a surly glare. Frafan wondered if his active imagination was working overtime again. Why would the rabbit be angry? Did it have anything to do with him and Janna being here, in a rabbit warren? He would go talk to this rabbit.

Just as Frafan started to ease his way toward the far wall, a very small male rabbit, nearly lost among many large furry bodies, pushed his way to the front of the group, right up to him and Janna.

The little fellow cleared his throat and said, "Ahem! I would like to officially greet our guests. I am Fastrip. I am Warden of this warren. I'm in charge of procedural things — sort of the right paw of the Governor, you might say. I do not brag when I say I have the best memory here. I know and remember all of the traditions and rules of this clan. Please call on me for any assistance you require."

Frafan was just about to express his thanks when, between the legs of a group of bigger rabbits, appeared a female cottontail, tinier yet than Fastrip. She was plumper than the little male, but of similar proportions.

"Warden! You a Warden! My fluffy tail you're a Warden!" she cried, sneering openly at Fastrip.

The two little rabbits confronted one another, eye to eye, snarling, right in front of Frafan and Janna.

"I am so the Warden! And you know it. Keep your disrespect to yourself, Sorghum," replied Fastrip.

"Oh...ah...please...I'm sure this can be settled to everyone's...ah..." Frafan glanced at the faces around him. They were all watching the small cottontails. No one paid him any heed.

"You get all the respect you deserve," said the small female. "Zero. Zip. And what's this 'Best Memory' nonsense? You'd forget your floppy ears in your nest if they weren't so firmly attached to your flat head."

Some subdued laughter came from the surrounding cottontails, only serving to embarrass Frafan even more.

"You're trying to upset me! You have no business trying to ruffle the Warden," said Fastrip, raising his nose.

"You're about as much a Warden as I am a blue and red snake," Sorghum shot back.

"I don't know about the blue and red part, but the rest of it fits," said Fastrip with an evil grin.

"You'd be the first to know what fits a snake," said Sorghum, "since they make up the bulk of your friends."

"Bulk? Speaking of bulk," said Fastrip, "we're going to have to widen the tunnels in the warden if you put on any more weight."

"Sure. When you know you're whipped just change the subject, you ninny."

The two little rabbits were sharp and quick of tongue. Their performance — for that's just what it was — was greeted by whistles and shouts of approval from their larger relatives. The small ones bowed and smiled and wiggled their ears at everyone. After their initial shock at Sorghum's outburst and the trading of insults, Frafan and Janna found themselves laughing along, angry faces against dark walls forgotten.

"I hope our little playacting didn't disturb you," said Sorghum to Frafan and Janna. "We feel, you see, that when one has had a frightening experience as you have, a dose of laughter is as badly needed as a mouthful of bluegrass and barley seeds."

"And," added Fastrip, "if it comes as a surprise, so much the better to make one feel full of breath and juice."

"We are actually mates, you see, and generally get along quite well," said Sorghum.

"Yes," agreed Fastrip, "see how I love her." And he hopped over to Sorghum and proceeded to give her a big hug.

"Get off my paws, you oaf!" she cried.

Everyone laughed again and Frafan said, "Thank you, Fastrip and Sorghum. I think your idea is on the mark. The laughter you provided was almost as valuable as the food. I feel much better."

"So do I," agreed Janna.

Frafan said, "One thing I did not understand was this thing you called a 'Governor.' Is there a funny story behind that word?"

A titter came from the cottontail and Fastrip glanced at Janna. She shrugged her shoulders and said to the rabbits, "I haven't really had a chance to tell him anything about the warren, you know."

"Well, then," said Fastrip, "it's not surprising that you don't know what a Governor is. But it is no joke. Rabbits, as you see, do not nest in small tree dens with one set of parents and maybe one or two sets of offspring nearby. Our way demands we have one rabbit who decides what is best for all of us, as your father or mother might. He or she calls Assembly in Gather Place, a meeting of all the rabbits in the warren, and answers their questions. He or she listens to disagreements among us and helps solve them. He or she interprets the will of the warren and sees that it is enforced. He or she must be the wisest and bravest among us. Our Governor is Mayberry."

Frafan turned to Mayberry and said, "Ephran didn't tell me that you were the leader of your warren."

"That is because he didn't know," said Mayberry.

"Well, from what he did tell me, I know he'd not be surprised." He looked out over the gathered cottontails. He could not find the angry face. "All of you, I can't thank you enough for your help and your welcome. I would not have breathed much longer out there. I still have many questions, though. For instance, how did you come to have my sister with you?"

"Much the same way you came to be here," said Truestar.

"Oh, Frafan," said Janna, "I was so frightened when the snow started to fall and the air became so strong and wild. I was lost almost at once. I couldn't find you or Phetra or..." She nearly choked. "Oh great bright stars! Phetra and Roselimb! In all the excitement I nearly forgot...Where..."

"Peace, Janna," said Frafan, and he put his foreleg about her neck and hugged her to himself. "Phetra and his mate left for their den a

37

long while ago. I'm sure they're safe and sound in their tree by now."

Mayberry said, "It is good news that Phetra and Roselimb are most probably secure in their nest. They are special friends. Truestar and I spent some time with them near the end of the warm season, you know...at Ephran's home on The Pond."

"Well, they were both running strongly through the branches when I last saw them," said Frafan.

Janna told how she'd finally left the trees when she could find no shelter in them and when to see, even to breathe, became nearly impossible. That act, foolish under most circumstances, almost certainly was her deliverance. At the bottom of the tree she found herself face to face with Highopper who, it so happened, was on his way back to the warren with a mouthful of last warm season's sweet clover. Although at first she was like her brother, distrustful of a shelter on the ground, she remembered Ephran's stories of rabbits, and storms, and safe places — and she followed the cottontail into his dark home.

"Do you feel up to a tour of the warren?" Mayberry asked when Janna had finished her story.

"I would love it!" said Frafan.

Though his legs felt sluggish and a heaviness lay deep behind his eyes, Frafan was too curious to pass up an offer to explore this unlikely and fascinating dwelling-place of the shorttails. For a squirrel, accustomed to a cozy den of leaves or a tight den inside a tree trunk, the rabbits' home seemed absolutely massive. Drafty as well. And every time he came to a corner in one of the long, dim, and twisting hallways he was afraid he might meet a hunter. The warren was built, after all, right on the earth.

Much skillful planning had gone into the place though. He had to admit that. The many dens and corridors through which they wandered were basically created by two large elms which had, according to Mayberry, fallen almost atop one another. They had crashed down, unto their own outstretched branches, into a dense thicket of elderberry bushes. Broken limbs and twisted groundcover held most of the elms' trunks and branches away from the earth. Leaves, small limbs, twigs and snow had formed a substantial roof. It kept the cold out (a good share of it anyway) and the warmth of earth and rabbit bodies in.

The rabbits had fashioned comfortable nests in the leaves and grass around the stems of bushes, loosely built against the nearest sturdy branch. Each rabbit family had its own private den, and all were interconnected by a maze of tunnels which zigzagged around broken limbs, dry tree roots, and particularly thick clumps of bushes. Being accustomed to the wide open and free spaces of the high branches, it was enough to completely befuddle Frafan and Janna. Unfortunately, the high branches were not the place to be right now.

There were many exits and entrances to the warren. None of them, it appeared to Frafan, very well hidden. Mayberry admitted that so many ways in or out seemed unwarranted, but he explained that if a small fox found his way in, the other openings were essential as escape routes. Drafts of chilly air were a necessary price for safety.

A cubicle near the entrance through which Frafan had first entered Great Woods Warren was nearly filled with food. He recognized the delicious smell as they approached it. The cottontails had done well in preparing for the cold season.

As they talked and the rabbits pointed out things which might be of interest or practical value to their guests, Sweetbud, Mayberry's daughter, suddenly appeared from around one of the sharp corners in the corridor. She hopped directly up to Mayberry, waited for a lull in the conversation, then leaned close and whispered in his ear.

"My mate and I have readied a resting place for you and your sister," Longrass said to Frafan, apparently ignoring his sister and her interruption. "Follow me and I will take you there."

When Sweetbud finished talking to him, Mayberry turned to the squirrels and said, "I hope you will forgive Sweetbud for this intrusion, and me for having to leave you for a short while. A matter has arisen that demands my attention. Please follow Longrass. We will talk soon, after you have had a chance to rest." His eyes were serious. "I know more of the story of Ephran and his disappearance than the crows told you, but I doubt it will be of great help. In any case, we will meet in Gather Place after you sleep. I will send someone for you."

With that, Mayberry and Highopper hopped after Sweetbud, down the dim corridor, around a bend, and out of sight.

"Come," said Longrass, as he turned down the hallway in the opposite direction.

Obediently, Frafan and Janna followed the young rabbit into near-darkness, white tail bouncing along in front like a beacon. Frafan wondered to himself what news Sweetbud might have had to cause such secrecy. The whole business came off as sort of discourteous. Oh well, he thought; Mayberry is, after all, Governor. He supposed that those in positions of authority were often bothered by little predicaments or quandaries about which he needn't worry.

He decided not to dwell on potential problems, and tried instead to keep track of the twists and turns, and the number of nests that they passed, some occupied by cottontails and some not.

"This is total confusion," he said to himself.

What difference did it make anyway? If danger came and he had to run, he would run. At a time like that he'd have no chance to remember corners and which turn led where. Squirrels couldn't think like that. He wondered if rabbits could. He understood Mayberry's point: thank Oak Trees and Budding Bushes there were so many holes to come and go! If he ran far enough he'd be sure to come across one of them. And that, of course, would depend on him being able to run fast enough — to keep ahead of the hunter.

Longrass stopped at the entrance to a most comfortable little den. The entryway was formed by a sizeable shattered branch, splinters of still-white wood sprouting in all directions on one side and the bent stems of elderberry bushes on the other. Overhead was a sturdy elm limb. It supported countless intertwined small branches, twigs, and dried elderberry leaves. As in Gather Place, muted light came from above, through cracks between wood and leaves filled with snow. The back of the den was formed by the crook of a branch. A bunch of soft leaves had been packed into the bend. The earth was covered with thick grass, some of it still green.

Janna carefully poked her head in. "Why, it's really nice in here!" she said.

Longrass smiled and said, "Why don't both of you rest. I'll be back when its time to eat and talk." He pivoted and silently hopped off down the corridor.

Janna touched her nose to her brother's neck and squeezed him close to her.

"Oww! Get off my paw!" he laughed, and hugged her back, even more tightly.

"I'm so glad we found you," she said.

"I am too. I could not have waited much longer." Frafan shook his head and sighed. "We were all so frightened for you, you know. We looked and looked. I'm sure Phetra and Roselimb think both of us are buried beneath drifts of snow. I wish there was some way we could let them know we're safe."

"But there is none. Right now there's no way we can reassure them. In a way they're right, we are actually buried in the snow. Although this is not my idea of a nice safe tree nest, I'm so tired I know I'll be able to sleep anyway. What about you, Frafan?"

"Just behind my eyes I think I am ready to collapse," he said. "I will sleep."

He didn't think he could stay awake even if he wanted to. As he told Mayberry, he'd been very near surrender out there in the frigid forest. Now that his stomach was full, his fur warm, and friendship in the air, to say nothing of the comfort of being near his sister, his eyes were near closing. He didn't want to cause her concern, so he didn't speak about what he was thinking. The petulant face against the back wall of Gather Place reappeared in his mind. Some of the residents of Great Woods Warren may not be especially happy with his and Janna's presence here. Not all enemies were necessarily outside these walls.

CHAPTER VI

ENEMIES AMONG FRIENDS

anna was totally drained. She admitted to Frafan that she hadn't slept at all during the storm, tormented with worry for her brothers and Roselimb. Truestar and Sweetbud had spent the night next to her, trying to calm her. She'd existed on sheer nervous energy for hours. Now, with one brother curled by her side, high hopes that the other was safe with his mate in his own den, friendly smells of rabbit and squirrel in warm air, and soft leaves tucked under her full stomach, she fell into a deep and peaceful sleep.

Frafan thought of asking her if she'd met any unpleasant rabbits before he got here. Had any of them said anything harsh or insulting to her, he wondered? But her tiny snores told him she was sound asleep and his questions went unasked.

He was as weary as his sister and desired nothing more than to close his lids. For some unnameable reason though, he felt he should stay alert. It was a feeling that something was amiss, something more than the fact this nest in which he lay was not the sort of which father and mother would approve, something more than unanswered questions and unresolved fears about Ephran and Kaahli. Despite all of it, his mind and body could no longer obey his will, and his eyes slowly closed.

He dreamed then. A dark and dreadful dream. If he weren't so exhausted, the unnaturally slow action, seen misty and wavering as through frozen water, might have pulled him up, squirming and mumbling loudly, from the deep vales of slumber.

He dreamed that he was running toward a black cavern, a massive cavity with a huge square mouth. At first it was unclear why he would stretch his legs with such determination to reach such a terrifying goal. All he could think was that he must get there in time, before the tremendous jaws clanged shut. Then, without knowing how he knew, he realized he must be the sacrifice. It was because the answer was there...the answer to Ephran and Kaahli's disappearance.

He felt himself being nudged awake, and not very gently either. He'd fallen asleep facing Janna and the first thing he saw was that her delicate lids were still closed. He was being pushed from behind, pushed so firmly that he had to plant a front paw in the thick matted grass to keep from sliding into his sleeping sister.

"Wake up! Wake up, troublemakers!"

Rolled up on his side and forced to his paws, Frafan turned sluggishly, trying to rouse himself, expecting to see Longrass. Governor's son or no Governor's son, this cottontail was going to get a lecture on the etiquette of awakening guests. To his surprise he found himself face to face with two strange rabbits.

Actually, he faced only one, the larger of the two, a male, who'd been using his big nose to do the pushing and shoving. The other, a female, stood back a little, away from her companion, near the wall of the tiny den. She was partly in shadow. "Wake your sister, intruder. And both you smelly and misplaced longtails get moving. We want you out of here."

The big rabbit's eyes glittered in the faint light. The glow was not the gentle and lively twinkle in the eyes of Mayberry or Truestar or Fastrip. It was an angry burning. On his left cheek a furless and jagged scar trailed down to his thick neck, pulling the eye out of round and giving him a wild and fierce look. He stood lopsided because one front leg was shorter than the other, and bent at an unusual angle. Frafan recognized this face. It was the face he'd seen against the far wall of Gather Place.

"Get moving? Get moving where? Is it time to eat and talk? Did Mayberry send you?" Frafan blinked and shook his head, trying to clear the heavy fog of sleep away.

"Never mind who sent us. As far as what time it is...it's time you and that female left this warren, that's what time it is. Get up and get out. And do it fast or I'll speed you up."

The rabbit's voice was not loud, but it was harsh and raspy. It forced its way into Janna's sleep. Without having to think, she jumped to her paws.

"What...what is it, Frafan?" she asked thickly.

"I don't know yet," he answered, without taking his eyes from the big rabbit.

"Who are you?" he asked, realizing that no rabbit sent by Ephran's good friend would be this rude.

"You ask too many questions." The big rabbit hopped toward the squirrels. "C'mon, Milkweed," he said to the other cottontail, who had not moved from the shadows, "these stupid treeclimbers seem to need some help in finding the way out."

"Please, Redthorn," pleaded the other rabbit in a soft voice, "let's go to our own nest."

Frafan felt Janna move to his side. He glanced at her. Her jaw was set and her eyes glittered. She was ready to fight. "Well, well," he thought. "So much for my ability to estimate who is and who is not faint of heart." If she was afraid, she was doing an admirable job of hiding it.

"Alright, Redthorn, that's enough! Back off!"

The sharp command, barked with authority by someone near the entrance to the den, froze the big rabbit where he stood. Whoever had called out was hidden from Frafan's view by the unpleasant rabbit whose name was evidently Redthorn.

"Mind your own business, Highopper," said Redthorn, without

42

turning. Despite the tone of his words, he spoke quietly, and Frafan could sense his uncertainty.

"I'm going to ask you nicely not to cause any more trouble," said Highopper. "Mayberry wants everyone in Gather Place for a meeting... Now!"

As Redthorn turned away to face Highopper, Frafan saw that four rabbits had squeezed into the den and he thought there might be more of them in the corridor. The rabbit who'd come with Redthorn, Milkweed he called her, held her tongue. She looked terror-stricken as she faced the other rabbits. The room was now stuffed with cottontails. For the moment at least, Frafan and Janna were ignored.

"Giving orders again, eh? You and your father are alike. Both of you real good at giving orders. I'm sick and tired of it. Orders backed by a bunch of cronies, too, I see. Afraid to come alone, I suppose."

"You know I'm not afraid of you, Redthorn," Highopper said in a very calm voice.

One of the new arrivals said, "Cronies? You call us cronies? I thought we were all supposed to be family. But if it's a fight you want, you'll get it."

"Redthorn," Milkweed pleaded, "this won't work. Don't give them an excuse to hurt you."

The big male whirled on his mate as though he was going to cuff her, but she didn't jump or even cower. She only looked at him with chin quivering.

"Have it your way then," Redthorn sneered. "Let's go to the big space. Let's find out if most members of this warren don't have better sense than you numbskulls. Let's see if they don't want these inferior types out of here."

One by one the rabbits hopped out of the little den and into the corridor. Frafan and Janna — amazed, confused, and more than a little bit frightened — stood side by side, right where they'd faced Redthorn. Highopper's face reappeared in the entrance. He smiled at them.

"Come along, folks. When Mayberry said all were to attend he certainly meant to include you. You're the reason for it in the first place."

When they arrived at Gather Place, Frafan was certain that it was even more crowded than when he'd been led there, nearly frozen and blinded, just a few hours ago. He'd never seen so many rabbits all in one place, and he didn't think there would be room for him and Janna. The crowd moved aside for them, however, and Sweetbud came forward to lead them toward the far end of the big open space. There, through a forest of long, pointed ears Frafan could see Mayberry seated above the rest. As he got closer it became obvious that the reason the Governor was visible from everywhere in Gather Place was because he was seated on a thick and twisted root. The root belonged to one of the fallen trees that formed the foundation of the warren.

Mayberry was in charge, there was no question of that. Seated on his high place, flanked by Highopper and Longrass, all he had to do was clear his throat and the murmuring and chattering ceased. It was as though all the rabbits lost their breath at the same instant.

Janna and Frafan were guided to a spot in front of Mayberry and just off to his right side. It was an uncomfortable position for a number of reasons. Gather Place, large as it was, was already overwarmed by too many bodies. Squeezing into the forefront, being the center of attention, didn't make things any cooler. He could feel many eyes watching. Watching for what, Frafan thought? For fear? Hostility? Confusion? There were certainly some of all those emotions inside him just now. Here they were, he and Janna, far from home and family, among creatures not of their own kind, in a shelter not of their making or liking. Most assuredly there were friends here. But how many enemies?

Sweetbud seated herself between Longrass and Janna. Frafan motioned to his sister to sit down. Across the width of Gather Place, and to Highopper's left sat Redthorn and Milkweed. Milkweed gazed up at Mayberry while Redthorn fixed the squirrels with a malicious glare.

Heaps of food had been placed at random locations and four or five rabbits were seated around each, in a crescent, facing their leader. Dried buds, seeds of various kinds, strips of green tree bark, and fragrant grasses — the food hadn't been touched. Everyone was looking at Mayberry. His voice broke the uneasy silence.

"Cottontails of Great Woods Warren," he began, "and our honored treeclimbing visitors..." He smiled at Janna and Frafan but Frafan thought his smile was forced. "Earlier this day, after Frafan, brother of Ephran, joined us, I determined that it would be good to gather here to eat and talk. To talk to the brother and sister of Ephran, who is my friend, who is friend to all the forest. I thought to help them, as we might, by discussing what we know of the disappearance of the noble treeclimber and his mate, to determine if a further search during the cold season is wise. And if it is, how we might best aid the searchers. Those topics still require our thought and, I think, our advice. However, a related subject that demands more immediate attention has arisen."

Mayberry faced Redthorn, who glared back defiantly. Milkweed kept her face in the food in front of her, not eating, and near tears again.

"As you all know," Mayberry continued, "any in Great Woods Warren may ask for audience in Gather Place, on any matter he or she considers important to our well-being. Redthorn has made it plain that he thinks he has something significant to discuss."

Frafan had been surprised that the rabbits started nibbling and chewing while Mayberry spoke. Then he realized that there was nothing disrespectful about it. Eating was just as important as talking, in most instances probably more important. It rarely mattered a whole lot what was being said. Often as not, Assembly gave somebody a chance to gripe about what most everybody else thought was a minor dissatisfaction, usually a pet peeve or something. That sort of talk could be very boring to listen to for any length of time.

However, if one could chew on nice sweet seeds or chewy grass, the whole business was quite bearable. The system had to be different for a large group of rabbits in one big warren from what it was for squirrel families in scattered nests throughout the entire woods. The way the rabbits of Great Woods Warren did it was actually a good deal less distracting than having many groups all talking at once. For the rabbits these sorts of meetings were a nice community meal...and a good way to govern themselves besides. None of them would dream of giving up the right to speak directly to their brothers and sisters. Sorghum told Frafan that the speakers at Assembly invariably felt relieved after unburdening themselves of what was itching under their fur. Often there was no arguing at all, everybody ending up laughing and eating together. If the sermon got a bit too windy, Mayberry and Truestar had some unique and diplomatic ways to cut it short.

As Redthorn turned, the long scar running down his face became more obvious than ever. It gave him a sinister look and made Frafan shiver. The assembled cottontails continued to rummage around in the stacks of food, searching for their favorite seed or grass.

"No discussion necessary," Redthorn said. "We got a problem here, a plain and simple problem I could have settled by myself if not for all the interference." He scowled in Highopper's direction. "It's not news to any of you that we got two treeclimbers in our warren. Two treeclimbers taking up space, chewing up our food, and putting off a real strong and bad smell. A smell hunters could easily follow. Squirrels have no business here. I say they're a danger to us." He looked at Janna and Frafan. "I say they leave. And if they put up a fight, I'll throw them out on their ugly tails."

The rumbling sounds made by the cottontails' chewing vanished. Wide eyes and open mouths met Redthorn's rude suggestion. They all knew the squirrels faced a very good possibility of starvation if left to roam the bitterly cold and snow-clogged woods.

Fastrip got to his paws. With a nod Mayberry said, "You may speak, Fastrip."

"Redthorn," said Fastrip, quickly swallowing a mouthful of grass, "you know it is our way to offer shelter and food to those in distress. The longtails were caught in a snowstorm."

"We take in those like ourselves: rabbits," retorted Redthorn. "That's all we've ever taken in. Not birds. Not snakes. Not squirrels.

Squirrels can't repay the favor, even if they wanted to. Rabbits can't climb trees. Besides, whose fault was it that they came to be out in a storm? The female herself told us they left their home to pursue this crazy quest against the advice of their own father."

"That's not the idea," said Fastrip.

"Then the idea should be changed," said Redthorn.

Another cottontail straightened its hindlegs.

"Yes, Darkbush," said Mayberry.

"Redthorn makes a valid point," said the new rabbit. "We can't just start taking in every lost or troubled creature in the woods. We've all worked hard to make this warren as comfortable and safe as possible. We've spent countless hours searching for and collecting all these seeds and grasses, enough to last us the cold season."

A female called Fairchance stood and was recognized.

"We're not necessarily done collecting food," she said, in a high, sweet voice. "There will come another opportunity to find seeds and buds. Everyone will have enough to eat. What if the air turns warm again, as it often does, and the snow becomes water? Then we can all go out and..."

"What if it doesn't?" snapped Redthorn.

"Not your turn!" cried Fastrip, trying to maintain order.

"Shut your face!" Redthorn shouted at the Warden.

Suddenly Gather Place was bedlam. Everybody was talking at once. Some were shouting in their neighbor's ear, some appeared angry and ready to bite, some just looked concerned and upset.

Janna and Frafan squeezed their bodies close to the ground, wishing they could crawl into it, like earthworms. They were baffled and appalled at the arguing and shouting among these animals they had considered so gentle and helpful. And they were thoroughly dismayed at the realization they were the cause of the commotion.

Then a sharp, high-pitched whistle filled the air in Gather Place. The uproar stopped as quickly as it had started. The rabbits held their paws to their ears and squinted their eyes to shut out the painful noise. Frafan and Janna were startled and might have bolted if the room hadn't been so full of rabbits that there was no place to bolt.

The sound, they saw, came from Truestar, who seemed to be creating it by blowing through her forepaws.

In the following calm Mayberry spoke. "I think we have all heard enough to understand the issue," he said softly. "Redthorn wishes us to revoke our vow of hospitality, except for other rabbits. Not that is has been abused — the last time we took in a stranger is when we welcomed Redthorn himself."

A murmur rose from the crowd. Redthorn bared his teeth.

"Before we try to settle anything," continued Mayberry, "I want to ask some questions. I want to ask all of you if you think that the scent of rabbit is less likely to attract a hunter than the scent of squirrel. Which of us has drawn air through the long snout of the fox? Could it be that our fragrance is in our own noses?

"Do you think that Frafan and Janna are at ease here...even before this fracas in a nest built on the earth began? Would they choose this sort of dwelling if they had any choice?

"Concerning food: You know we have always collected more than we can eat. When the snow melts we invariably throw out a great deal of it."

Sweetbud stood up. "Father," she said, "before we decide on one matter, we should discuss the other."

"That is true," Mayberry said, "you may continue."

All the rabbits turned to the pretty young female.

"While Mayberry was showing our guests through the warren," Sweetbud began, "I went to my parent's nest, thinking I would find my mother. She was not there. I was about to leave when I heard voices in the passageway. The voices belonged to Redthorn and Milkweed. Redthorn was speaking loudly."

"What did he say?" asked Mayberry.

"Evidently he had already been at your nest, father. He said you were hiding from him. He told Milkweed that the treeclimbers must leave and he said he knew you would not make them leave because you had this unnatural friendship with their brother. He was trying to convince Milkweed that the two of them would have to take care of the problem themselves."

"Did Milkweed speak?" asked Mayberry.

"I did not hear her speak."

Redthorn glowered at Sweetbud. Milkweed looked stunned.

"Is that when you came to tell me of Redthorn's plans?" Mayberry asked softly.

"Yes. As soon as they moved away I came out into the passageway and found you."

Mayberry lifted his face to the assembled rabbits and said, "When Sweetbud told me what she heard I set out to find Redthorn. I wanted to warn him not to take matters into his own paws. We are all aware of our own rule: We could not survive if each of us did as he or she willed. In any case, I could not find him and I realized he and Milkweed must have gone to the guest den. I sent Highopper there, accompanied by some of the young bucks. Highopper, tell us what you found in the guest den."

Highopper, young, strong, and proud as his father, stood and faced the assembly. "I found Redthorn and the treeclimbers confronting each other. I heard Redthorn tell them to leave the warren..."

"This whole thing is ridiculous!" shouted Redthorn. "All of you...see what's going on here: your corrupt Governor's got his daughter and son to join him in an attempt to embarrass me. You can see right through their act, can't you? I know you all feel as I do. We should throw Mayberry and his family out of the warren, along with the treeclimbers..."

"Sit down and be silent," Mayberry said sternly.

Redthorn swirled to face Mayberry on his high seat and snarled, "You sit down and be silent yourself. I'll close your mouth for you."

With that, the big rabbit leaped at Mayberry. His size and great strength dislodged the Governor from the seat of honor — and tumbled him from the twisted root.

Into the High Branches

His size and great strength
dislodged the governor from the seat of honor

49

CHAPTER VII
REDTHORN'S VOW

Mayberry used the very ferocity of Redthorn's charge to his advantage. His body relaxed as he let himself be thrown from his high seat. As they fell together, he fastened his teeth on one of Redthorn's ears and set a forepaw into the thick fur on the attacker's neck. He jerked and twisted his head while pushing with his paw and, in the wink of an eye, succeeded in flipping his adversary around in midair.

Meanwhile, Redthorn's teeth found in Mayberry's neck a passive and yielding target into which he was unable to sink his fangs. His front legs grabbed at Mayberry, trying to hold him still, but it was too late. The Governor landed solidly atop Redthorn, rear legs planted firmly on the bigger buck's soft underbelly.

Redthorn lay very still, head tilted in an unnatural position, red juice trickling down the side of his face from the ear that was still clenched firmly in Mayberry's teeth. Even Frafan knew that a rabbit's most dangerous weapons were their powerful hindlegs. One quick thrust of Mayberry's could instantly disembowel Redthorn. The defiance in the big rabbit's surprised eyes was gone. The hate and jealousy were not.

"Redthorn, you fool, you've attacked the Governor!" said Fastrip, breaking the breathless silence. "You must know what this means."

"Yes," said the rabbit called Darkbush, "I cannot support so stupid a rabbit, one that would try to force his opinion on all of us in this fashion."

Redthorn snarled in reply.

"You have taken matters into paws that do not govern. You do not have our consent. You've challenged the one we have chosen our leader," said Fastrip.

The residents of Great Woods Warren gathered around the two rabbits lying on the dirt floor, only a hop away from Frafan and Janna, who stood, stunned and motionless.

A voice from the crowd said, "We are the ones who are supposed to decide!"

Another cried, "Yes! Let us decide!"

Still another shouted, "Fastrip, call for resolution."

Darkbush shook his head at Redthorn. "Not a good way to go about things, Redthorn. Not a good way at all," he said.

The Warden said, "Hear that, Redthorn? Your warrenmates want resolution. Do you have anything more to say?"

Redthorn impaled Fastrip with a scowl but his lips did not part.

Fastrip then turned to the hushed rabbits and, with a voice louder than one would have expected from so small a cottontail, said,

"Resolution has been called for! First I call for resolution concerning Redthorn's attack on our Governor and whether you support it. All in favor..."

A low hissing noise began, and became louder and louder, like thin streams of air traversing a narrow place. The sound, coming from the rabbits themselves, was eerie enough in the tense semi-darkness that it came to Frafan's mind that even a fox, had one sneaked unbeknownst into Gather Place, might have been frightened into full retreat.

"Is there anyone who expresses dissent of the Governor? Or who thinks that the treeclimbers ought to be expelled?" Fastrip looked from face to face, from one set of wide eyes to another. Except for Redthorn's occasional grunt, the entire warren was now as still as the forest on a dark and frigid night.

Fastrip then turned to the still-entangled rivals and announced, "I say to you, Redthorn, that Great Woods Warren, here assembled, resolves against you. It must be you, not the treeclimbers, who leaves this place."

Mayberry slowly released his hold on his opponent's ear and put his rear paws back on the earth. Redthorn scrambled to his paws and glared alternately at Fastrip and Mayberry. But he yet held his tongue.

"Milkweed...," said Mayberry, his eyes remaining fastened on Redthorn, "you are mate to this troublemaker and have remained at his side during his forbidden actions. However, you have not participated. As Governor I offer you the choice of rejecting Redthorn, as we have, and staying here, or of leaving with him. If you go, consider yourself banished."

A tear rolled down the doe's cheek. "Your words are hard, Mayberry," she said in a quavering voice, "but they are just. They are no harsher than what my mate has said." She looked about the rabbits collected in Gather Place and said, "I know some of you remember why Redthorn is here. Some of the younger ones may not know the real story. I think most of you have forgotten what he was like when he came..."

"Save your breath, Milkweed," muttered Redthorn, "they don't care about us."

Milkweed seemed not to hear him, but she did not continue her story. Instead she looked at her sister. Knowing what was coming, Truestar's eyes filled with tears.

"I must stay with my mate," Milkweed said, "regardless of what that means."

The young bucks who were to accompany Redthorn and Milkweed to the main entrance moved into place. Redthorn snapped at his mate, "Come! These fools deserve their corrupt Governor and whatever he brings down on them. Let's get out of here."

He hopped off, looking straight ahead, red juice already drying on his wounded ear. The crowd parted before him. Milkweed followed meekly, Truestar at her side. Janna and Frafan were ushered into the line of rabbits which moved slowly and silently down the long corridor. Evidently, as the wronged parties, they were to be among the witnesses at the expulsion of the wrongdoers.

"Mayberry!" he called.

By the time Frafan reached the main entrance, formed of large elm branches and concealed by thick bushes on both sides, Redthorn and Milkweed were well beyond the protection of the warren, hopping off into the bitterly cold woods. Just as the thought occurred to him that it was strange that they didn't even look back, Redthorn stopped and turned toward the entrance.

"Mayberry!" he called.

"I am here," came the answer.

"You have made my ear crooked, as I did yours," said Redthorn. "This time you win. But I want you to know I will not rest until I bring sorrow...to you and especially to these treeclimbers. You'll see that they were not worth the trouble."

With that the big buck grabbed the doe roughly by the fur on her shoulder as a sign to follow him. Milkweed looked back once more, misery clouding her eyes. Despite that, she turned up the path after her mate. A sob broke from Truestar. Frafan glanced at Mayberry. The Governor looked very, very tired.

"Mayberry," said Frafan, "I greatly regret that Janna and I ever found ourselves in this part of the woods."

"Why do you say that, Frafan?" asked Mayberry.

"Because you are one of the last creatures in the forest I would wish this sort of trouble on."

"Ah," sighed Mayberry, "don't take it too much to heart, little friend. You bear no fault in any of this."

"Did he really make your ear crooked?" asked Janna.

"That happened some time ago — when I did not expect him to attack. I vowed then I would not be surprised by Redthorn again."

"Though it may be none of my affair, I can't help wonder how a rabbit like that stayed in a place like this with the rest of you," said Frafan. "Everyone else here is so friendly and helpful and...well...sincere."

"When Redthorn first arrived here he seemed brave, reasonable, and capable. Milkweed met him in a nearby field where a flock of grouse were trying to drive her and another doe from what the birds felt was their feeding place. Redthorn fought and chased them away. Milkweed was very taken with him."

"He was her hero," Truestar murmured.

"Anyway," continued Mayberry, "this episode was not the first difficulty he's caused — for me or for Great Woods Warren. Actually,

53

some time after Milkweed brought him back here I discovered that he'd been driven from another warren. That's the reason he was alone when he came upon Milkweed and her friend. It wasn't long before he started trying to impose his ideas on all of us."

Mayberry closed his eyes and slowly shook his head, as though trying to shake a cobweb from his ears. "It is better that he is gone. I just feel badly for Milkweed."

"But he threatened you!" said Frafan.

"I'm afraid it is you, more than me, that he wants to see harmed," replied Mayberry. "His hate runs deep. He may think revenge will be sweeter if exacted on you two. Watch for him. In any case, he is full of threats. As it happens, so is the entire forest. I think we will concern ourselves with him no more."

"Where will they go?" asked Janna.

"I do not know for certain. Rumor has it Redthorn was Governor of a small warren far from here. As best we could piece together the story from rabbits of other warrens, he was a very strict and uncompromising leader. He was forced to fight for his position of leadership many times, which accounts for his many scars and scratches. Apparently, he was finally driven out by a young buck. He and Milkweed may try to go there, but I cannot think those rabbits would take him back."

Janna's curiosity was not satisfied. "How did gentle Milkweed ever end up with him?" she asked.

"My poor sister!" sighed Truestar. "She made few friends and was often lonely. I think in Redthorn she found all the things she was not — loud, brash, and self-assured. I don't know if that explains anything."

"You said he was uncompromising," said Frafan. "What did you mean?"

Mayberry frowned for a moment and said, "Redthorn insisted that rabbits were the only forest animals of any consequence. All others, he said, were inferior. He'd have nothing to do with any of them and he preached that if given a chance to multiply, rabbits could and would rule the forest. It is a shame, you know. He is brave. He could have been a friend, a real ally.

"In any case, the whole reason for the Assembly was to have been a discussion concerning your brother and his mate, and your search for them. Let us return to Gather Place."

When they once again assembled in Gather Place, the mood was somber. It took Fastrip and Sorghum with their loud and insulting banter, along with a clumsy caricature of a brawl that ended in a tangle of legs and ears, to break the tension. Before long the cottontails were again chewing, if not cheerfully, at least with a certain degree of contentment.

The shorttails seemed to recover from the violent fight and the eviction of their relatives rapidly enough so that, at first, Frafan was astonished by their apparent insensitivity. Then he remembered discussing, with father and mother, how outsiders might consider rabbits an unfeeling lot, and how that was a kind of built-in protection.

"They have so many enemies, you know," Jafthuh had said.

"More than we?" Frafan asked.

"Perhaps not more, but more that can reach them. They aren't able to climb into the branches, you know."

"They cannot afford to dwell long on those problems they cannot control," added Odalee. "They would waste their entire existence at it."

"Mayberry," said Janna, as she sorted through the pile of seeds in front of her, "you said you knew something of Ephran and Kaahli's disappearance."

"Yes, I did. I helped search for them."

"Do you think searching again, now, would be worthwhile?" asked Frafan.

"If you mean a large search party, covering the same ground around Great Hill, only now deep with snow, I don't think so. I cannot imagine that kind of search would be of any help...what one might expect to find. But if you mean to look for more information, for clues, to speak to Klestra, then perhaps..."

"Did you have a chance to speak to Klestra when you looked for Ephran and Kaahli?" asked Frafan.

"No, I did not see Klestra. The crows told my rabbits he was off on his own search, along with chipmunks and rabbits from Bubbling Brook Warren. They were on the far side of Great Hill."

"Did you learn anything?" Janna's face was hopeful.

"I learned a great deal, Janna. The search, by every kind of creature available that time of season, was a fantastic lesson in itself. I learned again what amazing things can happen if just one forest animal makes the rest of us realize that we are all here together, simply trying to survive, to be at peace...if just one tries to help others, without a selfish motive. But, of course, that's not what you mean by what I learned. I'm afraid what we learned about the disappearance itself is rather meaningless."

"Maybe fresh ears can find some meaning," offered Frafan.

"That is true. "I will tell you what I know and perhaps you can find a message," said Mayberry, settling back on his tail. "It happened, while we were looking for clues, we came upon an old female chipmunk. She was very frightened of our large search party of rabbits and crows. I am sure she had never seen so many creatures, who normally do not associate with one another, all together. I had not either. In any case, what she did say made it obvious that she had been awake and had witnessed many of the events that took place the day that Ephran and

Kaahli disappeared. And so, though I didn't like the fact that we were upsetting her, I felt we had to learn all we could. She became more and more agitated as we spoke of Many Colored Ones. Eventually she ran off, into her hollow branch, and wouldn't come out."

"Did she see anything important?" asked Janna excitedly.

Mayberry rubbed his crooked ear. "I do not feel she was a dependable witness, so I would not assign much significance to what she said. However, flustered as her chatterings were, I am certain she said The Many Colored Ones left our part of the woods that day with their thundersticks — nothing more."

CHAPTER VIII

PATH TO THE POND

Frafan!

Janna's shriek yanked him from soft dreams of green leaves and fresh acorns. He jumped to his paws, heart pounding and eyes unfocused. It took a moment to remember these quarters, the place they'd slept now these seemingly endless cold nights. In the pale light that came from above, Frafan turned to face, in succession: the entrance, Janna, and then all four corners. He looked for glaring red eyes, a scarred face and shoulder, and a newly bent ear. But there was no movement, no suspicious shadows, and no menace. He sighed with relief.

"What is it, Janna?"

"Ohhhh!" she screamed again. "Another one! And...why, it's water! There's water falling on me!"

Tail curled tight, she had rolled herself into a ball just beneath the ceiling, in a place where light entered the room. As he stepped toward her he felt a chilling twinge on his own back, a stab so sudden and so cold that it took his breath away.

"Yipe!" he cried.

They looked at one another wide-eyed, then at the roof. Their mouths went from circles, to smiles, to outright laughter. There was only one explanation for the water. It had to be coming from the opaque snowpack over their heads.

"Janna," Frafan said, "I think this water is very good news. Let's see what's happening outside."

During these past days, while the air in the forest had remained stubbornly frigid, Frafan had used the idle hours to explore the rabbit warren. He'd come to know where all the entrances were, even though at one time he'd been convinced that it would be impossible for a runner of branches to master such a maze. He and Janna had visited each of them every day. And every day they scanned the quiet and bitterly cold woods and gazed longingly up into the big branches around them. It had seemed the dormant forest was permanently locked in the grip of the cold season. Perhaps now, at last, that dominion had been broken. Perhaps the air had finally changed.

They scampered purposefully through the tunnels, racing for the nearest entrance. When they reached one, partly hidden by a broken branch with leaves still attached, they found Highopper already there. He smiled and greeted them.

"The air is warm!" said Janna, pushing her nose past Highopper.

"Well, I wouldn't go so far as to say 'warm,'" said Highopper, squinting at her, "but certainly not as cold as it has been. And look, the snow has shrunk."

Indeed it had. Only a few days ago, when a more-than-half-frozen Frafan had stumbled into Great Woods Warren, the air had been brutally cold. And if he'd been able to stand up on his hind legs, the snow would have reached all the way to his nose, even in those places where it lay smooth and undrifted. Now, wonder of wonders, warm air had already shriveled it to a little over half that depth!

The sun shone gloriously down through bare tree limbs, casting dark shadows on wet, sparkling snow. Though Frafan knew its promise might be fleeting, he couldn't help feeling elated at the brightness and warmth. Excitement and hope grew in his heart and, before he could utter a word, Janna said to him, "Let's find Mayberry and tell him that we're leaving."

"How wonderful!" he thought, "She must be able to read my mind!" He could have cried for joy.

They scampered down dim hallways and around corners until they came to Mayberry's nest. Inside they found Mayberry and Truestar, talking quietly, nibbling on a breakfast of crunchy seeds and partly dried bluegrass.

"Pardon us," said Frafan, as he stuck his head inside the cozy den.

"Well, good morning," Truestar greeted them. "Come join us. Share our day's first food."

"Thank you," said Janna, her nose filled with the fragrant aroma, "I suddenly feel very hungry."

The squirrels usually ate their first meal in Gather Place with the rabbits. They now had a special invitation to eat in the Governor's quarters. It was the only nest outside of Gather Place in which food was allowed. Except, of course, for those soft nests filled with newborn cottontails.

As Frafan scratched through the pile of vegetation, seeking his favorite kind of seed, he announced, "Have you seen? The sun warms the forest and shrinks the snow."

"Yes," said Mayberry. "We have seen. Truestar and I were in the woods earlier this morning."

"If this air stays around for a bit we will see the earth itself showing its brown face again," said Janna.

Truestar smiled. "I wouldn't risk much on that. But perhaps Fairchance will yet find herself collecting more food. Though we rarely need it, she loves to have an excuse to harvest things the warren might need."

"We too will again be able to find things to eat," said Frafan, looking into the female cottontail's soft brown eyes. "Which leads me to tell you this is a time both happy and sad. We must leave, you know, and return to the branches where we belong. Our being able to climb and run once more is because of you and your offspring. My sister and I are more grateful than I can say."

"We are happy for you and for what we could offer." Then she raised her eyebrows. "You are going home, aren't you?" asked Truestar.

Her question caught him completely off guard. Frafan looked at Janna in surprise and confusion. When he had mentioned "leaving", he hadn't even considered "leaving" for the den of Jafthuh and Odalee. The only place he was interested in "leaving" for was The Pond, the only chance he asked was to find his brother.

Did Janna want to go home? Most likely. The search had been anything but a rousing success. Father had been right. His misgivings about the whole affair should have been accorded more weight. Frafan knew he must not think only of what he wanted to do. It would not be fair to his sister. Things may just as well get worse if the search went on. The cold season had barely begun. There had always been a host of enemies out there, besides the cold and snow. And now there was one more, one with a scarred ear and shoulder.

"Janna," he asked softly, "would you like to leave for father and mother's den?"

"Well...I suppose so...if you do," she said, disappointment in her eyes.

"Ha! My wonderful sister!" he nearly shouted. "You don't want to go home! I can see it in your face. I can hear it in your voice. You want to go on with the search, don't you?"

"Oh yes!" she beamed. "I'm not ready to give up yet. I was afraid that you were."

Truestar tried to frown, but found herself joining Mayberry's grin as their little longtailed guests hugged and giggled and danced a little dance.

"You are brother and sister to Ephran," said Mayberry, "so I expected this would be your plan. And I would not attempt to convince you otherwise. I would only remind you that, this time in the seasons, the sun's smile can be as misleading as that of the fox. I hope you have some of Ephran's talent for reading the sky and the movement of air. I only wish there was more I could do. Before the big snowstorm I and many of this warren helped search this part of the woods. I would go out again but..."

Mayberry glanced at Truestar and she looked back with a sad expression. Janna and Frafan understood the struggle in Mayberry's heart. On one paw he desperately wanted to learn what happened to his good friends, and to help them, if that was possible. On the other paw, as they'd discussed in Gather Place, there was really no place left to look around here. The perilous cold season was upon them, and Mayberry was responsible for the safety and well-being of the entire warren. Great Woods Warren was peaceful, but that could change very quickly.

"Mayberry," Janna said, "you've done more than your share for this squirrel family. When he was lost, so long ago, you helped Ephran find his way. Now he's disappeared and you've searched this entire part of the woods for him. You rescued my brother and me from certain starvation...and from Redthorn. Now those of us from the nest of Odalee must carry on."

Mayberry slumped wearily, as though he had carried a heavy burden a long way. Truestar moved close and nuzzled his thickly furred shoulder.

"Janna is right," said Frafan. "You are a true friend. Our brother did not forget you and neither shall we. You'll be the first to receive word when we have some idea of what has become of Ephran and Kaahli."

They left the Governor's quarters then, Truestar and Mayberry hopping slowly along. They went with Janna and Frafan toward the warren entrance, the same one Frafan limped through the day he arrived.

"If it turns stormy again," said Truestar, "and you are near Great Hill, remember that two of our young nest in the warren near Bubbling Brook. They will provide food and shelter — just tell them you know us — and please don't take any foolish risks in your quest."

"Keep an eye out for hunters," said Mayberry, "and take your food only in places from which you can see in all directions."

The squirrels nodded and mumbled their understanding. Frafan winked a secret little wink at Janna in the dark corridor. These dear and concerned cottontail sounded very much like father and mother.

They came to the entrance. Sunlight streamed into the darkness. Frafan and Janna turned to the rabbits one last time.

"We cannot truly thank you as we ought...," Janna began. Then she could speak no more. Truestar held her close.

"She means that speech isn't adequate to express our feelings," Frafan continued for his sister, despite a growing lump in his own throat, "but we can only tell you once more how much we appreciate everything you've done."

"For what we could share, you are most welcome," said Mayberry. "We wish the best of all things to you."

Frafan and Janna turned, scampered down the slushy rabbit track, wet snow splashing on their bellies. They jumped to the slender trunk of a young ash tree. After being on the ground and enclosed in the dark corridors and nests of the rabbit warren for what seemed such a very long time, the feeling they had as they reached the higher branches was nothing short of bliss. The brisk air was clean and fresh. It filled their

Into the High Branches

He raised his paw in salute
and Mayberry shouted "Find them!"

61

noses with a cool and invigorating sweetness. The sparkling and cloudless blue sky above soared away, over the treetops, in every direction they looked.

With an ear-to-ear grin, Frafan glanced back to the warren entrance, almost invisible unless you knew it was there, and to the two small figures far below, nearly lost in shadow. He raised his paw in salute and Mayberry shouted to him:

"Find them!"

* * * * *

"Do you think we're getting near The Pond yet?" Janna asked.

They hadn't traveled far, but the lazy days and nights in the rabbit warren had taken their toll. Their legs became weary very quickly, and they had stopped to rest again, this time at the base of a hill thickly wooded with elm and maple.

Frafan suspected that his sister's question was asked partly out of concern. She didn't want to be caught in another storm. He didn't either, of course. He thought they would both feel safer once they arrived at Ephran's nest, and at the same time realized he had no good reason to feel that way.

"I'm sure we're more than halfway there," he said, trying to keep the uncertainty out of his voice.

Janna looked at him hopefully.

Phetra's experience in having traveled the path to Great Hill was sorely missed. Frafan wished he and his brother would have discussed their planned route in more detail. Being able to interpret movement or changes in the sun, clouds, and air was a really valuable thing to be able to do and he was pleased that Ephran had taught him how. However, now he and Janna were at the stage where they needed more than general directions. Now they were looking for one particular hill, one particular pond. Yes indeed, recognition of one of those familiar landmarks would be very nice just now.

He would have asked more questions, naturally, but when the four of them started out from Phetra's den, they planned (or maybe just hoped), that they'd be together when the search got this far. And when they parted company that frigid day near Great Woods Warren they were all too cold to think clearly. Besides, Frafan hadn't imagined he'd need directions to go anywhere; he'd been quite certain he was just about done breathing. He knew Phetra and Roselimb had thought the same thing.

The sun was nearly halfway along its shortened path through the sky. Bright yellow beams reflected off the melting snow at an angle, making it difficult to look open-eyed at anything.

"Frafan," Janna's voice interrupted his thoughts, "what is that big mound over there?"

He squinted in the direction she pointed, toward a large and irregular hump arising from the earth. There were no trees nearby and the hump rose like a little mountain in the midst of a snowcovered clearing.

"Very interesting," said Frafan. He knew his comment did nothing to enlighten Janna, but there wasn't much else to say. He'd never seen anything like it before. "Let's go closer."

They moved away from the glare of the sun, getting as close as they could without leaving the trees. The mound was not snow. The snow that had fallen onto it or blown into it had melted. It was multicolored — gray and black, dull reds, pale blues and browns. It was made up of many large objects, some distinctly rounded, some angular...

"Stones!"

Janna put into words what Frafan was thinking. They were looking at a very sizeable pile of rocks! Only then did he hear the gentle sound of running water, water tumbling over smaller stones. Like one bolt of bright lightning following another, in an instant Frafan remembered...

"Rocky Point!" he shouted, with more enthusiasm than he'd shown since the beginning of the search.

Janna, concern they were lost growing by the moment, looked at her brother with dismay and confusion. This burst of excitement over a pile of stones was most unnatural.

"Rocky Point, Janna!"

Then, seeing she was perplexed, as quietly and slowly as he could he said, "Don't you remember Ephran's stories? Rocky Creek? Rocky Point? Water tumbling over stones? We've found it!"

"That's wonderful, I'm sure," Janna replied slowly, peering hard at the rocks, as though waiting for them to do something spectacular and amazing, like jumping up on flinty legs, beckoning to the treeclimbers, and then running off in the direction of The Pond.

"You don't remember, do you? I suspect you fell asleep while he was talking. Well, my dear sister, this is indeed a most wonderful discovery because, you see, Rocky Point is on Rocky Creek and..."

Janna leaned toward him. "Yes...what about Rocky Creek?"

"Rocky Creek, for your information, is connected to The Pond!" he said triumphantly.

"You mean...?"

"Of course," he crowed, "all we have to do to find Ephran's nest is to follow this happy little stream right to The Pond!"

They hugged and laughed. He tried to imitate the gurgling of the stream and they laughed and hugged again.

They set out once more, with lighter steps. Ice glittered along the banks of the creek and among the stems of wilted or sleeping bushes and bullrushes that stood in the cold water. Back from the shoreline, unnoticed by the happy treeclimbers, was another collection of rocks. That collection was not just a random heap of stones however. Something or someone had painstakingly arranged them to form a rectangular wall. The nearly snowless area encompassed by those rocks would have been obvious had they chanced to glance that way. It was too bad they didn't. Then again, they probably would not have seen the glittering eyes that watched their every move anyway.

They passed a little meadow of long, bowed grass, still partly buried in snow that had drifted thickly among the stems. On their other side stood bunches of tall wildflowers, heads brown and bent, no longer able to lift once bright and radiant faces to the distant ball of fire.

Brother and sister traveled along, initial exhilaration at finding Rocky Creek slowly eroded by the solitude of the woods around them. Now that they were more at ease about being on the right path — and all their attention was not diverted toward a search for landmarks — the unnatural quiet of the forest intimidated them. Not so much as a blackbird or a starling screeched from deserted thickets of tall weeds. No frogs croaked from the frozen wetland. Even the splashing of water as it tumbled over the uneven streambed seemed louder than it should. The sun's smile was indeed false; the warm season was gone.

While Frafan kept glancing from side to side, thinking and wondering about everything he saw, Janna stuck to business and kept her eyes on the path ahead. "Look, Frafan, Rocky Creek splits in two!"

He looked up. So it did. One problem followed in the pawprints of another! Ephran had not mentioned a fork in the stream. Which one led to The Pond? One of the waterways seemed to cut, with a certain air of authority, through the trees to their left. Going that way would be following, more or less, the same general route they'd been traveling. The other branch meandered off in nearly the opposite direction, toward the place from which came the warm winds. The decision seemed obvious.

"Frafan, we can't afford to take the wrong path. We don't have the time." Janna glanced at the cloudless sky. "Anyway, it's clear that we should follow the stream going the direction we've been traveling. It gives me the feeling that it knows where it's going."

Frafan frowned at the water. "It may know where it's going, but the water doesn't," he whispered to himself.

"What?" she said. "What are you mumbling about?"

"Look at the water, Janna."

At first it meant nothing to her. Then she realized that the water in the streambed she wanted to follow was very nearly still, maybe trying to run toward her, while the water in Rocky Creek was traveling away. Then she understood; the running water itself, not the streambed, was showing them the way! Water in this stream was supposed to flow into The Pond, not out of it.

They set out, turning sharply with the stream that bent away from their path. They passed another meadow, this of long, wind-blown prairie grass, broken sow thistle, and deserted and leafless bushes. Now and again, in the willowy branches, a tiny and forlorn bird's nest might be seen. Then, just as Janna was about to ask, for the sixth time, how far he thought they might have to go, something ahead glistened.

Through the naked trees was a small body of water, sparkling like dew drops in the cold late afternoon sunlight. When they saw it, at the same time, they could only look at one another. Voices could not be trusted. Frafan's heart fluttered. There was no doubt; this had to be the place. This had to be Ephran's Pond.

Sometimes there's answers.
Sometimes there ain't.
Never hurts t'ask the question.

Rennigan, from his nest on High Hill

CHAPTER IX

KLESTRA'S STORY

H ello!

The voice belonged to a male red squirrel, who appeared unexpectedly on a decrepit box elder tree. He eyed the gray squirrels alertly, perching himself on a dry branch attached to the tree by a flimsy strand of bark. Frafan and Janna's first impulse was to ignore the little troublemaker, as father had taught them, and continue to look for Ephran's nest. Old notions clouded their minds...and for a moment they forgot who they'd come looking for in the first place.

Memory jogged, Frafan answered, "Hello to you of red fur. Might you be who I think you are?"

"That's a very strange question," replied the red squirrel. "The answer, I believe, is I being who you think I should be has the same likelihood as you being who I think you must be."

"You're Klestra!" cried Janna.

"Yes, I am Klestra. And, unless I'm very wide of the mark, you are the kin of Ephran."

"I'm Janna, one of Ephran's second sisters, and this is..."

"I know," Klestra interrupted, beaming at them, "I can guess who this is. This would be Frafan, second brother of Ephran: observer, searcher, teacher, and explorer. Ephran talked a great deal about both of you. I would not have had the courage to send word with the crows had I not felt as though I knew you. Welcome to The Pond and to..." Klestra hesitated for a moment and his smile faded. "...our home."

He took a quick breath and said, "Come, I'm sure you're tired and hungry. We will go to the nest of Ephran and Kaahli. It is large and tightly woven...a good place to eat and talk. Ephran liked to say that he thought he constructed a good nest until Kaahli made it better."

Klestra led the way through unadorned trees and along the edge of The Pond, where the water had frozen into a thin, sparkling sheet. Many muskrat dens were visible, scattered here and there. Like everything else, they looked deserted. One could only imagine how wonderfully bright and cheery this place might be during the warm season. Now it was quiet and desolate. Frafan suddenly felt a flood of relief that they'd found Klestra. Or that he'd found them.

There were so many things to look at, to try to remember. Ephran had described all of this. There was The Hedge...the duck nest...Great Hill, of course...and before he knew it the next tree held a squirrel's nest. Ephran's home.

The nest was big and solid, tucked securely in the crotch of three large boughs. Janna's attention was drawn to what she first thought was a slender and discolored leaf, hanging dejectedly near the entrance to the nest. As they moved closer she realized it was a feather.

"We'll all fit comfortably," Klestra reassured them, as he led the way into the nest. "You'll be happy to know there are many nuts and seeds inside. I did a little relocating, from where Kaahli had hidden a great many of them near the tree's roots."

"Do you stay in Ephran and Kaahli's nest now?" asked Janna.

"Sometimes. When I'm on this side of The Pond. I keep hoping that I'll wake up one morning and... Well, come inside."

The nest was spacious, much larger than their den near Corncrib Farm. The walls and floor were thick and firm, supported by heavy limbs outside. Though neither Frafan or Janna had spent much time in other squirrels' homes, and even though they'd never been inside a nest constructed of nothing but sticks and leaves, this nest felt as solid and secure as any tree den they could imagine.

"This seems very much like our nest in Great Woods Warren," Janna said to Frafan.

"Yes it does," he agreed, "only it feels much better to be up and away from the earth."

Klestra cocked his head at them. "Are you speaking of Mayberry's warren?"

"Yes," said Frafan. "Do you know it?"

"I know where it is. I've been that way a few times. You sound as though you've been inside."

"That we have. We spent quite some time there actually. After the big storm. When the air became so cold."

"You stayed in a rabbit warren?" asked Klestra.

"Not much choice," said Janna. "It was very interesting. And, as it turned out, almost as dangerous as the woods itself."

Klestra shook his head. "I don't know why I'm surprised. You are brother and sister to Ephran, after all. Later I will have to hear all about this. And about Mayberry and Truestar."

It was dark in the nest until Klestra, standing on a barkless branch protruding from the wall, opened a most ingenious flap of interwoven sticks, vines, and wild grape leaves that made up part of the roof. It was much like Blackie's door in the den of her Many Colored Ones at Corncrib Farm, thought Frafan, only this door opened to the sky, not the earth. And it opened only a little way, but enough to let in just the right amount of light and brisk outside air.

"How clever!" Janna remarked.

"Whose idea was that?" asked Frafan.

"I'm not certain," said Klestra. "It could have been either's. They built such a fine nest that a tree den was really unnecessary. I wish they wouldn't have felt the need to find one. Anyway, I didn't know about this opening to the sky until I came in here after Ephran and Kaahli left..."

"Left? You think they just 'left'?" interrupted Frafan, a surprised look on his face. He wasn't sure if it was a question or a statement.

"I guess I don't know what to think," said Klestra. "I suppose I said 'left' because that's what I hope happened." He rubbed his nose. "Anyway, I'm puzzled and fresh out of ideas. That's why it's so good of you to come. I especially appreciate it because I know how dangerous a long trip through the woods can be. I purposely avoided mentioning to the crows that I wanted someone here. It's very unfortunate most of Ephran and Kaahli's friends are either asleep or have flown far away. Though I must admit I don't know if having all the birds and animals of the forest here would help solve this mystery."

He rambled on. He seemed to be thinking aloud, a funny little habit Frafan recognized. Clearly, Klestra needed someone besides the impassive crows to talk to. Even more than sympathy for his agitation, which Frafan and Janna certainly had, they felt a sense of wonder. This animal, member of a family known to be unfriendly if not downright hostile toward gray squirrels, most surely loved Ephran and Kaahli as much as any brother or sister could.

"Can you tell us what happened here, Klestra?" Janna said softly.

Klestra cleared his throat, collecting his thoughts. He peered up at the rapidly waning light coming in through the trapdoor in the ceiling, lay down an acorn from which he'd taken one bite, told Janna and Frafan to help themselves from the many nuts on the floor of the nest, and began his story.

"It was the day of the first snow. I remember that clearly. Ephran and I had gone over Great Hill to look for a tree den. I guess Ephran and Kaahli thought they'd feel safer if they had solid wood around them. In any case, after we got to the other side, Ephran decided he wanted Kaahli along, to help pick a tree. So we came back to get her. That's when we saw two Many Colored Ones, only a few jumps from this very nest. I suppose They were the same Ones who'd been here before, the Ones who hurt Cloudchaser, Ephran's mallard friend, and caused him to fly into Lomarsh...the Ones who took Cloudchaser's son away with Them."

Klestra took a deep breath. "Anyway, They carried thundersticks. Kaahli was trying to hide from Them. They would surely have found her if Ephran hadn't purposely distracted Them. He ran away through the branches, chattering like a snapping turtle had him by the tail..." Klestra chuckled quietly but his eyes were sad. "The Many Colored Ones followed, running along the ground, pointing their thundersticks up into the branches, making an awful racket.

"Kaahli and I watched him run and jump. It was something to

see, I can tell you, even for treeclimbers who are used to such things. His jumps were so long and smooth. So very graceful. He nearly flew..."

Klestra looked at them with a tight smile. "Your brother wanted very much to fly, you know. But it turned out he couldn't. He was far away when he fell. If there would have been leaves on the trees we wouldn't even have been able to see him fall."

Klestra's voice cracked. Without shame he wiped both eyes with the backsides of his paws. He picked up the acorn again, took a small bite, and chewed slowly.

"I suppose all of this is a waste of time," he finally said. "I had no business sending the crows to you. Animals of the forest..." He cleared his throat again and said more loudly than he needed to, "Animals of the forest fall every day. And are never seen again. I know that. I just can't accept the fact that Ephran and Kaahli are gone."

"Can you remember anything else?" asked Janna.

"Not much. I went to look for him of course. After The Many Colored Ones went away. When I came back I found that Kaahli's mind had closed. Her eyes saw things only in other places. Other times. She would not speak to me. I had to lead her back to her own nest. And I wasn't in much better shape than she, I'm afraid. I was so upset and confused I'm not even sure I looked for Ephran in the right place."

"Did you find any...any red juice...or anything?" asked Frafan.

"No, no juice, but it was snowing, you see. Everything was covered with a layer of snow. The only strange thing, now that I think back, was a bright green feather caught in the branches of a gooseberry bush. I thought at the time it was such a rare and unlikely green among the bare brown branches and white snow. Kaahli would have loved it. I suppose it had been there since the warm season."

"Did you see if The Many Colored Ones took anything with Them when They left?" asked Janna. She was hoping that the crows' message had not left out a terrible fact and that Mayberry's frightened chipmunk had not been mistaken.

"They searched for a while, I believe, but at the time They left I was trying to comfort Kaahli and get her back to the nest. I have no idea what The Many Colored Ones took with Them."

The squirrels sat and ate silently, preoccupied with their own thoughts. Klestra wanted to be sure he hadn't left anything out of his tale, no clue that might be helpful. Frafan and Janna tried to digest what they'd just heard.

"The crows and I searched until it grew dark, far away and over Great Hill," said Klestra. "We finally gave up when we could not see. I came back to be with Kaahli. To my amazement there was no sign of her in the nest or anywhere about. I've been looking for both of them ever since."

"Mayberry and a good part of his warren were here looking too, you know," said Janna.

"Yes, I know. We looked in different places. I had no chance to speak to him. The crows carried messages between us, but there was precious little to tell."

Klestra heaved another deep and melancholy sigh. "I don't think any purpose would be served by looking around Great Hill anymore. This whole area has been explored better than the inside of a walnut in the paws of a starving treeclimber. Maybe there's no use to search anywhere. Any of us could have walked right by him..." Klestra swallowed hard. He struggled to find his voice.

"Any of us could have walked right by his snow-covered body and not even seen it. You know, if it was just Ephran gone, and there had been no word for this long a time, the conclusion would be obvious. But Kaahli's disappearance, there's the real puzzle! The Many Colored Ones were long gone by the time she disappeared. I keep asking myself: was she so grief-stricken that her mind gave up? Did she run off, thinking to join her mother? Did she just wander off in a daze? I can't understand it."

"Or...," said Frafan, "might she have set out to find her father?"

Klestra sat up with such an expression of surprise Frafan wondered for a moment if he might have been bitten on the backside by a large beetle. He dropped his acorn.

"That's it!" he cried. "Of course! Why didn't I think of that? I forgot completely about her father. That is precisely what she must have done! Where else would she go to seek help and advice? She must have set out for the peaceful Spring...to find Aden!"

CHAPTER X

AMBUSH IN THE ROCKS

Klestra was so excited it took both Frafan and Janna to calm him and persuade him it was foolishness to even consider starting out for The Spring before morning. The more he chattered the more he convinced himself that, not only had Kaahli probably set off for that peaceful place where the water came from the earth, but she had most likely followed Ephran. Ephran, perhaps confused, perhaps slightly injured by the thundersticks, must have run off in that direction.

Why else would she leave without telling her friends where she was going? What sight, other than her beloved mate, body yet filled with breath, could inspire her so that she would scamper off in such eager haste? Indeed, what else?

Janna scratched her ear and thought it sort of fit together. Although the whole business seemed a bit far-fetched, even Frafan began to think it was at least a reasonable theory. Especially if Ephran had been stunned by the thundersticks. Anyway, none of them could come up with a better explanation. Not unless they admitted the thing they didn't want to admit.

They stayed in the nest of Ephran and Kaahli that night. It turned out to be a most restless night. Another leg of their journey was about to be undertaken at a time when most everyone, except hunters, was sound asleep or far away in warmer places. It really didn't make a whole lot of sense, this chasing wild ideas around the forest, but then that's precisely what Jafthuh had told them. In any case, they'd come this far...and the puzzle was still far from solved. If anything, the search had become more confusing. At least now they'd be traveling with Klestra. The red squirrel had some familiarity with the territory. Food and shelter shouldn't be a problem. Not unless they had to go beyond the landmarks he knew.

These thoughts, along with many others, tumbled through Frafan's mind and filled most of the dark hours. He knew he wasn't alone in his worries.

They woke from fitful sleep to find the air outside the nest moving in great gusts, swirling around the tree trunks. Showers of crisp leaves, freed from ice and snow, and swept away from sheltered resting places among thick-stemmed sumac and gooseberry bushes, skittered in frenzied, rustling vortices along the forest floor. No hint of blue could be seen through the sullen gray clouds moving rapidly overhead. It seemed cheerful days and perilous missions did not keep company.

Frafan and Janna followed Klestra along the shore of The Pond, they in the high branches, he in the low. It was, at the same time, both thrilling and depressing for Frafan to realize that he was traveling the same route, through the very same branches, where Ephran had placed his paws so many times. Where had he stopped to rest? Which bough did he favor? What did he look at as he passed this way?

Ahead, not far from the frozen shoreline, four crows perched in the limbs of a young birch, their jet black feathers a stark contrast to the pure white tree. As the squirrels drew closer Frafan and Janna recognized Kartag and Mulken.

"Halloo, forestwatchers!" Klestra hailed them.

"Eeyah, treek limers," said one of the crows.

"Mulken! Kartag! Do you remember us?" asked Janna. Frafan thought her greeting was more a matter of pride that she recognized them than it was delight at seeing those bearers of sad tidings.

"Yes, smalt reek limer, weem ember," said Mulken.

"Haf only theestew young cumtu serchfer ther own?" asked Kartag.

Before either of the gray squirrels could answer, Klestra said, "They will be sufficient."

"Where duther two?" Mulken asked.

"The other two? Oh, you mean Phetra and Roselimb! They went back to their nest," said Frafan.

"Ummm. Las track you'n greats torm," said Mulken.

"You lost track of us? We didn't even know you were watching us!" Janna was incredulous.

"You not spected knoweewatch..." Kartag almost smiled. "'Less we wishuknow."

Klestra was of the opinion that crows' reports regarding activities in the forest, valuable as they could be, were generally haphazard, often inaccurate, and sometimes more than a bit exaggerated. They liked a good story. And if it wasn't exciting enough, they'd spice it up. He wondered how Janna, if she was paying any attention to what was going on, could miss a large black bird flapping around in the sky or perched on bare tree limbs. Crows would have a hard time hiding this time of season, even if they wanted to. He interrupted their boasting.

"Have you any news for us?" he asked.

"Weef no worduf Ephran," said Kartag.

"No hunter in disp artuf woods," added Mulken.

"Thank you," said Klestra. "If you see anything we should be made aware of we will be traveling up Rocky Creek to a place called The Spring."

The crows nodded soberly.

Kartag said, "We will knowhere u'are."

The squirrels left the crows as they found them, feathers fluffed out against the cold wind. They came to the place where Rocky Creek emptied into The Pond. Klestra showed them his tree and Janna thought how untidy, yet relaxing and peaceful, the whole area around his den looked. Any passing hunter would certainly be aware that a red squirrel had a home nearby. Klestra evidently didn't care, maybe because he wasn't there most of the time. They had no urge to linger, but immediately set out along the waterway, retracing Frafan and Janna's steps of yesterday.

Lunch was provided from one of Klestra's food caches near the stream, this one carefully hidden near a huge rotted elm stump at the edge of the forest. Although a few stale and soggy hickory nuts were dug out of the hole, pinecones made up the main course, and Klestra attacked them hungrily. Frafan and Janna were not especially excited about pinecones, but they ate gratefully, knowing they could not afford to be choosy at the beginning of this most menacing time, the very long and dreary cold season.

All conversation and chewing ceased when, at the same time, they detected the far-off "OUNK, OUNK" of a flock of white swans. The treeclimbers sat very still, eyes and ears directed to the sky. Then the huge birds appeared, soaring gracefully over the treetops near The Meadow. They flew in two ragged formations, mighty wings pushing them through the air. Their long necks stretched toward warmer water far away, while cold gusts pushed against their tailfeathers. They called back and forth to one another with a cry so utterly wild and absolutely forlorn it made Frafan shiver. The sky behind them would be empty.

The passing of the swans left everyone feeling a bit depressed. The lack of sunshine didn't help matters. They moved along the creek in silence for a while, sometimes forced to stop and close their eyes — when an especially strong gust of wind whipped through the trees, cutting them with shards of dried leaves and crystals of ice.

"Frafan, what is that sound that hurts my ears?"

He hadn't been paying much attention, talking to himself, trying to imagine other possibilities to explain what could have happened to Ephran and Kaahli. Janna's question brought him back to attention. He picked up his ears.

She did indeed hear something out of place. Above or through the restless whistling of the wind came an intermittent high-pitched screech, carried to them on the blustery air. He looked to Klestra, whose wide-eyed attention was focused on the wavering cry. It seemed to be coming from somewhere just ahead.

"Rabbit," Klestra finally said.

"Rabbit?" Janna repeated, not understanding.

"Yes, the crying. It's a rabbit," said Klestra.

"Are you certain?" asked Frafan, finding the sinister shriek very unrabbitlike.

Klestra ignored him initially, intent on listening especially closely the next time the wind brought the eerie sound. There it was again!

"That's what it is all right," Klestra said grimly, nodding his head slowly, "that's the sound they make when they're trapped or hurt."

Though they glanced at one another for agreement, there was never any doubt they would have to interrupt the search. It was what Ephran would have done.

Rocky Point was only a short distance ahead, and the closer they got the more certain they became that the squeals were coming from that fallow place. They were nearly at the end of the trees. A bar of stones stretched in front of them. The lament came to their ears once more, weaker this time.

Frafan tried to locate the origin of the cries, hoping they weren't coming from the barren area just ahead. There was only a bit of scattered vegetation here, a few wispy tufts of stiff and frozen grass and some type of stunted bush.

The place lived up to its name. It was dominated by rocks...rocks of all sizes and shapes. A thick carpet of pebbles ran down to, and well into, the water. The pile of massive boulders, high as a young sapling, Frafan and Janna remembered seeing earlier. Immovable that stack of stones stood, as it may have from ages past, just beyond the outjutting of land that gave Rocky Point the second part of its name.

Back to their left, along a high ridge of earth, there was a grouping of rocks of considerable size. All eyes focused there as a feeble whimper, barely more than a part of the wind's whistling, now most definitely came from the midst of those rocks.

The ridge was well away from the water and a good distance from any trees as well. Not so much as a spruce grew close enough to afford an overview of who or what was hidden by the great stones.

They had come this far. There was no need to discuss what had to be done next. They hesitated only a moment before leaving the branches. Frafan and Janna followed Klestra as he ran down the trunk of a sturdy little poplar tree and onto the flinty soil.

They approached the roughly circular cluster of rocks as cautiously as they could. Many of these boulders were large enough to hide any number of hunters. And every step took them further and further from safety in the branches.

The crying had ceased. There was no sound save the moaning of the wind, brushing rough granite and sandstone.

The massed rocks formed a wall. The manner they fit together, flat edge to flat edge, concave to convex, seemed unnatural to Frafan. But then, nothing about this place, devoid of beloved trees, seemed quite right. Unless one wished to think of scrambling over the wall, there appeared, from this angle at least, to be only one place where the boulders were far enough apart to allow passage beyond. The time for caution was over. What thought of prudence might have remained was thrown to the gusty wind. All three ran together, through the opening.

They found themselves in an oblong fortress of mosscovered boulders, surrounded by walls from five to seven taillengths in height. There were gray rocks, red rocks, and blue rocks, one atop another, bigger near the earth, smaller at the top. Gaps, like missing teeth, appeared in the upper row, holes where stones had fallen and rolled to a more stable resting place. Here and there bunches of now-frozen grass had grown from under the protection of those that had fallen.

Laying in front of a long, undulating hillock against one side of the enclosure was the object of their concern, the apparent source of the pitiful screams. A very large male rabbit raised himself from his huddled position against the earth and stood on his forelegs. The expression on his face was not one of pain or surprise. It was anything but the sort of expression they would have expected. It could only be described as a sneer, and it appeared on the rabbit's face just as the squirrels' mad dash into the stone-surrounded arena came to a confounded, skidding halt.

For the shortest part of a moment Frafan and Klestra had the same thought: the crooked ear was the mark of the Governor of Great Woods Warren. But Klestra could not know, and Frafan momentarily forgot, another cottontail now bore that scar.

Janna's gasp was clearly audible in this quiet place, protected as it was from the whistling wind. And the horror on her face ignited his memory.

"Redthorn!" breathed Frafan.

A bewildered Klestra looked at his unbelieving companions, at the grinning rabbit, and back again to Frafan and Janna.

"You know this cottontail?" he asked.

"We didn't have time to tell you...," began Frafan.

"Oh, they know me all right," said Redthorn.

Klestra felt excluded, almost as though he was invisible. The rabbit's attention was fixed on the gray squirrels, and theirs on him.

"Are you hurt?" asked Klestra, trying to break the obscure and frightening preoccupation the cottontail and his friends had with each other.

Redthorn's evil gaze shifted to the little red squirrel and he said, "What is a red treeclimber doing running with grays? Figures, I guess. Inferior species attract one another." He lifted his nose. "To answer your question: No, I'm not hurt. Your worthless friends, and even more worthless you, are the ones who are going to be hurt."

"Why...?" began Klestra, but he was interrupted by Frafan.

"Do you mean to fight all of us?" asked Frafan. No doubt the big cottontail was a match for any one squirrel and maybe even two. But three separate battlefronts would be very difficult to cover.

"Fight? Are you all looney?" asked an increasingly agitated Klestra, "Why in the Great Green Woods would you want to fight?"

"I don't plan to bother myself much with any of you. I'm going to have help, you see," said Redthorn.

Just as the words left his tongue they all heard another curious sound on the restless air. Holding their breath, straining, they recognized what it was at the same moment. Barking! There was only one animal that Frafan knew of that sounded like that. A dog was moving in their direction, and it must be moving very fast!

Klestra knew full well what a dog was. He was much more a traveler than were his friends, and he'd seen his share of dogs. He'd always dismissed them as "hunters without teeth." Not that he thought their mouths were empty except for their tongue — he called them that because the dogs he'd seen were noisy and apparently careless. They almost never looked up into the trees, probably because they were unable to climb. However, since the nearest tree was just now a good distance away, the menace of a dog closing in on them took on new and grave significance.

Janna and Frafan had not seen a dog, but they knew a little about them. Blackie had made reference to them, usually rather unkind remarks. Ephran and Mianta had spoken about this sort of animal in general and had described one dog in particular... right down to some fascinating imitations of the barking noises it made.

"I don't know what this is all about, or what it is you have against us," said Klestra, as the barking grew louder and louder, "but those stones are too big and slippery for us to climb easily and you have no chance of leaping over them. If the dog comes in here, you will be trapped just as surely as we are."

"I take it the gray longtails haven't told you about their misadventures in the rabbit warren, have they?" This time Redthorn was speaking directly to Klestra. "Too bad. Not surprising, though. They sure didn't do anything there to brag about. Through their own stupidity they interfered where they weren't wanted and endangered a peaceful family of cottontails. I really don't have the time to explain it all just now. And I'm afraid you won't survive to hear about it later.

"As to my getting trapped in here by the dog, I think not." With that, Redthorn moved aside just enough to allow the flustered squirrels a glimpse of a sizeable black hole in the ridge of earth behind him.

"You see? I have a shelter in the earth. One that treeclimbers would not dare enter. Even if they found courage enough to run under the ground, I will be down there, in a narrow tunnel, to greet them."

Action was called for, but surprise and confusion numbed their minds and paralyzed their legs.

Just as the dog reached the opening in the rocks, puffing and panting, the air was pierced by an agonized squeal of pain. The wild cry filled the rocky arena and so startled the animals they froze where they stood.

The scream, Frafan realized, had burst from Redthorn's throat. This time he was not pretending. He was no longer trying to bait the trap.

A very large badger had appeared in the hole behind the rabbit. The ferocious hunter had evidently been awakened from delicate sleep by Redthorn's faked cries. Powerful jaws were locked on the cottontail's right hindquarter. The badger's eyes were tightly closed against the showers of dirt and pebbles being kicked up by the rabbit's free left hindleg.

The badger tugged mightily, attempting to drag Redthorn into the deep, dark recesses of its den while the cottontail, stunned and terrified, tried to escaped the viselike grip. Despite Redthorn's respectable size and strength, the struggle seemed desperate, painful, and futile. It would have been just that if it weren't for help, help given by the very individual upon whom Redthorn had counted.

With two long leaps, the dog sailed over the heads of the befuddled squirrels, toward Redthorn who was silently but rapidly losing the struggle for his breath, to the entrance of the badger den. Without hesitation, and with a dull thump, the dog's paw came solidly down on the badger's scalp.

The dog's claw raked across the flat skull, pulling out tufts of black and white fur. With a violent shake of its massive head, the badger opened eyes and mouth at the same time. The red liquid that stained its lips and teeth was Redthorn's, but the scarlet rivulet that ran into its eye had already welled up from deep cuts inflicted by the dog.

Teeth bared, the badger crouched in the sandy dirt, snarling and hissing. Undaunted, the dog stood over its opponent, a low, frightening rumble coming from its throat. Long and yellowed fangs were bared. The dog lunged suddenly and sent the badger scurrying into the deep tunnel.

Redthorn had dragged himself away from the fracas. He lay very still on a tuft of dry brown grass. The treeclimbers gathered around him, not knowing what to say or do. Indeed, there was precious little to be done. The cottontail's right hindleg was broken and dislocated. A puddle of red had dripped from his matted fur and discolored the parched grass. With its last tug, the badger had torn a dreadful gash in Redthorn's lower abdomen and upper thigh. Muscles had been torn loose and the belly cavity lay hideously exposed.

Redthorn's eyes fluttered open and he scanned the three

"The air was pierced by an agonized squeal of pain!"

concerned faces clustered around him. Then he craned his neck to look for the dog. The shaggy animal had quietly stretched out on the earth, head between paws, just behind Janna.

The rabbit lay his head back down and, with considerable effort, whispered, "Seems...seems I don't know much about hunters after all."

"Didn't you check out the hole in the earth?" asked a shocked Janna, with a treeclimber's natural aversion to damp, dark places in the ground.

"Not much time," Redthorn murmured. "It looked deserted...loose, sandy earth...badger shouldn't of been there. A mistake...I made a mistake about the badger. But the dog..."

He extended his neck once more, to see if the big yellow hound had moved. Or if the dim-witted beast might finally consider the possibility of attacking the treeclimbers. But it just lay there, watching with sad brown eyes and listening with floppy ears.

"Why doesn't the dog..."

At that moment everyone's head turned as another rabbit came rushing through the entrance to the enclosure, swerved to miss the dog's legs, and came to a sliding stop against the stone wall.

"Milkweed!" cried Janna.

"You know this one, too?" asked an open-mouthed Klestra.

Milkweed's eyes skipped from Janna and Frafan, to her mate, to Klestra, and finally to the dog. Without hesitation, she hopped slowly to Redthorn and lay down beside him.

"I thought I sent you home to your sister," Redthorn said in a soft voice.

"I didn't leave right away," she said. "I wasn't sure what I should do. Before I made up my mind, I heard cries — obviously yours. I had trouble following them in the gusty wind..." Her eyes found his deep wounds and she cried aloud, "The dog has finished you!"

"Dog didn't do it," he whispered. "Badger. I was too near the hole over there." He nodded his head toward the badger den, then looked at the dog, a thin smile on his lips. "Can't understand that one."

Milkweed took in her surroundings: the stone enclosure with only one way in or out, the dark hole in the earth, her mortally wounded mate. She said to the dog, "I understand now what his plan was. He expected you to do his dirty work for him. He wanted you to destroy the treeclimbers. He thought he could escape down the hole. He can't comprehend why you didn't attack them. Or him. Or me. I don't understand either."

"Suppose I shouldn'ta chased anybody," said the dog, surprising everybody by speaking. "Sorta promised I wouldn't. Gives the wrong compression. Not much of a hunter, see? Got more important things t'do."

"Then how did you happen to chase Redthorn here?" asked

Klestra.

"Well, digbone it, I wasn't gonna! That rabbit kept runnin' right in front a me. Was tryin' to mind my own business, just headin' downstream. And here he comes...runnin' right across m'path — two times!"

"He did that purposely," said Milkweed.

"Purposely?..." Klestra was still having trouble putting the whole affair together. Why one of the hunted would try to get itself and others trapped like this went beyond anything he'd ever experienced — or even heard of.

"The dog's telling the truth. That's what I did," said Redthorn, without opening his eyes. "Since we left the warren, Milkweed and I have been looking for a place to spend the cold season. I thought I'd wait until the snow melted before I took my revenge on the gray squirrels, and eventually on Mayberry. But yesterday, when Milkweed and I rested outside these rocks, I watched you two running along the creek..." Redthorn pointed to Janna and Frafan "...then this morning, after I saw this crazy dog, the three of you passed by, heading this way. I knew how nosy and what do-gooders you are, and of your deranged brother's habit of getting involved in everybody else's problems. I didn't figure you'd pass up a chance to help a rabbit in distress, especially since it was rabbits who were stupid enough to shelter you in their warren. I decided, if I ran quickly ahead of you, got the dog's attention, and timed things right...then my revenge was at paw."

As fretful air groaned around the stones, Redthorn grimaced. With great effort he fought off the pain.

"I asked Milkweed if she wanted to help me teach you a lesson," he continued, "but she kept asking me what kind of lesson. I wouldn't tell her. At that point I wasn't sure myself. I should have known she wouldn't have helped me anyway. I finally left her upstream. Told her to go find her way back to Great Woods Warren. I ran here and began my distress calls about the time I thought you'd come within hearing distance. It should have worked."

Redthorn glared at the dog. "Something wrong with you, dog," he said, in a voice as loud as he could muster, "Something very wrong. Why don't you hunt? Who told you not to chase? And what took you so long to get here?"

"Told ya I don't hafta hunt," said the dog defensively. "Get plenty ta eat. Reason I didn't follow ya in here real quick was that I saw this here chipmunk, ya know?... Kinda disappeared on me. Spent some time lookin' fer 'im. As fer chasin', I promised some friends not t'chase...not longtails or shorttails."

"Friends?" Frafan's face lit up.

"Yeh. Gave m'word ta some treeclimbers...like yerselves. P'raps ya know 'em. Call themselves Ephran and Kaahli."

CHAPTER XI
OLD FRIEND AND HUNTER

J should have guessed," groaned Redthorn.

As soon as the yellow hound jumped right over the heads of squirrels and attacked a badger, Frafan knew this was not your nuts-and-shells hunter. He would almost have to be the same animal who had frightened the wits out of Mianta and had been, in a very real sense, the cause of her becoming mate to Laslum. He was the dog who had found pleasure in the company of Ephran and Kaahli. This was the creature who had come to consider treeclimbers his friends.

"Fred!" cried Janna, "You have to be Fred!"

"Yep, guess I hafta be. How'd ya know my name?"

Janna's excitement and Fred's question were interrupted by a low moan. They both turned toward Redthorn. A gurgling sigh erupted from deep inside the tormented rabbit. Milkweed had not left his side and now she bent low to comfort him and to hear his words.

Though he couldn't speak above a low whisper they all heard him say, quite clearly; "I think...that it's not just hunters I don't understand. Milkweed...Treeclimbers...I've made...I've made a mistake. I can only ask that you..." His eyes grew wide for a moment and his intact left leg straightened. His head slowly bowed and he slumped in the grass.

Milkweed choked back a sob and put her face deep into Redthorn's thick fur. "He...he wasn't always... When I met him he was brave. And good to me..."

They all sat quietly while Milkweed mourned. Though Klestra didn't know Redthorn, and notwithstanding the fact that Frafan and Janna had little reason to be upset about the end of this particular rabbit's breath, the treeclimbers felt a unified sense of regret. They couldn't help feeling sorry for Milkweed, who apparently loved Redthorn despite his shortcomings. And to some degree they were saddened by his last words; he hadn't been able to finish what he was going to say, but it seemed likely that he was going to ask pardon for his thoughtless hatred of squirrels. And of almost everyone else. The larger part of their grief was because one of the hunted had again fallen victim to a hunter.

Milkweed did not want her mate fought over by carrion eaters. Though it was not the custom of rabbits, she asked Fred to help, and the two of them dug a shallow hole. They carefully slid Redthorn's body into it. Milkweed covered him with the loose dirt, using her hindpaws, and Fred pushed a few stones, as many as he could manage using his tender nose, over the hole. Milkweed lingered a while. The others waited for her by the entrance. Finally they left the rocky enclosure together.

Though they were accompanied by a dog, a hunter to be feared by most other hunters, Milkweed and the squirrels were uncomfortable in the blustery open expanse of Rocky Point. They scurried toward the woods while Fred loped along behind, sniffing here and there, stopping to dig around an especially large rock. Milkweed and the squirrels sat down under the trees. Nobody said anything for a while. None of them knew quite how to begin. Janna broke the silence.

"I'm sorry, Milkweed, for your loss."

It seemed a very small thing to say.

"Thank you," replied Milkweed, "but I needn't tell you my mate had grown sour as moldy clover on a hot day. I hope you know I do not feel about treeclimbers as he did. His heart was full of jealousy and hate, you know, and he convinced himself that what he wanted was best for the entire warren. It was unacceptable to take his frustrations out on his own kind so he attacked outsiders."

Frafan and Janna could still think of nothing to say and, after a moment or two, a dejected look appeared on Milkweed's face.

"I understand why you don't speak. I can't say I blame you. You are thinking: 'Suddenly this shorttailed female is all sadness and apology. Where was she while her mate threatened, and pushed, and finally tried to have us gnawed apart?' And you are correct, of course. I was right there, at his side. I let him bully you. I have no excuse except he was my mate and friendless but for me. And...I was afraid of him too. I will admit that." She breathed deeply and raised her chin. "But this is not a worthy apology. Not really. All I can say is that I finally realized what had to be done when I understood his plans for you.

"As he said, we saw you longtails and the dog earlier, after we had traveled a good distance upstream. We were looking, you see, for a small group of outcast cottontails who Redthorn insisted had a warren somewhere around here. He said we'd be welcome there."

Klestra frowned. He'd seen his share of rabbits during his travels along Rocky Creek, but a warren of exiled rabbits? He thought maybe Redthorn was confused. Then again, without spending some time getting to know them, how would a red squirrel manage to tell a reasonably well-situated sort of rabbit from a fugitive anyway?

Milkweed looked back, checking Fred's location, and went on: "The dog was on the other side of the water when we first saw him. We hid and waited a long while until he passed by. As you can see...," she glanced back at Fred, "he wastes a great deal of time, digging at every stone and sniffing around every bush. Redthorn seemed relieved when the dog went on his way, but after we saw the three of you he said he had an idea; he would have his revenge on the longtails after all. I wanted nothing more to do with revenge, and hate, and plots, and so he told me

84

to go back to Great Woods Warren and beg forgiveness from my sister's mate. Then he left me. For a time all I could think of was how wonderful it would be to be back home. It took a while to forget my selfishness and to know, this time, I must try to stop him. I ran as quickly as I could."

She looked at Janna and said, "I was going to warn you. I really was. I had even decided I would fight him if I had to."

Then the poor doe broke down entirely. Sobs racked her body. Frafan did not want to doubt her sincerity, even though he knew she might have come on the run only because she thought her mate was really hurt or trapped. But what did she have to gain by the detailed confession she'd just made? Was it a fabrication to make friends? Did she think they would somehow gain her re-entrance to Great Woods Warren? Or did she believe they had some strange power over the dog and she could still find herself in trouble if they turned on her?

The answer, if there was a simple one, was known only to Milkweed. Frafan and Janna looked at one another. Frafan, seeing his sister's sad expression, knew what she was thinking and nodded his silent approval to what she wanted to say.

"We believe you, Milkweed," said Janna, "and we forgive you. Thank you for trying to help us."

The cottontail lifted her tear-stained face to them with a relieved smile.

"What will you do now, Milkweed?" asked Frafan.

"While the air remains gentle, I plan to do just what Redthorn suggested. I will return to Great Woods Warren and beg entry." She dried her eyes with her paws. "I only hope that Mayberry's usual generous spirit is still upon him when he sees me at the entrance."

"I don't think I'd worry about that," said Frafan.

"Please tell Mayberry that we found Klestra and are on our way to find Aden, father of Kaahli," said Janna. "There is hope our brother and his mate are at The Spring."

"I will give him your message," replied Milkweed. "I wish you success in your search. From all I've heard, Ephran and Kaahli must be worth finding."

Fred sauntered up just as the cottontail turned to leave.

"I still don't understand you, dog," she said, "but I know you tried to rescue my mate and I thank you for that."

"Didn't help much, I guess," said Fred, wrinkling his nose.

"Have a safe journey, Milkweed," said Frafan.

"You also," said Milkweed, and she hopped off through the grass beneath the bare branches.

Fred sat down facing Frafan and Janna. "Never finished our talk. Still don't know how ya knew m'name," he said.

"Our brother told us all about you," said Janna.

"Yer brother?"

"Yes. Our brother is your friend, Ephran," said Frafan.

"Yer Ephran's little brother'n'sister?" smiled Fred, eyes growing wide. "Well, I'll be tied and teased! That's just who I was lookin' for!"

Klestra had been quiet, listening to the conversation, trying to make some sense of this whole affair. The red squirrel knew better than to be surprised at anything concerning Ephran. But to be tricked into a frightening situation by a vengeful cottontail, only to be saved by a badger and a dog...! This business boggled even his healthy imagination.

At the end of the warm season, when Ephran and Kaahli returned to The Pond, Kaahli had mentioned something about meeting a yellow dog in their travels. Klestra had missed most of the story because he had been preoccupied with how he was going to tell his friends about a tragedy — the terrible fate that had befallen Cloudchaser, their mallard drake friend.

"You're looking for Ephran?" asked Klestra.

"Yep. Lookin' for Ephran," confirmed Fred, eyeing Klestra suspiciously. "What're you to him?"

"I like to think I'm his best friend."

Fred looked to Frafan and Janna with a questioning expression. They nodded their sober affirmation.

"Fred, meet Klestra," said Janna.

"H'lo, Klester. Spose shouldn't be real surprised at Ephran's friends," he mumbled.

"I would think not," muttered Klestra.

"Ephran and Kaahli are both missing, you know," said Janna.

"Both? Knew Ephran was lost, but not Kaahli."

"How did you know about Ephran?" asked Klestra.

"Heard some other gray longtails talkin'."

"Where was that? Where did you hear gray squirrels talking?" asked Frafan.

"Right near my place," replied Fred.

"And where is that?"

Fred leaned to one side, lifted his paw, and scratched vigorously around a floppy ear. A lopsided grin appeared on his face.

"Well...where is your place?" repeated Frafan.

"Don't rightly know," said Fred.

"You don't know where your den is?" Janna asked.

"Well, I sorta know," Fred said. "If I follow this here stream back a stretch I can find my way. I think."

Klestra thought he might know why a hunter like this would not know his way around the woods.

"You stay with Many Colored Ones, don't you?" he asked.

"Hey, that's good, Klester! You're a smart feller. Yes, indeed. I do keep these ol' bones warm in a den with a Many Colored One. In a place where there are lots 'n lots a dens just like his."

Klestra spoke to Frafan and Janna. "His nest is in one of those warrens of many dens. Do you know of them?"

"Mother told us," replied Janna. "But we've never seen a lot of them all together in one place. She always said not to go close to their dens."

"Not all of us listened, I'm afraid," Frafan murmured to himself.

"Let's get back to those gray squirrels you overheard, Fred," said Klestra. "Exactly where did you hear them talking? In a woods near your den?"

"No woods around my den, Klester. No, I heard 'em in some little maple trees, right next to my place. I wasn't snoopin', ya unnerstand. There was this here cat down th'way, ya know. Was gonna give that old tabby somethin' to worry 'bout. Anyway, heard one of 'em squirrels say somethin' about a treeclimber from the woods, a treeclimber would fight with skyhunters if need be, a treeclimber had skunks and ducks fer friends..." Fred hesitated and looked at Klestra. "And red treeclimbers, too, now as I think on it. Anyway, that sure sounded like Ephran to me. So I listened up real careful and this one particler sassy little treeclimber what acted like he knew somethin' the others didn't, he says somethin' about this special treeclimber bein' hunted by Many Colored Ones and now nobody could find him."

Fred suddenly attacked his rear quarter, scratching and biting. Then he sneezed and snorted for a minute or two.

"Bug, I guess," he explained. "Well, as ya might figure, I had a few questions fer them longtails. But when I got their 'tention and tried to get a little infermation, they got scairt. They was well outa my reach, but they got scairt anyways. They run off through the branches and the more I hollered the faster they run. So I had no choice. Had to come and look fer myself. Had to try and find out what's goin' on with Ephran."

"Are you trying to tell us treeclimbers nest in the branches near your Master's den? Right there among Many Colored Ones?" Klestra was flabbergasted.

"Sure. Mostly gray ones. Some of those orangish ones. Ain't seen no red ones though."

Though the squirrels might doubt his instincts and tracking ability, there was no real question about Fred's honesty. His announcement, about squirrels nesting right in among a whole lot of Many Colored Ones, would have to be digested. It ran counter to everything they'd been taught.

"How did you get this far all alone?" asked Janna.

"Got some help," admitted Fred. "Just watchin' Ephran last

warm season helped. That fella sure knows how ta find his way around. Anaway, I know the path my Master takes to the woods. Followed that a ways. Got a little messed up, but ya don't wanna hear about that. Ended up near a purty place where water runs outa the ground. Met a friend who set me goin' the right way again. Friend of Ephran's too, by the way. Called Aden."

"Aden!" gasped Frafan. "You found Aden?"

"Sure. He's the one told me ta follow this here stream 'til I get to a place called The Pond."

Klestra's voice was heavy. "Ephran and Kaahli aren't with Aden then?"

"Nope. Were they sposed ta be?"

"We were hoping...," said Frafan, and he closed his eyes for a moment. "Had Aden heard or seen anything of them?"

"Don't think so. Didn't say too much to him. Didn't even tell him that Ephran was missin'. Didn't want to worry him, ya see. Just kinda let him think I was goin' callin'."

It was a severe shock. Their flimsy dream was torn to shreds by the dog's simple and forthright answers. Kaahli and Ephran were not at The Spring. Kaahli and Ephran may not have come in this direction at all. Except for being further from Ephran's nest, they were in about the same fix as they'd been in when they started out...nowhere. Worse really. At this time, at the beginning of the cold season, they were at far greater risk than they had been at The Pond. What could they do? They would simply have to go back, that's all they could do. The brave quest had received a blow, very possibly a fatal blow.

"Not much to go calling on at The Pond, Fred," said Frafan. "Ephran and Kaahli are not there either."

"Oh," said the dog, "howdja know that?"

"Because we just came from there," said Klestra.

"Oh."

Fred scratched his ear again. Frafan noticed that Klestra started to do the same thing, then caught himself, and put his paw back on the ground. Janna gazed off into the trees.

"Is there anything you might have seen? Anything strange? Anything that might give us an idea of where to look for Ephran and Kaahli?" Frafan knew he was asking desperate questions of the dog. It was foolish to ask such things of one who was not even a native of the woods. How would the hound know if something was amiss out here? Then again, his Master brought him hunting sometimes.

Fred shook his head dejectedly. "Na. Didn't see nothin' strange. And I still can't figure how to find anything to eat out here. Good thing I run inta one of them dens where Many Colored Ones nest in the woods. They fed me. Was real nice ta me..." He smiled and tilted his head to the side. "Hey! There was sumthin' kinda funny, now's you mention it. Not that They fed a strange dog, though that's queer 'nuff... but those Many Colored Ones had quite a bunch a animals around their place. All kinds a animals and birds. Not just cows and such either."

Klestra's head came up.

"Where?" he asked, with rising excitement. "Where is this den of Many Colored Ones? This place with many animals?"

CHAPTER XII

TALES OF SHINING WINGS

It seemed fitting that the clouds began to break apart as they started upstream, the direction from which Fred had come. Klestra was ecstatic and Janna was infected with his happiness. Fred wore a big grin as he jogged along beneath them. He wasn't quite sure what he'd said to make them so joyful, but he was pleased to have been of service.

Frafan was not convinced celebrating was called for. He didn't care to be thought of as a perpetual pessimist but this situation reminded him of when they left The Pond. On that occasion Klestra was certain he knew where Ephran and Kaahli had disappeared to. Now, once again, he'd persuaded himself he was hot on their trail. And he had no better reason this time than he had the other.

So somewhere ahead was a farmsite with many animals...so what? From what mother had said, farms always had animals. Some had more and some had less. Jafthuh would say red squirrels tended to hasty judgments. "Snatching at milkweed seeds," he'd say. Anyway, Frafan knew that hurried decisions often had troublesome consequences. He also knew both father and Ephran sometimes made them. He might do it himself. Once in a great while.

"Let's not get our hopes real high," Frafan said quietly. But they were used to him talking to himself and neither of his companions were listening. They were jabbering too loudly to hear him anyway.

"We've come about as far along Rocky Creek as I've ever been," said Klestra. "I have only one more stock of food hidden and that's just ahead."

The food was pretty much the same as it had been last time — only the amount was less. It looked as though the stash had been discovered by a chipmunk with a hearty appetite. Klestra said he'd left a number of acorns, but if he had, they were gone. What there was they ate slowly, knowing, from here on, a lot of luck was going to be needed to keep stomachs from growling.

Expressing what all of them were thinking Frafan said, "If the snow holds off we'll be all right."

"Yes," agreed Klestra. "There are lots of places where warm air has cleared the snow from the earth. Our noses can still lead us to food hidden under the leaves."

The squirrels offered Fred whatever he might find to his liking but, after sniffing around the seeds, nuts, and pine cones for a minute he said, "Thanks anaway", and lay down at the base of a white pine.

"Fred," said Janna, working hard to scrape a little food from the inside of a dry shell, "do you think you can lead us to this farm where you saw the animals?"

"Dunno," replied the dog. "Sure hope so. Gettin' awful hungry."

Frafan scanned the sky and surrounding bare trees for crows. He remembered Aden and Ephran telling the story about helping Fred find his Master's den on the shore of Blue Lake. The memory did not tend to build confidence in Fred's leadership ability. But crows would know if a farm was nearby. It would be nice to see a crow just now. As seemed so often the case, however, they were never around when you wanted them.

"Say, look who's coming!" said Klestra, pointing to a pair of whitetail deer. The graceful animals were browsing on what greenery they could find, moving slowly through the trees in the squirrels' direction.

"Hello there!" Klestra shouted to them.

The smaller of the two, a pretty doe with big eyes, looked up into the branches, smiled, and said, "Hello yourself, little treeclimber. What brings you out on such a cold and blustery day? Are you lost?"

"No, no," laughed Klestra. "We're not lost. Just in need of some guidance. I and my friends here are trying to locate a farmsite..."

Fred picked that moment to stand up. Where he'd been laying he'd been unable to see who Klestra was talking to...and he was curious. As soon as he poked his shaggy head up, above the tops of thick bushes, the deer spied the movement. In the next instant they realized what they were looking at.

"Wait! Wait!" Klestra shouted. "He's not what you think!"

But words meant nothing now. He could only watch two bouncing white tails disappear among thick brown tree trunks.

"Aw, shucks!" said Fred. "S'pose they were scairt a me."

"S'pose," said a chagrined Klestra.

"I wonder what they'll tell their friends," mused Frafan. "Can't you hear them? 'Two gray treeclimbers, along with a red one, traveling through the woods with, believe it or not, a yellow dog as a companion! And they wanted directions to a farm!'"

"No one will believe them," laughed Janna.

"They'll think it's some sorta joke," giggled Fred.

"Pretty close to the truth," Klestra said under his breath.

"Say, Klester," said Fred, looking up at the red squirrel, "what'ya mean when ya told 'em I'm not whut they think?"

"Obviously they thought you were a hunter," said Klestra, "and I'm not sure if they were right or wrong."

The conversation was interrupted by the strident cawing of two crows overhead. Klestra chattered loudly to attract their attention. The crows circled and settled into the branches of a tall tamarack. One of them was Mulken. The other was a stranger.

"Mulken!" called Klestra, "where were you when we needed

"Wait!, Wait!," Klestra shouted,
"He's not what you think!"

93

you?"

"Eeyah! Neet me?" asked Mulken, as he looked directly at Fred. "See what mean, red longtail, but dog not thret you. Or me. No climb. No wing."

"I'm not referring to the dog. He's a friend. Sort of. I'm talking about the rabbit who tried to ambush us. Why didn't you give us warning?"

The crows looked at each other with puzzled expressions, then back at Klestra. The unknown crow said, "Umm, sawt ooe cottontels. No ideeou 'aunt warn uv rabbits. Youbin eatena rotten seets?"

Mulken said, "Me an dis one, call 'im Darkeye, we fly back Pond wunt ime. Udder tings see 'n do. What you 'spect? What you talk 'bout?"

"Never mind for now," replied Klestra. "Sometime I will tell you about it. I know how much you like peculiar stories."

An idea popped into Frafan's head. It had occurred to him earlier that Phetra and Roselimb, if they made it back to the lakes, and then to Corncrib Farm, would have brought very disturbing news to his parents.

"Mulken," he said, "can you take news back to the den of Jafthuh and Odalee for us? Can you tell the squirrels there Frafan and Janna are safe? That they are with Klestra — and carrying on the search for Ephran and Kaahli?"

Mulken shrugged. "Many names to 'member. No promise. If air 'appens tublow tha tway...ge tunder wing...maybe..."

"That's all I ask...," said Frafan, "if the air pushes you in that direction. And make it simple. Just tell them Frafan says, 'Everyone safe. So far, so good.'"

Klestra said, "Just now we need information that requires no work. No extra flying. It's very important for us to know if there is a farm nearby."

"Firm? You meana den of Meneek Uler Duns? Where dey grof 'ood, kee plots a'animals?"

"Yes. Lots of animals. That's what we're looking for."

The other crow, Darkeye, dropped from the higher limbs to join Mulken. With obvious excitement he said, "There iss! There iss a place! But yoonno go. No gok loose."

"Why shouldn't we go close?" asked Frafan.

"No, no. Danjerus. Much danjerus," said Mulken. "Crow stafe are way from dis un."

"Why do you fear this particular farmsite?" asked Klestra. "I thought you forestwatchers felt comfortable near dens of The Many Colored Ones."

"No tis un," repeated Mulken, shaking his black head. "Crow

94

always careful ner den Meneek Uler Duns. But dis un, stafe arr way. Here fierse skyhunter; skyhunter tree times big as s'awk, one wi twing shine bry tin sun, wing spread bik un wite, not move. Flifast, cry, whine — mose t'rrible voice! Circle round'n'round, looksee anyting sneak upon a den. All while, one dem Meneek Uler Dun stan b'low, watchahunter, way't frit find someting...somebudy."

Frafan was appalled. "I've never heard of such a bird," he said, "a bird with shiny wings. Does it fly there all the time?"

"Na tall times," replied Darkeye. "Sumptimes watch far way, not see it. But sumptimes cumup reelfast. No know when."

"What do you make of that, Klestra," asked Frafan.

"Amazing story. I don't know what to make of it."

Klestra eyed the crows, trying to tell if this might be some sort of trick, and wondering what reason they could possibly have for fabricating such a preposterous story.

"Nogo dere," repeated Mulken seriously, shaking his head slowly to and fro. "Skyhunter see us fersh yure in bareb ranches."

"I think," said Klestra, "our search takes us that way. After hearing your story I must ask if it isn't the two of you who have been pecking on rotten seeds."

The birds remained silent.

"We knew there would be danger," said Janna shakily, as much to convince herself as anyone.

"Please tell us where we can find this very strange farm," said Frafan.

Mulken looked at his fellow crow, who ruffled the thick black feathers on his back in a sort of shrug.

"As you 'ish," said Mulken, "but ute ake grey trisk." He lifted one black wing and pointed upstream. "Follow Rock Eek Reek small way. Bigs edar. No green last warmtime. Look ahwhere inta coal dwind. Seem eadow. Dens Meneek Uler Duns acrossag rass."

"If go der, crow snot see," said Darkeye.

"Yes, we understand," said Klestra, "you will not follow us. You won't be able to see what happens to us."

The crows rose from the branches and sailed off in the gusty air. As Frafan watched them slip away into the gray mist, a tiny idea, a faint glimmer, crept into the outermost fringes of his thoughts. The crows said they would not go near the farm. For how long? For how long had this peculiar farmsite been a blindspot for those blackfeathered watchers of the forest?

Frafan saw the red cedar first. It was huge, but its size is not what made it stand out from its neighbors. No more than a conical skeleton, withered branches should have been green, even at the beginning of the cold season.

"Well," sighed Klestra, "there stands the guidepost the crows gave us...and yonder lies my last landmark, Spruce Hill, Kaahli's old home. I guess this is our last look at Rocky Creek. For a while at least."

"Spruce Hill!" said Janna. "I remember Kaahli telling of the nest she built here, the nest she stayed in until you brought her to Ephran. Could they have come back here? Might she and Ephran be inside the nest?"

"I thought of that some time ago," said Klestra. "I was so desperate to find them that I've had the crows look twice. According to them, there was no one here either time. I suppose it wouldn't hurt to take a peek for ourselves, one more time."

The closer they got, the more apparent it was that the cozy nest was deserted...deserted and forlorn among the bare branches. Janna climbed into the brittle leaves to be certain no one lay asleep in the chilly interior, but she emerged almost immediately with a sad shake of her head.

They traveled slowly along the meadow's edge, where thin and crusty snow lay still and unbroken. Though still a long way ahead, the big dens they sought could be seen through the trees. Every time Fred spied a likely-looking clump of thistle or a patch of briar bushes he would gallop out into the meadow, scattering brown grass, sticks and snow in all directions. He was hoping to flush a sleeping grouse or pheasant, hoping to see it explode into the air in a flurry of feathers and a cloud of snow. However, he found no birds to frighten.

He would stand for a moment, disappointed, then roll his head to the side with a little "Woof" and jog back to his friends, a crooked smile on his face.

After a slow and careful time, with many stops to look all around, they drew close enough to make out details of the farm. Even though he was sitting on it, Fred's tail was trying to wag. Limp tongue hanging from drooling mouth, Frafan knew that the dog's thoughts had turned to the meal he imagined he might smell, even from this distance.

"Les go," Fred said. "No skyhunter 'round now. T'weren't any the last time I wuz here either."

It looked peaceful alright. No threat to be seen or heard, on the ground or in the air. A blanket of unruffled snow lay all about the collection of dens. There was a big red den and a smaller yellow one. There were others, smaller, scattered here and there around the farm.

The snow, thawed away in open and high places, was deepest where it had drifted in a grove of little trees Frafan recognized as a kind that bore apples. Near the yellow den, standing alone, was a stiff and motionless figure. It looked something like Them — The Many Colored Ones — except it did not have their exceptionally long rear legs. Actually, it had no legs at all. It was three balls of snow, stacked one atop the other, largest on the bottom and smallest on top. From the middle ball a single crooked branch stuck out to either side. Frafan decided it must be harmless.

"I guess we'll have to get closer," said Klestra. "We won't learn much from this distance."

With a common bond of discomfort the squirrels set out through the trees. Below them, a totally empty stomach and visions of food finally overwhelmed poor Fred. He could no longer bear it.

"Arf!" he barked gleefully, and galloped off toward the yellow den with its big shiny squares of darkness.

"Fred, wait! Where are the animals you spoke of?"

Klestra's shouted question was asked too late. Fred was already out of earshot. He was making too much racket to hear anything but himself anyway. They watched as he ran right up to the den entrance, yapping all the way, tail flailing like a supple willow branch in a squall. He stood at the entrance, looked back at them, and waved with a front paw. They were dazzled by his audacity.

Frafan held his breath. It took long enough so that he thought perhaps the den was empty, but suddenly the entrance opened and a small and fragile-looking Many Colored One burst out as though flung by a springy green branch. Its long forelegs reached out and grabbed for Fred. Janna gasped, but the little Many Colored One only dug its claws into Fred's fur and coddled the dog. Suddenly another small One appeared, this One sturdier than the Other. It held something round and blue and flat above its head. Frafan had seen this sort of thing before, through the windows at Corncrib Farm. And Blackie ate from one. It was called a "dish." Fred barked the louder, leaping and frolicking about it's legs. As soon as the dish was placed on the earth Fred stopped yelping, pounced, and stuck his snout into what must be his long-awaited meal. The small Creatures stood there while the dog ate, making soft sorts of sounds.

"Have you ever seen anything so strange?" asked Klestra.

"Never," said Janna, wide-eyed.

"Well," said Frafan under his breath, "I've seen Blackie eat, but with less excitement and a lot more manners."

As Fred ate, apparently ignoring the ungainly Beings standing right next to him, Frafan pondered the scene. Familiar somehow. Not Fred eating from a flat blue dish. It was the large red den...and the smaller yellow one. Two diminutive Many Colored Ones. An apple orchard. Even the slender likeness of a bird atop the red den. This had all been described to him... Or else he'd dreamt it. Kaahli! Kaahli had spoken of these dens...and of the apple trees...

"Klestra! Janna!" he choked.

"What is it, Frafan!" said Janna in alarm, looking at his excited face.

"This is where Aden and Laslum were kept prisoner," he blurted.

"Kaahli's father and brother? Are you certain?" asked Klestra.

"It has to be..."

"Yes! Yes!" Janna's face lit up. "You're right, Frafan. A yellow den. Two small Many Colored Ones..."

Klestra scowled. "Are you saying this is where Ephran and Kaahli found Kaahli's family?"

"That's right," said Janna. "Kaahli told us of this farm. About that den, color of the blossoms of the water lily, and about the bigger red den. Even those small Many Colored Ones... They must be the Ones who were with Aden and Laslum when Ephran and Kaahli first arrived here."

"You know, none of our family, even Aden and Laslum, who were here for some time, mentioned a skyhunter with long silver wings," said Frafan skeptically.

No one had an answer for that, and they sat in the branches for a time, watching as The Many Colored Ones danced around Fred, who was licking the dish clean with his big wet tongue.

"This is very bad news," Klestra finally said.

"I agree," said Frafan. "I doubt Ephran or his mate would return to such a place of their own accord."

"But look how gentle They are with Fred," said Janna hopefully.

"Fred is a pet of Many Colored Ones," said Frafan. "Even these Creatures evidently treat their pets kindly."

"What about the animals Fred said he saw here?" asked Janna. She did not want to believe they might have come all this way for nothing, that the search had taken a terribly false path. She did not want to consider the possibility they were far from safety and shelter and food, to say nothing of being at least as far from an answer to the disappearance of her first brother and his mate.

"This may or may not be the same farm Fred stopped at before. There may or may not have been other animals. If there are other animals, they may or may not be prisoners in the big red den," said Klestra.

At that all eyes turned to the huge den. It stood, solitary and desolate, at the edge of a tangled field of tall brown weeds, cocklebur, tall thistles, and tree stumps. To squirrels, it was about the most awesome and terrible structure they could imagine.

"Oh dear!" said Janna. "Do you really think there might be animals in there?"

"Well," said Klestra, "if this is the right farm, it's a reasonable guess."

"I hope we haven't come all this way just to sit here and guess," said Frafan. "We haven't learned a solitary thing yet. We have to go inside. Besides, we're going to want shelter."

Klestra wrinkled his nose. "Why is that?"

"Because the clouds are going to spill snow. I don't know about you, Klestra, but Janna and I would just as soon not be caught in another snowstorm."

CHAPTER XIII

CONCERNING ONE-SIDED CONVERSATIONS

It took a lot of persuading to get Janna to move toward the big red den. At first she thought of using the excuse of not wanting to leave Fred, but that didn't make a whole lot of sense. The dog was obviously where he wanted to be, doing what he wanted to do. Klestra was in no hurry either. Frafan himself wasn't especially delighted with the idea of looking for a way in, but he knew what had to be done and he cajoled the other two along, telling them it would be warm inside...and safe. He didn't know for certain it would be either.

It occurred to Frafan that Blackie had talked about the place she called "barn" on Corncrib Farm, and she told him how animals had once nested in the barn, long before the squirrel family moved into the hole in the old oak. She hadn't offered to show him around the huge and dilapidated place, and Frafan had never really taken the time to explore it. He'd peeked inside once, saw it was deserted, and decided there was nothing to learn by hanging around. Besides, it was dark, hollow, and altogether too quiet in there.

Janna remembered nothing of barns, if she ever knew anything about them. What she hadn't forgotten was what happened the last time she got separated from companions in a snowstorm. Both she and Klestra found it easier to move as the first tiny flakes of snow appeared in the air.

The big black openings in the side of the barn, covered with a glaze that looked like ice, were actually each made up of four smaller coverings, separated by two crossed wooden sticks. Frafan knew what they were called. Blackie had told him that too. They were "windows," and though the cat did not know the stuff they were made of, there was no doubt they were another sign of the amazing ingenuity of The Many Colored Ones — ice that never melted.

One of the windows did not reflect light as the others did. Frafan understood immediately why this was so. It was because the see-through covering was gone. Broken or removed. Whatever. He understood what a hole was. It was a way in. Whether they wanted to be in or not was unimportant.

Though Klestra had been leader of the quest up to the time they'd met Fred, the territory he knew best was the deep woods around The Pond. He'd never nested anywhere near Many Colored Ones. He remembered the awe in Ephran's voice when he told of Frafan's frequent visits to the dens of The Many Colored Ones on Corncrib Farm. Frafan had learned a great deal about Those who walked on their hindlegs. Klestra knew the time had come to yield command to someone who hopefully had a sharper vision of the path ahead.

"Frafan," said Klestra, as they approached the end of the trees, "do you think it wise to just go running right in? Is there some way we can determine how safe it is?"

"I wish I knew a way, Klestra. These sorts of dens are meant for animals, so I can't believe there's anything basically harmful in the place itself. It depends on what's inside." Frafan's lips pulled tight over his teeth and he whispered to himself, "I hope we can see what's inside before we go in."

Outside the barn and leaning up against it, just below the broken window, was a clumsy-looking object made of sliced trees. The wood had been shaped to form a sort of platform, supported in front by a round piece of wood, and with two branches pointing backward. Frafan had seen Blackie's Many Colored Ones use a similar thing, stacking objects they wanted to move from one place to another on its flat surface, picking up the two wooden branches in their forepaws, and pushing it ahead of Them, round wooden piece rolling smoothly across the ground.

White flakes were now flying thicker and thicker. Frafan ran the last few leaps across the flattened and brown grass and jumped up on the wooden thing, one of whose branches stuck up high in the air. He ran to the very end of it, stood on his hindlegs, and peered through the broken window.

"What do you see?" asked Klestra from the earth, casting quick nervous glances at the corners of the barn, tail twitching from side to side.

"Do you think it's safe?" asked Janna, her teeth chattering more from fright than cold.

"I don't really know," answered Frafan. "All I can see is a large stack of dry grass."

"Any cages?" asked Klestra.

"Not that I can see from here."

"Any animals?" Janna's voice was hopeful.

"No."

As Frafan stretched to try to get a better view, a gust of bitter wind swept around the corner of the barn and nearly blew him from his perch.

He steadied himself and said, "We'll have to hope that what I can see is more important than what I can't." With a short and graceful jump, he vanished into the black hole.

Janna looked over to a confused and doubtful Klestra. No scream of pain came back to their ears through the hole. No chattered warning rose above the whistling of the wind. No glaring monster peered back through the broken window. With a deep breath, she followed her brother and leaped through the square hole. No good being out here all alone, thought Klestra, and he clambered up the side of the barn, through the hole, and fell onto the other side...right into a soft pile of dry weeds.

Frafan and Janna were there, hearts still beating fast but breath coming more evenly.

"Are we unhurt?" whispered Frafan.

Janna and Klestra nodded.

They stood together, trying not to tremble, trying not to breathe, trying to adjust their eyes to the dim light. All they could be certain of was that it was definitely warmer inside these walls than it was outside, and that the big red den smelled of dried vegetation — and animals. Many animals. Some of the animal smells were familiar, some not.

So far, so good. Frafan's pulse was already slowing. He was reminded of his first moments in Mayberry's warren.

As their vision improved they realized they occupied a small space within a large space, like Frafan and Janna's private nest inside Great Woods Warren. The cubicle was filled with sweet alfalfa and, except for a narrow gap to their right, was closed off from the rest of the barn by a high wall of rough wood. They could have climbed the wall, of course, but of one mind, and nearly falling all over one another in the process, they started for the gap at the same instant.

For a moment they stood silently, drinking in sights none of them had seen before. Sights their parents and grandparents had never seen. Sights no one would believe unless they had seen for themselves. Klestra and Janna, especially, were totally dazzled.

The inside of the red den was immense. It was even larger than they had imagined, looking at it, as they had, from a distance. Above them was a sky of long and thin wooden slices, fitted tightly together. Huge squared spars, like trees without bark, supported the ceiling and spanned the great distance between far-off walls. These in turn were supported by equally massive timbers set into the ground. Actually, the floor from which these "trees" sprouted was not earth. It was a hard, smooth, discolored white surface Klestra could tell contained some sand.

Gentle light fell from the widely spaced and badly stained windows in the side of the barn. In the weak illumination the awed treeclimbers beheld the barn's inhabitants. To their left was a series of wooden stalls, each filled by a single huge animal. Though none of the squirrels had ever been this close before, there was no question what kind of animals these were. These were cows.

The only sound to be heard, except for the sighing of the wind outside, was the slow rhythm of chewing. Back and forth, up and down, the cows' jaws worked on mouthfuls of dried grass and alfalfa plucked with their lips and teeth from a stack in front of them.

To Frafan's right rose a dark wall. At first, without thinking it through, he assumed it was the other outside wall of the barn.

"There's nothing in here but cows," said a disappointed Klestra.

"I don't see any cages," said Janna. "Where did Fred imagine he saw all those animals?"

"Well," said Frafan, "I can't say where they are. But I think we can assume the animals Fred saw are not all inside the den of The Many Colored Ones themselves."

"Could he have been telling us...a tall story, knowing we'd want to investigate?" wondered Klestra.

"You mean so we'd help him find his way to food?" asked Frafan. "I don't think so. I can't imagine Fred being underpawed. Furthermore, I think we're being misled by the darkness. It's deceiving. There's more to this den than we're seeing from here."

Frafan's curiosity about Many Colored Ones and their dens, especially how They nested and moved around inside, gave him an advantage. If this den was constructed along the lines of the ones he'd peeked into, then the interior size should closely match the exterior ones. It was not at all like a squirrel den in a thick tree. This den should be mostly hollow space. Long before he jumped into the dry alfalfa he realized there was a good deal of barn to both sides of the window through which they'd entered. All they'd seen so far was one end, a small corner, the part the cows occupied.

"See!" he whispered loudly to Janna and Klestra, "Here is a way to the rest of this den."

A large slab of wood hung ajar, incompletely closing off a big squarish hole in the wall. Frafan recognized what it was immediately and Janna thought she understood what her brother was getting at. There was a similar slab of wood on the nearby yellow den and, of course, on the outside of the den at Corncrib Farm. It was Klestra who was having trouble understanding what doors were all about.

"Frafan!" hissed Klestra, "wait a bit."

Frafan began to creep toward the door and it made Klestra nervous.

"Let's speak to the cows," Klestra continued, "Maybe we can find out from them what's on the other side of that big piece of wood."

"Yes," agreed Janna, "That's a fine idea! Let's talk to the cows."

"'Talk to the cows?'" repeated Frafan, his eyes focused on the partly open door and the darkness beyond. "Good luck. You don't know much about cows if you think..."

His words, spoken softly, were once again lost on his companions. They had already tiptoed off, intent on the nearest cow. If they would have looked back they would have been puzzled by the huge smile that appeared on Frafan's face. "Well, why not? Stress time. Time for a little Fastrip-and-Sorghum act," he thought, as he ran to watch the fun.

Klestra and Janna crept silently around a large female cow, until they stood face to face with her. They could only gape at the great, round animal in her stall, slender tail switching slowly from side to side, massive head surrounded by a wooden frame. Her white face was down, snout buried in a trough filled with dried grain. When she first lifted her head she seemed not to see them. Her eyes were unfocused and her mouth slid back and forth, chewing her food with unconscious contentment.

"Hello there!" cried Klestra.

The cow's mouth stopped moving and her big brown eyes came to rest on the tiny creatures in front of her.

"I say," said the red squirrel, "my name is Klestra. This is Janna and, back there...," he pointed at Frafan, "is her brother Frafan. We've come a long way, you see, at considerable risk. We are looking for another pair of gray treeclimbers. We think they could have passed this way. I wonder if we might interrupt your meal just long enough to obtain a bit of information?"

The cow stared at him.

After a very long pause Klestra nervously said, "It can wait, of course. Go on eating, if you wish."

The cow began chewing again. Her eyes did not waver from the two little animals in front of her.

"Klestra!" hissed Frafan.

"Shhh," said Klestra, smiling up at the cow, his eyes glued to hers. "We can wait. She doesn't care to talk while she eats. Touch of class. Dignity. Manners. Have to respect that."

"But..."

"Pleeese!" Klestra said sharply through his teeth, waving his paw in Frafan's direction, but still not looking at him, "I understand that you have more experience with Many Colored Ones, but here we have a real animal. Let me handle this." He beamed at the cow again, his most charming smile.

The squirrels sat on the cold floor, like obedient little students. Only when she bent over to get another mouthful of grass did the cow take her eyes from them. Time was wasting. Klestra glanced at his friends. Janna's gaze was still fixed anxiously on the cow. Frafan was grinning at him... Grinning!

"I say...," Frafan tried again.

Once more Klestra cut him short. "All right, all right, my young friend! I've been around a bit too, you know. And for considerably longer than you have. I said I'd handle this situation...and I will." He got up and moved a step or two closer, which caused the cow to tilt its head, focusing one big eye on the little red squirrel.

Klestra cleared his throat and began, "My good cow-creature,

"My good cow creature," Klestra began. "Lovely resident of the meadow."

lovely resident of the open meadow that you are...graceful occupant of grassy fields: I cannot help but comment on the beauty of your eyes...ah...so big...so brown...so...so expressive. And your tail...not bushy and unsightly like mine, picking up dust and wood chips all the time, but so neat...so useful for chasing bugs. Then we come to your legs. Ah yes, your legs..."

"Your legs are too skinny for your big fat body, and so filthy that even a toad would avoid being seen near them," Frafan said loudly.

Janna gasped. Klestra's mouth fell open.

"Frafan!" Klestra cried, and ran to where Frafan was sitting, off to the side. The cow continued to watch Janna. "Now you've done it! Now we'll never get any help or advice!"

"We wouldn't have anyway." Frafan could not hold the laughter inside any longer. "Look at her." he managed, as laughter gurgled up from his belly.

Klestra and Janna turned back to the cow. Her expression hadn't changed one bit. It finally dawned on them: She had not understood one word they said.

CHAPTER XIV
CREATURES IN CAGES

Frafan had to admit to Klestra the only reason he knew cows did not communicate in the common language, if they communicated at all, was that Blackie had told him. He did not make the discovery on his own because, by the time he opened his eyes last warm season, cows and pigs no longer inhabited the little barn on Corncrib Farm. The corncrib, with its dwindling supply of yellow treats, was a relic.

Frafan's confession that a lot of what he knew came from a cat, of all unlikely creatures, made it easier for Klestra to laugh along. What kind of a deep woods creature would learn from a cat? Besides, he conceded he had made himself the fool by his stubborn insistence that he could carry on a conversation with a cow...even though he knew nothing about cows.

"Do you think they might speak to each other in some fashion we don't understand?" wondered Janna.

"They make noises, I know that much at least," said Klestra. "It may mean something. Then again, some sounds are empty."

Frafan said, "I think the only way we'd learn the answer to that question is to stay around cows for a while."

"I hope we aren't here long enough to find out," said Klestra. "And speaking of being in one place long enough, I suppose we'd better be moving on. There seems to be nothing more to learn where we are."

"We're going to have to go through that big hole, aren't we? Without any idea of what's on the other side." Janna's voice trembled.

"Don't be frightened, Janna. I'll go first," said Klestra. "It's my turn. If I bump into anything really bad I'll let you know. Then you can hide. Or run back the way we came."

"Nice try, Klestra," said Janna, with a weak smile, "but I don't know where we could hide in here anyway. If some sort of terrible thing nests in this place, it would certainly know its own den better than we. And I hardly want to go back out into another snowstorm."

"Janna's right. We might as well do this the same way we've done everything else during this journey — all at once and without a clear idea of what we're getting into," said Frafan.

Together they stepped through the hole. The part of the barn they found themselves in was even darker than the part they left. There were fewer windows, and just enough light entered to outline vague shapes. Though the area was smaller than the cows' place, it was still enormous. It was so huge you could almost imagine you were still out in the woods on a dark night. Frafan couldn't help but think how much of it was wasted space. It was not like a squirrel den. There was nothing snug or cozy about it. Even the simplest birds understood that floors should be constructed of soft and warm materials. Even animals that lived in the cold earth knew walls should be close together to conserve body warmth. Strange creatures, these Many Colored Ones. So clever in some ways...

Off to their right were four stalls, bigger than those the cows occupied. In each of these Frafan could make out a large shape, taller than the cows. They had to be animals. Like cows in some ways, but longer of leg and more graceful in appearance.

Directly across, in light fainter yet, was, no doubt of it, cages. Rows of cages. Large and small cages. Square and oblong cages. Dens to close creatures in, prisons made of familiar and beloved wood, wood cut into spars and slices. And stretched between the pieces of wood — the new and nameless — the thin but extremely tough and carefully woven web Ephran and Laslum had described so well. It was the net that prevented entering or leaving, the tendril that could not be chewed, the entwinement that meant the end of freedom.

"Frafan," said Janna in a faltering voice, "Do you see...?"

"Yes," he said as calmly as he could, "I see the cages."

"I think we should leave," she said.

"Leave? Leave for where?" asked Klestra. "We've been through that. You convinced me that there's nowhere to go."

Janna shrugged, shivered, and said nothing.

Frafan strained to see more detail. This barn was most amazing. Many Colored Ones had built it as a place to keep their pets. And, apparently, their prisoners. It was nothing like the den at Corncrib Farm, the one Blackie's Many Colored Ones made their own nests in. There was no luxury here. No fuzzy, colored pelt covering the floor. No nest within a nest for sleeping and dreaming. No tiny bright suns gleaming from walls or roof. No padded and pelted furnishings to sit or lay on.

"Frafan! Something moved!"

Janna's cry broke into his thoughts and echoed from the wall behind him. One of the big animals turned its head toward the treeclimbers. Then, from the far side of the barn came a voice:

"Who speaks from over there?"

The question seemed to float in the still near-darkness, a voice with no source. It most definitely had not come from one of the large animals in the stalls.

Klestra turned to Frafan, wide-eyed, as Janna squeaked, "Ohh, Frafan, please! Let's leave. Snow or no snow."

"No, Janna. We haven't been hurt. Or even threatened. Whoever spoke must be in a cage. Let's see if we can help."

Klestra, scared half-silly himself, could barely suppress a giddy giggle. "This," he thought, "is truly Ephran's brother. Curiosity before suspicion, courage over fear...'Let's go help' he'd said." It was almost like being with Ephran again. Klestra ran after Frafan toward the darker side of the barn, Janna at his heels.

Most of the cages were clean and empty except for bits of dried grass. A stained and perfectly round silver dish lay on each scuffed floor, the same kind of dish they'd seen Fred eat from. However, near a wall with broad shelves of wood, and beneath a smudged window, were at least two occupied cages.

The silhouette of one of the prisoners, a big bird, was unmistakable. It was a rooster pheasant. Nearby, in a slightly bigger cage, a four-legged animal paced back and forth.

"Frafan," barked Janna once more, "Wait!"

The two males had run ahead, toward the captives. She had hung back, trying to foresee any threat, trying to assess these frightening and alien surroundings.

"Wait? Wait for what?" asked Frafan as Janna crept up to him, her eyes darting to and fro. "Don't fret, Janna. From Aden and Laslum we've learned enough about cages to know these creatures cannot escape and harm us."

"I'm aware of that," replied Janna, "I just don't want you two big brave explorers to run headlong into a trap of your own. Laslum did, you know."

"Oh...Yes, that's right...I remember the story now," said Frafan, the impatience in his voice fading. He and Klestra squinted at the cages with considerably more attention than they had before.

"No need to worry at this point," came a precise voice from the bird's cage, "though I totally agree with the young female treeclimber's cautious approach to these matters. You are in no serious danger as long as The Many Colored Ones stay inside their own den. Or, at least as long as they do not come inside this one."

Klestra had heard the clipped chirpy voice of a pheasant before, but it had been a long while. Frafan and Janna remembered the distinctive crowing from the edge of a meadow of high weeds and thick grass near home. In answer to a barrage of questions, their mother, Odalee, had told them about these big birds called pheasants; the drab brown females and the roosters with brightly colored heads.

She said that pheasants claimed that their ancestors had come to these fields and meadows from a land far away. A land so different and strange that the animals of the forest would have difficulty believing them...even if they could believe in a place other than an extension of their woods. The mere thought of far-away lands opened up all sorts of puzzling and frightening possibilities.

To make their story even more farfetched, pheasants insisted that their history, passed from one generation to the next, was that they did not fly here from those faroff territories. No, they claimed their great-great grandparents, far removed, had been carried here! Carried by Many Colored Ones!

After he'd heard of them, and listened to their voice, Frafan had searched for a pheasant. Unfortunately, they seemed to prefer thick grass and dense brush to tall trees, and so their domain was not his. And though Jafthuh laughed at the pheasants' story, Frafan felt it could all be true. Their appearance was unique among birds. And their song, if it could be called that, had a special sort of a faraway and exotic sound.

The strongest testimony to the truth of their tale was the way they used their wings. Unlike other birds, they never flew great distances, even when frightened or hunted. Perhaps, Frafan thought, they were too proud to feel or admit fear. But even when the cold season settled on the woods, they did not fly far away. Perhaps their wings were not made for long flights. Perhaps, even if they'd wanted to, they could not have flown here from a distant place.

In any case, at last he was going to meet a pheasant! He was about to speak when Klestra asked, "How often do The Many Colored Ones enter this den?"

"Unpredictable. Totally unpredictable," answered the pheasant. "They come and go as They choose."

Another voice said, "Most likely They won't come out here now...not while it snows and blows."

The voice was soft but the squirrels were startled nonetheless. They whirled to face the speaker, the animal in the nearby cage. They were close enough to see its little eyes, surrounded by dark halos, peering at them through the webbing.

"Allow me to introduce us cagedwellers," said the pheasant. "The young raccoon goes by the name of Farnsworth. I am known as Ruckaru. I would bid you welcome but, under the circumstances, it seems somehow inappropriate."

"Nice to know you, I'm sure. My name is Frafan. The female is my sister, Janna, and the red treeclimber answers to Klestra."

"A distinct pleasure all around," said Ruckaru, "though I must admit that conversing with squirrels has not been an everyday occurrence with me. But then, circumstances make all the difference, don't they?"

"How did you come to be in cages?" blurted Janna.

Ruckaru cocked his head to one side and smiled. "Ah, this one you call Janna advances more quickly with her tongue than with her paws. A fair question, however. I think I can honestly say we came to be here quite by accident. And I daresay our reason for being where we are is probably far less interesting than the reason you come unbidden."

"Probably just to escape the snow and cold," the little raccoon said in a very quiet voice.

"That's true, Farnsworth," Klestra said. "Our unfortunate excuse for being in this den is to seek shelter."

"Unfortunate?" said Ruckaru. "Aha! I knew I smelled a good story. Please tell me why it is unfortunate that you found refuge from the snow and cold? 'Any clump of weeds in rough air' is what my father always said. And, though I suppose I risk giving offense, I cannot help ponder why a red treeclimber and two gray ones enter here together. Not exactly your most common trio, I think you will agree. I get the definite impression that your being together is no accident of wind and snow."

"You're quite right, Ruckaru," said Klestra. "Strange as it might seem, we three are friends. We have been traveling together. But that's a long story."

"Plenty of time for stories," said Ruckaru, smiling widely. He turned and brushed at the dust with one wing before settling down on the floor of his cage.

Frafan glanced at Klestra, who shrugged and said, "Why not? What else is there to do but talk and learn what we can."

With one more look around, to be sure no other surprises were in store, Frafan curled his tail around him and sat on the cold floor. Janna did likewise.

"Well," he began, "the unfortunate part of our story is that we sought this place hoping we might find my brother and his mate here. When we saw these Many Colored Ones' dens and apple trees we realized my brother had told us of them. They were here last warm season. They would have known of the cages. They would not have come back."

"But they might have come back," said Janna. "We don't know they didn't. There might have been reason." She was suddenly short of breath as she looked up at Ruckaru. "Might you know of squirrels here?"

Ruckaru shook his head. "Sorry. I have been here for but a short time. My black-eyed friend, Farnsworth, less yet. There have been no treeclimbers here during my stay. Until yourselves, of course."

"We were told there were many animals here," said Janna, disappointment in her voice, "not just cows and..."

She glanced over at the large animals in their wooden stalls. They had not uttered a sound. As far as she knew they were like the cows, unable to understand a word of the common language. However, they seemed to be listening attentively.

"More and more fascinating, eh, Farnsworth?" said Ruckaru. "You will be interested to know that I too have been given to understand that there were a goodly number of animals here — and not too long ago either. Everything from a chipmunk to a large mallard duck. But they are gone now. Do not ask when or why so many creatures of the field and forest might have been here. It would not be fair for me to guess about a matter of so much obvious importance to you." He smiled at Janna. "By the way, my dear, those large and sleek animals you eye so suspiciously are called horses. They represent no danger to us, unless we find ourselves under their hooves...I understand they are extremely heavy. The Many Colored Ones ride on them."

"'Ride on them!'?" three voices squeaked.

"That's what I said. Ride on them. I'm amazed...have you never seen a Many Colored One canter about astride one of these noble creatures?"

Three furry heads shook from side to side.

"Bright Days and Seed-filled Fields! Where have you been? It is quite a sight, I can assure you; one large creature seated atop another, prancing around the meadow as though they were up to something of great import."

Recovering enough to speak, Klestra said, "We are of the deep woods, you know. I have seen Many Colored Ones rarely...and these things you call horses, never. Can you say why they ride like that, one upon the other's back?"

"I have wondered the same thing. Not to get from one place to another, as far as I can tell," said Ruckaru. "Many Colored Ones have more efficient ways to do that. I suspect that They, The Many Colored Ones, do it for enjoyment. Just as I might fly over a deep and dark valley for the strange feeling I get in my belly as I pass over the edge. As you might, just for the thrill of jumping from one high branch to another."

"Are you saying They think it's fun to ride on a horse's back?" asked Janna.

"I am just supposing. I never actually asked one of Them." Ruckaru squawked and snorted at his own joke, flapping his wings, raising a cloud of dust and straw from the floor of his cage.

"Is it so very funny They ride for pleasure?" came a deep voice. "Does everything done by squirrels and pheasants have serious purpose?"

"You can speak!" cried Janna.

The rumbling voice had come from the chest of the largest horse, a brown stallion.

"Of course we can speak."

"Oh, dear. I'm so sorry. I thought perhaps you were... maybe...sort of...like the cows on the other side there..."

"Cows inhabit their own world. Like pigs," said the horse.

"Ruckaru! Why didn't you tell me horses could speak?" she demanded angrily.

The pheasant grinned and shrugged.

"Janna meant no offense," Frafan said to the horse.

"None taken — at that mistake. We understand you are of the deep woods. Few of us have been there. I suppose we might be surprised at much of what we saw and heard if we found ourselves in the place you dwell."

"Thank you for being so understanding," said Frafan.

"Have you horses been here a long time?" asked Klestra.

"Longer than the pheasant or the raccoon."

"May I ask: have you seen any squirrels here, inside this place...in cages?" asked Frafan.

"Doves, chipmunks, a small deer...even a fox," replied the horse, "but not a treeclimber. If they were, when would your brother and his mate have been here?"

"About the time of the first snow," said Frafan.

"Ah, well! We can be of no help then. Until well after the first snow we spend our time in the meadow. During the warm season, you see, we go back and forth between this place, called a barn, and where fresh grass grows. We would not have been back here, in the barn, at the time of the first snow."

"So when the air becomes very cold you are here, in this place you call a barn, surrounded by wood," Klestra said thoughtfully, "and in the warm season you are surrounded by the long shiny vines with many thorns, strung from tree to tree. Like cows, you are kept by The Many Colored Ones both inside and outside their dens."

"I object to being called 'kept'," said the horse. "And I certainly don't like being compared to cows."

"They take care of us, you see," said the golden-haired horse in the next stall. "They see to our needs."

"They take care of you? Why do They do that?" asked Janna.

"Well...," said the golden-haired one, turning to the horse in the next stall, and looking a bit confused, "I told you. It seems to make Them happy to ride on our backs."

"And what about you? Do you find it enjoyable to have those big creatures mounted on you?" asked Klestra.

The horses exchanged another glance. The golden horse said, "Does a red squirrel find it enjoyable to find itself in danger searching for a pair of gray squirrels? That is your story, is it not? What do you call that sort of sacrifice?"

"Well, that's called friendship," said Klestra. "A totally different thing. You can't mean you think of Many Colored Ones as friends!"

"Not quite friends, I suppose, but not so very different," said the golden horse.

"I think I understand. A little bit anyway," said Janna. "Ephran told of other creatures who might care and help. And how they might not always be found in the same sort of pelts we wear."

The horses nodded slowly. Klestra looked at them as though trying to see through them. He said nothing. Neither did they.

"Thank you for your help," Janna finally said to the horses. She turned her face to the raccoon. "And how about you, Farnsworth? How did you come to be here?"

"Well...I was going fishing with my father. One more outing before the water froze, you know. We were close to Spring Creek when Many Colored Ones attacked us. Father ran in one direction and I in another. They made a great racket with their thundersticks and I..." Farnsworth choked and a tear ran down his cheek.

"Was it these Many Colored Ones that did this...?" asked Klestra. "The Ones whose barn we are in right now? Was it They who pointed thundersticks at you?"

Janna put a paw on Klestra's shoulder. "I don't think Farnsworth cares to talk about this any more," she said.

"Oh yes I do," said the raccoon, sniffing back his tears and steadying his voice. "Something I know might be important for all of us. I want to tell you the rest of my story." He took a deep breath. "To answer your question, Klestra, I have not seen the particular Many Colored Ones who chased us here, in this place. I don't think These are the same as Those. I could be wrong, of course. They all look alike except for size and pelt color. But I'm fairly certain I escaped Those who were after me. My leg was hurt though. The loud noise from the sticks made it feel numb. I could barely run. I got very tired. So tired I couldn't even climb a tree. And I couldn't find a hole to crawl into. I guess I finally fell asleep. I don't remember much after that. I don't know how I got here. All I know is when I woke, I was here. In this cage. With a very strange and sticky leaf attached to a deep scratch in my side."

He turned to show the squirrels a grayish covering, just above his leg. It looked to Frafan as though some of the fur had been removed. Most unusual.

"You know, a similar thing happened to me," said Ruckaru, "though Farnsworth and I haven't really discussed it before. I too was injured. A fox surprised me in tall grass. The wily thing grabbed my wing in his teeth. I barely managed to pull loose. I made myself rise into the air and I sailed as far as I could, to the edge of the short grass near The Many Colored Ones' den. I was so exhausted I didn't even care when a little One came and picked me up in its paws..."

Ruckaru abruptly stopped talking. "Shhh!" he said. "Something is coming!"

Sure enough. They could all hear it. Through the massive wooden walls and above the sighing of the wind came a sharp yelping sound.

116

Barking! A familiar kind of barking...to the squirrels at least. Fred was just outside the barn!

But he was not alone.

CHAPTER XV

THE RIGHT PATH

*T*he squirrels had no time to run and hide among the empty cages against the back wall. They may not have chosen to do so in any case, but they hardly had time to hide at all. As the slab of wood that shielded them from the outside world swung wide, they rushed to conceal themselves as best they could.

Klestra and Janna jumped behind Ruckaru's cage. Frafan scrambled behind a thick timber that rose from the floor and soared to the ceiling. Cold air poured over Frafan as he caught a glimpse of gigantic snowflakes filling the opening and bright light outlining a tall figure standing above Fred. As quickly as the door opened, it closed again.

At first all Frafan heard was Fred's coarse breathing and the scraping of paws on the hard floor. Then there was a sound, a voice perhaps, a most unusual voice, soft and garbled. Fred responded with happy whimpers and tiny yelps. The large Thing appeared out of the shadows, looming high above Frafan, crouched in his hiding place.

It was exactly what he knew It would be, a Many Colored One. He was far closer than he'd ever wanted to be. He must stay hidden, he must move around the big timber and keep out of sight. At the same time he wanted to watch, to see what It was up to. The fuzzy light, his total fascination and subsequent lack of any movement, along with the fact he was not expected or looked for — these things may well have saved him from being noticed.

The Many Colored One wore a bulky pelt with thick fur around the neck and the forepaws. Drab brown and gray in color, It looked almost like a forest animal, except what forest animal walked around on its hindlegs? The face was in shadow, but blue eyes glittered when It faced the glow from the windows. Fur grew beneath a sharp little snout and completely covered the top of its head. Frafan was not surprised when It stripped the fur covering from its forepaws, revealing slender white digits. He knew there would be no red juice.

Frafan could not imagine what the Creature was doing or what It intended to do. At the moment It seemed preoccupied with Fred's neck. Working away, It twittered and whistled like no bird Frafan had ever heard. Finished with the dog, It straightened up and walked, with nary a wobble, to the shelves of wood beyond Ruckaru's and Farnsworth's cages. Standing as high as possible on long hindlegs, It rummaged about with a front paw in the dusty debris on the top shelf. Meanwhile, the other forepaw reached out and pulled on a slender white vine that hung from the ceiling.

Into the High Branches

Frafan caught a glimpse of...
light outlining a tall figure...

A bright light flashed on at the very moment that something fell or jumped from the top shelf. "Bang!" What in the name of Green Grasshoppers!... Frafan's heart nearly stopped. In that instant, Janna bolted from behind the pheasant's cage.

The room was suddenly bathed in the same peculiar yellow light Frafan knew so well — artificial sort of light that filled the den of Many Other Colored Ones at Corncrib Farm. Janna's frantic scramble across the barn floor, toward the far wall and a row of roundish and squarish objects stacked there, apparently went totally unnoticed by The Many Colored One.

The object which had fallen from the shelf was a sort of dish, like the one Fred had eaten from, only larger, flatter, and silver in color. It hit the floor with a loud clang, immediately followed by a shout from The Many Colored One. It reached out and grasped the dish with a forepaw while the dish spun and quivered on the dusty floor.

Frafan wondered where Klestra was, and what he might be thinking. He could not see the little red squirrel from where he crouched behind the wooden post, but he guessed Ephran's good friend, accustomed to the deep woods, must be nearly crazy with fright.

The sudden light and noise had obviously been one too many surprise for Janna. Frafan wished he would have taken her with him, to his branch overlooking the den of The Many Colored Ones at Corncrib Farm. He knew now she would have been brave enough to go with him. If she had come along then, she would not be so terrified now, of these tiny round suns that The Many Colored Ones could cause to light or unlight as They wished. She would have seen dishes. She would have understood that Many Colored Ones tended to sudden and strange actions. Luckily, she had not been detected.

Or had she? The huge Creature, humming sounds to Itself, headed in her direction, dish in its forepaw. Almost without thinking, Frafan stepped out into the open, behind the back of The Many Colored One, who was moving away from him. He heard low hissing from Ruckaru and Klestra, even a tiny yelp from Fred.

It was not their warnings that kept him from chattering and warning his sister: it was the fact that this strange Animal, the builder of this den, was not approaching Janna's hiding place as a hunter would. There was no stealthy movement, no attempt at silence, no obvious interest in the dark place to which she'd run. On the contrary, It was being very noisy — making low musical sounds with its mouth. It acted somehow...harmless. Frafan knew better, of course. They were anything but harmless. They caused trees to fall when the air was still. With their thundersticks they took breath, once and for all, from Cloudchaser's son. They hunted Kaahli. Who knew what They might have done to Ephran? Yet...

121

It bent down, over one of the lumpy things against the far wall, apparently a container of some sort, like a cache of nuts, dipping the dish in, pulling it out again, now filled with a chunky material. Fred was watching too, and he barked with delight.

Frafan ducked back behind his post just as The Many Colored One pivoted toward him. It sauntered casually back to Fred, set the dish in front of the dog, and went once more to the shelves. It returned with a thicker and deeper dish and walked to a curved and shiny branch extending out of the wall behind Fred. With one forepaw It grasped and twisted.

Water poured from the branch! The deep dish was obviously hollow. When the dish was full the branch was twisted again ...and the water stopped flowing! The water was placed in front of Fred, who was, amazingly enough, happily sizing up the food that had been placed in front of him. Frafan wondered what sort of immense stomach this yellow dog must possess!

The Many Colored One then walked over to Ruckaru and Farnsworth, peering at them closely through the mesh of their cages, murmuring softly. Quickly It stood, reached one paw over its head, and pulled the vine. The little sun immediately darkened. It moved quickly, opened the door a crack and, as suddenly as It had appeared, was gone.

Klestra crept out from behind the cages, eyes fixed to the wall where The Many Colored One had disappeared. Janna wouldn't come out into the open at first, until Frafan had assured her that it was all right.

"Well," said Klestra, with a long, quiet whistle, "that was about the most amazing series of events I've ever seen. Frightening, too, being as how it all took place so close at paw." He looked first at the tiny white globe above, dark now, and then at the branch in the wall.

"Oh Fred," said Janna, "how are you?"

"Okay. Far as I kin tell."

"The Many Colored Ones didn't harm you, did They?" asked Frafan.

"Nah. Just keep feedin' me. As you kin see. Knew They would."

"They didn't hurt you?" asked Janna, closely inspecting the dog, as though he might not be telling the truth.

"Just played 'round. The little Ones, ya know? Didja find anything out in here? Anything 'bout Ephran and Kaahli?"

"We found many things, but not what we were looking for," replied Klestra. With distrust he looked again at the silvery branch in the wall, from where the water appeared, and where a tiny drop yet hung. "Frafan, did you see water come from this branch? Hazel Nuts on an Elm Tree! I've never seen such amazing contraptions!"

Frafan smiled and shrugged. "That is amazing, no doubt. But

They are capable of all sorts of mindboggling things." He turned to the dog. "Fred, the only animals in this den are a lot of cows, a few horses, one pheasant and one raccoon. No treeclimbers except us. The other animals you saw here are gone."

"Gone, huh?"

"Yes. We're the only free ones here...except for you."

Fred looked mortified. "Not me either," he said. "I ain't free."

For the first time Frafan saw the slender vine. It was attached to a sturdy peg on the wall behind Fred, not far from the branch of water. And it led directly to the dog's neck.

"Fred," cried Janna, "you're all tangled up!"

"Yeah. I know."

"How in the High Blue Sky did you manage to do that?" asked Klestra with a snort and a shake of his head. And, without waiting for explanations, the red squirrel scampered over.

"Do you think we can gnaw through this vine?" Frafan asked Klestra, who had a length of the long cord trapped on the floor, between his paws.

Klestra frowned. "I don't think so. This vine is made of the same hard and shiny stuff as the cages."

"Don't chew on that," said Fred. "You'll just end up breakin' yer teeth."

Frafan sat back, trying to think of something to do, studying the long looping line, running from Fred's neck to the wall of the barn. The dog's legs were free and the vine wasn't twisted around anything. The truth occurred to him in a flash. "You didn't tangle yourself in that vine, did you?"

"Ummm... Not really."

"The Many Colored One attached you to the vine, didn't It?"

"Ahhh, could be...could be."

"You let that big animal attach you to the wall and didn't even try to escape?" Janna said, disbelief in her voice.

"Well...," Fred began — then hung his head and closed his mouth.

Frafan had not noticed the collar encircling Fred's neck before this moment and it irritated him that he had been so unobservant. Until you knew it was there, the ring of brown and silver was hard to see, buried in the thick yellow fur of Fred's neck. Now that he could see it, gleaming in the faint light, he found it fascinating. It bore a strange design with many deep scratches and swirls in its surface, unlike anything he'd seen in the woods. The terrible vine was attached to the collar.

"You've been tethered like this before, haven't you?" Frafan asked gently.

"Yeah."

"Does your Master do this to you?"

"Sometimes." Fred did not look up.

"Do you know why?"

"Dunno. Guess just ta keep track of where I am."

"Well, I'll tell you this," interjected Ruckaru, "I don't understand horses or dogs. Both are big and strong enough to give any Many Colored One a real battle. Instead of fighting for your rights you humor Them, play with Them, work with Them. As sure as high corn means food and cover, I've been hunted by dogs running with Many Colored Ones. I don't see why you do it."

The deep voice of the brown horse said, "Maybe it's not my business to interfere, but you small folk are making a big issue of this business of being tied. Obviously, none of you understand and, just as obviously, the dog is unable to explain. You of the woods seem to think that The Many Colored Ones who built this den are some sort of monsters. I tell you..."

Once again the horse's speech was cut short, and the discussion postponed indefinitely, by the frantic flurry of wingbeats overhead, accompanied by a shower of wet snow and feathers.

Three female pigeons; one pure white, one speckled brown and white, and one a splash of colors, perched on a rafter high above the treeclimbers, smoothing and drying their feathers. Directly above the birds' heads Frafan could see where they had entered the barn; a square hole in the wall. Exactly like Blackie's hole! Only far above the earth...and without a covering of wood.

The white pigeon flapped her wings a few times and noticed many eyes peering up at her. "Well, well," she observed, "a whole new group of visitors."

"Fuzzy feathers!" said the speckled bird, "it seems every time we leave..."

"We come back to a bunch of fresh faces," said the one with different colored feathers.

Ruckaru cleared his throat.

"Frafan...Janna...Klestra," he said as he faced each of them in turn, "I would like you to meet Flutterby...", the white bird nodded her head, "...Peppercorn...", the speckled one winked at them, "...and Payslee,..." The multicolored bird smiled. "...the three lovely sisters," Ruckaru concluded.

"Ruckaru," said Flutterby, "you are the most blatant flatterer we've ever had as a guest in this place."

"We don't know what you seek," said Payslee.

"We told you that we are unable to open your cage," said Peppercorn.

124

"Ha!" Ruckaru laughed, "I do not seek impossible gifts. I say you are lovely because you are. You must realize, of course, that I am somewhat prejudiced. I favor feathers over fur."

"You didn't...," said Peppercorn.

"...introduce...," said Flutterby,

"...the dog," said Payslee.

"So I didn't," replied Ruckaru, "And for a rather good reason actually. I don't know him myself. If you desire an introduction, perhaps one of the treeclimbers would accommodate you. They seem to be his friend."

Peppercorn fluttered down from the high rafters to perch on the top shelf behind the cages.

"How very curious...," she said.

"Yes, a dog and treeclimbers...," said Payslee.

"And friends yet, the old pheasant claims," said Flutterby.

"It's true. He is our friend. He helped us find this place," said Janna. "His name is Fred."

Fred nodded. The pigeons did likewise, looking a bit perplexed.

"The whole affair is very odd," said Ruckaru. "In any case...," and he turned to the squirrels, "this answers one of your questions. The pigeons are the reason I know that other animals were here earlier. This place is home to these wondrous birds a reasonable share of the time, you see. At least considerably more of the time than the horses."

"Ah, so that's the reason...," said Flutterby.

"That uncaged treeclimbers are found in the big den...," said Peppercorn.

"Because you seek a previous visitor," said Payslee.

"That's right," said Frafan. "we seek our brother...the red treeclimber's friend. When we find him we hope to find his mate as well."

"Ah, yes," said Flutterby.

"I see," said Payslee.

"Exactly," added Peppercorn.

From their high roost the pigeons peered down, waiting for the next question. It took a long time. Finally, with a quaver in her voice, Janna did the asking.

"Have there been any gray squirrels here?"

"Oh, indeed...," said Payslee.

"At any one time or another one might find...," added Flutterby.

"...a gray treeclimber or two in this barn," finished Peppercorn.

Frafan craned his neck toward the pigeons. Why did everything seem to hang on the words of birds lately? First crows, then a pheasant, now pigeons. It was these birds, sitting far above, that held the secret. They knew what he feared to discover.

"Might there have been two gray squirrels here about the time of the first snow...a male and a female?" he asked slowly.

"There was..."

"There were..."

"There has been..."

Janna fairly shouted, "Were their names Ephran and Kaahli?"

The pigeons looked at one another, then back at the squirrels below them.

"Sorry," said Peppercorn. "There were a pair of squirrels here, in a cage..."

"They were very quiet. The male slept a great deal...," said Payslee.

"And the female just lay by his side," said Flutterby. "We did not ask their names."

Janna's face fell. "It doesn't sound much like the Ephran and Kaahli I know," she said.

"Still," said Frafan, "if he was hurt..."

"I'm sorry we can't be of more help," said Flutterby.

"But the season you inquire about is a time when we do as much flying as we can," said Peppercorn.

"There is still food to find then. We leave the barn early — and return late. We don't get a chance to visit with those in cages then as we do now," said Payslee.

Klestra was silent. Janna's face was a mask of disappointment. Frafan knew he had to say something.

"Well, I think we have to assume it was them. We have to go on from here."

"Come, Frafan. How could they have traveled this far from The Pond?" muttered Klestra. "A badly hurt male and a half-crazed female? Impossible."

"Who knows what is and what is not possible? How can we find out who they were unless those squirrels are still somewhere about, somewhere they can be found. The quest is not over." Frafan hesitated and turned his face toward the pigeons. "Can you tell us where they might be now?"

"No! No!" Ruckaru screeched. "I don't want to listen!"

Everyone turned to the rooster who had spun away from the mesh and run to far corner of his cage. For the first time Frafan noticed a thin stick fastened to the underside of one of the bird's wings, which Ruckaru had raised over his head.

"What in the world...," said Payslee.

"...ails you," said Peppercorn.

"...you silly old pheasant?" asked Flutterby.

"He's afraid to find out what happens to birds and animals who are held in cages," said Farnsworth softly.

The brown horse snorted.

Peppercorn grimaced. "Quite ridiculous," she said.

"Yes," agreed Payslee, "No wonder he never wanted to speak of the creatures who..."

"...inhabited these cages before him," said Flutterby.

"I can't say that I blame him," said Frafan. "I'm not certain that I want to hear the answer to my own question."

"I hate to disappoint you, but I don't think any of us can give you an answer," said Peppercorn.

"Again, you must understand that we are not here much of the time," said Flutterby.

"Though we sleep in this place almost always, and eat here frequently, we do fly away to many other places," said Payslee.

"So I'm sadly afraid we can't tell you where all the guests in the cages end up," Peppercorn said.

"However, Ruckaru, you old goose, I have seen many caged birds and animals freed," said Flutterby. "I've seen them fly and run off, over or through the trees. One day early last warm season we even saw squirrels releasing squirrels from a cage among the apple trees."

The pheasant dropped one wing slowly and peered sheepishly beneath the other. "'Squirrels releasing squirrels'?" he asked quietly.

"You...you were here then...the day Ephran and Kaahli set Kaahli's father and brother free," murmured Frafan.

"Flutterby, did you recognize the pair of squirrels who were here in cages as the ones who opened the other squirrels' cage?" Klestra asked excitedly.

"Too far away...," said Flutterby.

"From the apple trees...," said Payslee.

"To be sure," said Peppercorn.

"Could they possibly have been the same squirrels?" Janna was practically begging.

"Never occurred...," said Payslee.

"To us...," said Flutterby.

"To ask," said Peppercorn.

Frafan sighed and shook his head. Every question seemed to lead to a hole without depth. "When did you last see these two gray squirrels, the ones who lay in a cage in this barn?" he asked.

"One brisk morning, as I remember...," said Payslee.

"But when we returned that evening...," said Peppercorn.

"They were gone," said Flutterby.

"Could they have been set free?" asked Klestra.

"Perhaps," replied Peppercorn, "but we saw neither of them again."

"Yes," agreed Payslee, "And I don't think they could have traveled far..."

"Wait! Wait!" Flutterby flapped a damp wing at her sisters. "Could they have been taken away...in the blue carrier?"

"Yes. Yes, now that you mention it. Entirely possible," said Peppercorn. "That would explain why we did not see them again."

"Definitely. They could have been placed in the blue carrier and taken away," nodded Payslee.

"It has been done before," said Flutterby, and the pigeons nodded solemnly at one another.

"Stop this! Please!" shouted Ruckaru. "What are you talking about? What in the world is a 'blue carrier'?"

Flutterby said, "Why, the blue carrier is the big shiny container that The Many Colored Ones travel in. Surely you've seen them. Not all are blue, of course. Like Those that use them, carriers are many colored."

She glanced at the upturned faces. It was quite obvious that the squirrels had no idea what she was talking about.

"Come now!" she continued, "No animal which lives anywhere near The Many Colored Ones can miss seeing these huge objects that carry Them about! When They don't walk or, I suspect, when They want to get somewhere far away very quickly, They climb into this big cage..."

"...A 'carrier'," said Peppercorn. "You know...a shiny thing with four round black legs along its belly. Once The Many Colored Ones are inside of it the legs roll over the earth with great speed..."

"...Faster than we can flap our wings," said Payslee. "And The Many Colored Ones, within their little shelter, scoot off along those grassless ribbons of ground: those smooth paths that lead to the edge of the earth."

Fred, who'd been silent ever since the pigeons arrived, lifted his head and said, "Cars 'n trucks! I know whut ya mean! Now you're talkin' stuff I know somethin' about."

CHAPTER XVI

DRINKERS OF THE PALE RED JUICE

hey talked for a long while after that, as the world outside the big barn grew dark. They talked first of the astounding "carriers", those movers of Many Colored Ones called "cars" and "trucks" and "vans". Suddenly Fred was the most knowledgeable among them. Even Klestra was impressed.

And carriers were only the beginning of what was discussed. Fred's observations during the long time he'd nested with a Many Colored One added to what Frafan had seen in his trips to the white den and what Blackie had told him. The other creatures in the barn were as much amused as they were fascinated by Frafan's excitement when he realized what words like "boxes" and "doors" and "shelves" and "steps" really meant. He squirmed and gurgled like a thirsty worm on dry earth in a hot sun.

In his experience Klestra had seen a car only once, and then at a great distance. Janna remembered seeing one that belonged to the Inhabitants of the white den at Corncrib Farm. Obedient daughter that she was, she never got close enough to the dangerous dens to learn anything about the noisy, smoke-breathing things. Not that she'd wanted to anyway.

Frafan, explorer and seeker, had seen the green car with the fat round legs, kept in a small dark den with but a single opening, on the far side of Blackie's nest. It terrified him. It sneaked up on him once, surprising him while he was poking around the place. Chugging and sputtering, it nearly caused him to run headlong into a stump. He'd not go near the thing's hiding place after that.

Luckily, the likes of these car things were rarely seen or heard near the nest. Jafthuh and Odalee, born and raised in the deep woods, could tell their young ones nothing about them. Frafan wanted to learn all he could, but he had decided these ugly, smelly, gigantic creatures were a little beyond what he thought he'd ever need to know. He was wrong. Fred would have to be their source of information.

"Do they breathe?" asked Frafan.

"Must," said Fred. "Sure blow some foul smellin' air out their backsides."

"What do they eat?" asked Janna.

"Don't rightly know if they eat," admitted Fred. "Know they drink though. Master stuffs a vine into the side of his truck. Old black vine. Hollow inside. Juice comes out. Red stuff. Not the same juice inside a you'n me. Thinner stuff. Lighter color. Terrible smellin'. You know what I mean. Anyway, right inta the truck she goes. Glub, glub, glub."

"They have a mouth in their side?" Once again, Klestra was having trouble with what he was hearing.

"Yup."

Unknown and frightening as they might be, cars and trucks took on great importance if one of them transported Ephran and Kaahli away from this place. Unfortunately, the horses, who might have something to add, had fallen asleep — or at least weren't answering any questions, even if asked in fairly loud voices. And so the conversation slowly drifted to other topics.

That the identity of the gray squirrels who'd been in the barn was unknown was a disheartening fact, but Frafan was determined to make the best of it. Something inside insisted it had to have been Ephran and Kaahli. The timing had been right; the squirrels in question were here when it first snowed.

But he could not imagine how to answer Klestra's question: How indeed would two treeclimbers, neither in any shape to travel, have made it all this way...to the very farm where they had freed Aden and Laslum from a cage? And, of course, there was at least as great a problem in imagining why they would come here of their own free will, even if they were able to travel.

"So we know there were squirrels here," said Klestra, "and that's all well and good. They may or may not have been Ephran and Kaahli. Whoever they were, they may have left this place in one of those car or truck things. But how can we find out who they were, if they did, and where they went?"

"...Or were taken," Janna corrected.

"I think no one can answer that except The Many Colored Ones," said Frafan with a sigh.

The treeclimbers lay down on the dusty floor, mulling over what they'd heard. The pigeons could be of no further help. At first Frafan felt frustrated that Flutterby, Peppercorn, and Payslee hadn't paid more attention to what was happening around them, for not being more interested in what became of those squirrels, and what their names were. Then he told himself this was the way of things. Most birds and animals found looking out for themselves about as much an undertaking as they could manage. Ephran and Kaahli's whereabouts may have been uppermost in his thoughts and dreams for days, but why should it be among theirs?

"I'm getting hungry," Janna said.

"Now that you mention it, so am I," said Klestra.

"Hunger is not a problem in this den," said Flutterby.

"Come over here...," said Peppercorn, fluttering down to one of those roundish lumps propped against the wall, very near where The Many Colored One had obtained food for Fred.

"...And peek inside," said Payslee.

"What is it?" asked Frafan.

"Things to eat...," said Peppercorn.

"Called 'bag'," said Fred, before the other two pigeons could say a word.

Klestra cautiously approached the bag. He stuck his nose out and sniffed. "Smells like corn," he said with a big smile directed at Frafan and Janna. He jumped to the rough surface. Pulling with his front claws, the floppy upper part of the bag opened wide and spilled cracked corn and oats onto the floor.

"Food!" Janna and Frafan said together. Klestra slid down and the three squirrels attacked the grain as though they hadn't eaten since early that morning which, when they stopped to think of it, was precisely the case.

After some serious and silent munching, Frafan sat back, sighed, and licked a bit of corn dust from Janna's ear. "My, oh my, that was wonderful. Bags are fine things indeed. Now then, I have to bring up another matter that still bothers me," he said.

"What..." asked Flutterby.

"Might..." said Payslee.

"That be?" finished Peppercorn.

"The crows who helped find this place warned us about a huge, ferocious, and very noisy skyhunter. From their description, I know they weren't referring to pigeons."

"Yeh," said Fred, "big silver wings, they said. Hardly ever flapped 'em, they said."

Flutterby's quizzical look turned into a big smile. "See!" she said to Payslee and Peppercorn, "I told you those old black thieves were frightened off by the shiny winged one!"

"Do you mean to say that some kind of terrible skyhunter does actually nest here?" asked Janna.

"Oh, the crows were not imagining things," confirmed Flutterby with a hearty laugh.

"Is it a hawk?" asked a nervous Klestra.

"No," replied Payslee.

"An owl then," said Frafan.

"Not an owl," said Peppercorn.

"Come sisters," said Flutterby, "enough teasing. I will introduce our treeclimbing friends to the noisy and mysterious skyhunter."

"Introduce us?" squeaked Klestra, his tail forming a large curl above his head.

Wide-eyed, the squirrels watched as the pigeons flapped through the air and came to rest on a half wall. On the other side of the wall, behind the horse stalls and near the door that led outside, was a small and

131

very dark place.

"Don't go over there," growled Fred.

"I must see what frightened crows so badly and what pigeons seem not to fear," said Frafan as he took a few steps toward the wall.

"I wish you could come with us," Janna said in a small voice to Fred, knowing she'd feel a great deal safer with the big dog at her side.

"Really," the white pigeon said, "don't be afraid. Come along now."

"You must trust us," said Peppercorn.

"The terrible skyhunter is fast asleep," said Payslee.

Frafan looked up at the pigeons. Why would they lie? It was foolish to be afraid. There was something to learn here. And it must not be dangerous. Nevertheless, he noticed his paws were shaking as he crept toward the dimly lit part of the barn where the birds waited. And he realized he was talking to himself again, mumbling over and over that there was nothing to be afraid of. Janna and Klestra followed him with even slower steps.

He peeped around the corner and into darkness. At first he could make out only vague shadows. More slabs of wood, shelves, stacked with unknown objects of various shapes, and long sticks of different sizes leaning against the near wall, some with flat ends, some with spindly claws, some with long spiny whiskers. Dust and spider webs were everywhere. He noticed a ghastly smell. It burned his nostrils.

As his eyes adjusted to the faint light, a large object on the floor slowly became visible. The thing seemed to glow in the darkness with a dull silver sheen. It had immensely long wings, spread wide, not tucked in as one would expect in a sleeping bird. It rested on two spindly legs, rounded at the end where they met the floor. A comically twisted stick was attached sideways to its nose and its tail was three flat appendages, one standing straight up and the other two pointing outward on either side. There were no feathers.

"That's no skyhunter!" said Klestra, who had peeked over Frafan's shoulder and now jumped out in the open.

"What is it then?" asked Janna.

"I've seen things like this...in the sky...over the woods," said Frafan, moving closer, scampering around to look at the skyhunter from behind.

"Certainly," agreed Klestra, "I've seen them too. I was obviously correct when I surmised they must be a toy of The Many Colored Ones."

"Do you mean there are many hunters like this?" said Janna, still perplexed.

"Oh, yes!" said Payslee.

"This is not the only one of its kind," said Peppercorn.

"As his eyes adjusted to the light,
a large object became visible."

"But there are no more of them here," said Flutterby.

"When I've seen these winged things, high over the woods, I thought they were much larger than this one," said Frafan.

"The ones that fly over the woods are much larger," nodded Flutterby. "They fly so high, so very far above where even we can fly, it is difficult to imagine how very big they really are..."

"As I said, this one is just a toy," said Payslee. "It is much smaller than the real thing..."

"Those who live in the yellow den cause this one to fly," said Peppercorn, "but They stay on the earth and direct it in its flight."

"They built this thing, then, with their paws?" said Klestra.

"Yes."

"Amazing," said the red squirrel. "Simply amazing."

"Whut's goin' on over there?" shouted Fred. All three of his friends had disappeared and everyone was speaking too softly for him to hear.

Klestra ran back, out unto the barn floor where Fred could see him, and said, "Very interesting lesson over here, Fred. Actually," he mused, "more of a mystery than a lesson."

"Yes," agreed Frafan. "Everything we learn about Them seems to lead to new questions."

They all talked and laughed then, and told Fred of the trick The Many Colored Ones apparently unwittingly played on the crows. A toy skyhunter, of all things! Who would have guessed? A toy which apparently derived its energy from the awful-smelling red fluid. A toy that roared like thunder. A toy that flew like a bird but left smoke and not song in its wake. A toy that played in the clouds and yet could be controlled from the earth. It was nothing short of astounding. What would be next?

Finally they tried to get down to business, to formulate a plan of action, a few ideas of where to go from here. New ideas, however, refused to budge from sleepy heads.

Ruckaru and Farnsworth fell asleep on the floors of their cages. Fred curled up near the wall where his silvery vine was attached. The pigeons, on a high rafter, tucked their heads under their wings. The horses stood silently in wooden stalls. Frafan could not tell if their eyes were closed. The squirrels found a wonderfully warm and soft resting place in a large pile of old brown bags that smelled of green grass, golden corn, and the sweetness of black earth.

Frafan had many dreams that night, but he was so tired and his sleep was so very deep he could never make sense of any of them. They would remain one jumbled mosaic of scenes and shapes and sounds.

He would vaguely recall cruel laughter coming from a misshapen face with redstained teeth and long ears. A rabbit? Birds:

crows and pigeons together, along with a large Many Colored One, perched in a straight and uncomfortable-looking row, on what at first seemed to be a large rock. Perhaps the back of a horse. Or was it a dog? And he and Ephran, seated in a leafy elm, watching one of the winged skyhunters of The Many Colored Ones over the forest. As it swung low over the trees, graceful and hardly mumbling, he could see someone inside. Surprise of surprises: it was himself...looking quite at ease and bored with the whole affair!

He woke to muted sunlight coming through the barn windows. The pigeons were gone, apparently off seeing what the new day had to offer. Klestra was still asleep, but Janna was not to be seen. After the first quick thrust of fright in his chest, and before the cold fear reached his mind, he heard her voice.

"Oh good! You're awake," she said. "Come up here, Frafan, and look out."

She stood atop a stack of stained brown boxes, looking down at him. He got to his paws, waking Klestra who yawned and stretched. Frafan shook the dust from his fur and clambered up beside her.

Through the very dirty window he could make out the neat yellow den, home of The Many Colored Ones. The earth between the barn and their den was barely covered with snow. It occurred to him that the storm he smelled before they sought shelter in the barn had weakened considerably. As it turned out, they would not have had to seek shelter in here after all. His weather-forecasting ability was not as awesome as Phetra thought. Only time would tell if the decision to jump through the window had been good or bad.

Two of The Many Colored Ones stood outside their den. A large One, male he thought, the One who had brought Fred into the barn, and a much smaller One — the One who had fed the dog. Father and son, almost certainly. A Third stood near the entrance to the den, forelegs folded across its chest...smaller than the large One, bigger than the small One...longer hair... more delicate features. A female. It must be a female. When She went inside, the two Males disappeared into a smaller den which stood between the barn and the yellow den.

The air grew very quiet. Sun glistened from white earth. A pair of sparrows fluttered about, looking for seeds in the shallow snow.

"What do you suppose They're doing in there?" asked Klestra, who'd shaken the sleep from his head and found a seat next to them.

"I don't know," said Janna, "but I suspect..."

A coughing and snorting sound cut her comments short. The squirrels watched in unblinking silence as something long, blue, and shiny rolled slowly out of the den. What was this? It was big...huge, actually. He didn't pretend to be an expert, but this creature, or whatever it was, did not look like any of the "cars" Frafan had seen before. It didn't look like anything he'd ever seen, period! Suddenly, its side split open, and the little Male jumped from the thing's very innards, and began to run toward the barn.

"It's coming this way!" gasped Klestra.

"What's coming this way?" asked Ruckaru, standing with his back against the webbing of his cage.

"Small Many Colored One," said Frafan curtly. "It's leading a long blue monster...car, truck, whatever it is...right to us." He scrambled down from his perch.

"'A long blue monster...?'" Klestra repeated, tail twitching from side to side.

"What shall we do?" squeaked Janna.

"Hide again. Those of us who are able will have to find a place to hide," said Frafan.

CHAPTER XVII

INTO THE DARKNESS

The squirrels had barely enough time to conceal themselves before two parts of the wall swung away from each other, screeching painfully. One entire side of the barn seemed to disappear, revealing a vast expanse of white earth, fields, and bare trees. Frafan squinted as bright light once again flooded the interior of the barn.

From around the corner appeared the monstrous thing Fred called a van, rolling along on plump black legs that flattened the thin layer of snow beneath them with a crunching sound. Its heading changed slightly, toward the gaping hole where the barn, only a moment earlier, had seemed a solid wall.

As it turned, and even amid the awe and excitement, Frafan could not help but wonder at the streaks of white on the monster's flanks. They formed unnatural yet graceful arcs and lines. Could they be scratches in what he knew was a very hard and shiny pelt? If they were, they bore a striking resemblance to the kind on the collar Fred wore around his neck.

The dog sat on his tail, tongue hanging, unafraid. Could it really be that these mind-boggling vans were old stuff to Fred? Or was it that the gentle and simple dog simply did not appreciate danger? Klestra lay on the floor, behind an unopened bag of grain, eyes fixed on the van. Frafan's heart pounded against his chest as though it was trying to escape. Janna was emitting little yelps, almost silent, apparently not even aware she was doing so. Or perhaps — Frafan couldn't be sure — she might have hiccups.

The blue monster rolled slowly up to the doorway and stopped. Now he could hear it growling; a low, steady rumble. At the same time, clouds of graywhite smoke rose from its underside. Two red eyes, one on either side of matched clear ones, flickered brightly for an instant. The rumbling ceased. One last wisp of smoke was swept away by a gust of air.

Part of the van opened wide. Frafan was sure it was the side opposite the one that he saw split open before. A door? Did such a horrendous monster have a door? The large Many Colored One stepped to the ground. The smaller One, who had apparently opened the side of the barn, skipped into the shadows ahead of his bigger companion. What a strange way to move!

"Woof!" said Fred.

The small Many Colored One made a gurgling sound, ran to the dog, and squatted on his hindlegs. He put his front paws into the fur on Fred's back.

The squirrels cowered near the silver skyhunter. Immobilized by fear and fascination, intent on every move of The Many Colored Ones, they were ready to bolt at any movement in their direction. While the little male One hugged and petted Fred, the larger One walked to the blue van, which nearly filled the opening to the barn. He stood between its dull red eyes and, somehow, tickling or pushing with its forepaws, coaxed the shiny monster into opening its massive jaws.

Frafan choked. He knew he must be brave. He knew this had to be just another of The Many Color Ones' amazing toys. He told himself that this thing did not really breath and actually eat food as the animals of the forest did. He wanted, so badly, to believe that it could not see, or think, or feel. Would Fred laugh if he knew how near panic the brother of Ephran was?

He couldn't help himself. This thing; this huffing, puffing, grumbling, blinking terror that might have taken Ephran and Kaahli away, was too much to face. The huge jaws parted, but not up and down as with every other creature Frafan had ever seen. These jaws opened from side to side! And their parting revealed an enormous black cavern. It was too dark inside to discern whether or not there might be teeth.

The large One left the van with its gigantic mouth standing open. Frafan sniffed for the acrid smell and listened for the hissing sound of hunter's breath, but no sickening odor came to his nostrils and no wheezing to his ears. The longlegged One then walked to last night's bed of empty bags and picked them up with a single swipe of his forepaw. He then walked back to the gaping mouth and pushed his load into it.

"Is It feeding that...terrible thing?" whispered Klestra.

"If It is, the thing isn't satisfied," said Janna. It was true, the jaws made no move to close, no move to chew. Had the thing just swallowed, in one big bundle, that mass of soft brown material?

The small One made a sound in the direction of the large One, who answered with a grunt. The two of Them moved to Farnsworth's cage. Each on an end, They picked it up with their front legs and slowly carried it, along with its little prisoner, toward the mouth.

"Ohhh...No!" whimpered Janna.

Farnsworth made not a sound. His eyes were closed as he and his cage slid out of sight into the darkness.

Then They removed the vine that led to Fred's neck. The dog was led by his collar to a large empty cage.

"Don't let Them do it, Fred," Klestra whispered under his breath.

But he did. The mesh door was opened and Fred was pushed, gently but unceremoniously, inside. Frafan noticed an amazing thing: Fred's tail was still wagging! The dog was heavy and his cage was big. With obvious effort The Many Colored Ones carried the squirrels' gentle friend to the sacrifice.

138

"We have to do something!" said Klestra.

"What do you suggest?" Frafan asked, the old unfriendly lump of fright back in his throat.

Fred followed Farnsworth into the dark cavern. The last Janna saw of him was a slightly puzzled and bemused look on his face. His tail was still moving, but slowly, almost absentmindedly.

The Many Colored Ones stood fearlessly between the squirrels and their lost friends, right next to the awful opening, exchanging unintelligible sounds. Suddenly the large One walked to the side of the van, stepped inside, and pulled the opening shut behind Him. The small One scampered off into the far recesses of the barn.

The blue monster woke with a roar, a flash of lights, and a puff of gray smoke.

Ruckaru was curled in the farthest corner of his cage, both wings over his head. The horses stood in their stalls, faces like masks. Flutterby, Peppercorn, and Payslee had quietly returned, slipping through their little door. Now they perched quietly in a row, high overhead, peering down. Klestra and Janna looked like they wanted to crawl under the hard floor. Janna's eyes held bulging tears.

The jaws stood wide open. Frafan realized that there was nothing between him and the awesome cavity. In that instant he remembered his dream...the one he'd had in Great Woods Warren... the one that Redthorn had waked him from...the one where he faced the gaping jaws...

"Klestra," he said, "I have to go."

"What...?"

"I don't have time to explain. I'll be back." He wondered if he believed himself. "Take care of each other. Tell Mayberry I think I'm close to the answer. Good-bye, Janna."

He ignored the utter astonishment on their faces and took a deep breath. Then he stood on trembling legs and ran as fast as he could, trying not to think, trying not to listen to the voice inside his head that shrieked he was running the wrong way, that freedom lay through the open wall of the barn, past the blue monster, and up the nearest tall tree.

Just as the small Many Colored One reappeared from the shadows, Frafan leaped through wide blue jaws — and into the black unknown.

"Trafan leaped through wide blue jaws - and into the black unknown"

CHAPTER XVIII

INSIDE THE BLUE MONSTER

(T)he small male Many Colored One struggled with the object He grasped in his front paws; half carrying, half dragging. It looked like the same material the squirrels had used for a nest the previous night; a bag, only filled with other bags. He boosted it unto the lower lip of the monster and pushed it into the waiting mouth. He stroked one big jaw, then the other, and they slammed shut with a resounding "Bang!".

"Frafan....," whimpered Janna.

Klestra had not moved. He and Janna continued to watch, with cold fascination and horror, as the van rolled slowly away. The large One came out of the van once more, pulled on the doors, and closed off the outside world. The interior of the barn once again became dim.

Ruckaru lifted his wing, peered around him, took a deep breath and peeped, "They didn't take me!" He sounded as though he didn't know whether to be delighted or disappointed.

"Quickly, Janna," said Klestra. "We must find our way out of this place! We must follow the blue van!"

"No use, no use. It runs too fast for you," said the white pigeon.

"If it decides to go far, I doubt that even those of us with wings can keep pace," said Payslee.

"But we can try," said Peppercorn.

With that, all three pigeons slipped through the little trap door, spread their wings, and sailed away in pursuit of the van.

* * * * *

Frafan found himself standing, legs apart, on a smooth and slippery surface. The light was very dim. He noted, with considerable amazement, that he no longer felt afraid. Actually, he was quite calm. Then he wondered if he might not be so frightened that he had passed into that state father spoke of — wherein his mind had decided that loss of breath, forever, was so near and so certain that it was no longer possible to concern oneself with a thing like fear. Or else he might have suspected all along this peculiar and alien "van" would not really harm him. As Ephran had told him: "Many of the things that frighten us the most have no interest in helping or harming. They don't even know we exist."

In any case, by the time he opened his eyes, waiting for the blow that refused to fall, the massive blue jaws had closed without ruffling the fur on the back of his neck.

"Fred?" he whispered hoarsely.

"Yep. I'm here."

"Farnsworth?"

"Yes. I'm fine," came a soft voice.

The van moved ahead and daylight streamed in from either side. Bright beams shone in as well from what he had thought might be some kind of big buggy eyes in the jaws. Now he understood they were all openings to see outside, made of the same smooth stuff as the openings through which he spied on The Many Colored Ones at Corncrib Farm, the openings that were not always openings; called windows.

There were no teeth inside the monster. Where he stood was cold and dry, not moist and warm as one would expect inside the mouth or belly of a hungry hunter. A flush of embarrassment washed over him.

The part of the van he and Fred and Farnsworth occupied was closed off from the two Many Colored Ones. Those strange creatures were enclosed in their own little nest somewhere in the part that took the lead in this crazy ride. Fred's story the previous night was that The Many Colored Ones sit in the front of trucks and vans and cars...and control where They go. His words had been hard to understand, but obviously true. Frafan's heart came up into his throat as they took a sharp turn. He, along with the cages, skidded toward one side. Lest it surprise him again, he spread his legs apart for balance.

"Fred," he asked, "do you have any idea where we are being taken?"

"Not sure," said Fred, "least 'bout you folks. Suspek it's takin' me home."

"Home?" Frafan was having a hard time thinking, or at least keeping his mind on one subject. There were so many things he wanted to ask about just now, and he had no idea how much time he had to find them out. Besides, the swaying and lurching of the van was very distracting and worrisome.

"Sure. Been taken home before," Fred said matter-of- factly.

"Are you telling me these Many Colored Ones know your Master's den is at Blue Lake?" asked Frafan.

"Nah. We don't nest much in that den, just during the warm season, sometimes in huntin' season," said Fred. "Got another den, one we stay in mosta the time, in a place where there's lotsa Many Colored Ones." The dog looked at Frafan's befuddled face and broke into a crooked smile. "Oh, wait, I see whut's confusin' you! It ain't these here Ones actually know my Master. Oh, no. It's the thing aroun' my neck. The straight and squiggly scratches on her seem ta mean somethin' to 'em. Tells 'em things. Like where I come from."

"Preposterous!" thought Frafan, but he didn't say it aloud. Fred must be very upset about what had happened so far today. Maybe he wasn't so accustomed to being tied and in a cage as he said, especially when the cagers were unfamiliar Many Colored Ones. Could he be so agitated that he'd utter such foolish remarks and think they made sense? All Frafan saw when he looked into Fred's eyes was honest simplicity.

Then again, maybe the scratches did have a pattern. Maybe Fred meant they could be understood in some way, as Ephran taught Frafan to understand the sky and the wind. The whole idea was intriguing. But this was not the time. There were more immediate problems.

Frafan turned and said, "Farnsworth, I'm going to try and get you out of that cage." He moved carefully toward the raccoon on the slippery floor.

"Never mind, Frafan," said Farnsworth. "I've had some time to look these cages over. There's no way you or I can open it. I'd rather you climb up on Fred's cage. Maybe you can see outside and get a clue as to where we are...and where we're going."

"I think you're right, Farnsworth," agreed Frafan, after examining the cage door for a few moments. "No use wasting time. I'll take a look outside."

The hard, thick webbing made for easy climbing, and Fred's big cage had slid under one of the windows. Just above Fred's head Frafan got his balance and peered out, into the sunlit morning countryside. He gasped.

Round black legs beneath him must be turning incredibly fast! As fast as any whitetailed deer in a big hurry. Maybe as fast as a hawk in a steep dive. Trees alongside the flat and smooth path the van followed were fairly flying past. Then, suddenly, the trees were gone. The sun, behind the van, cast short shadows on a huge barren field of white snow and clods of black dirt. The field stretched far away, to the edge of the sky itself.

Whistling past at regular intervals were those strange trees, one after another, like huge sticks without branches, trees without limbs or bark, trees all connected together by long vines, stretching from the top of one to the top of the next, trees like those supporting the vines near Corncrib Farm. Then came a slough, a little frozen puddle thick with brown cattails. Scenes flashed by, one after another, so fast that it made him dizzy. He lay down on the mesh of the cage and looked down at Fred.

"Well," said the dog, "what's goin' on out there?"

"The world is sliding by, Fred," he whispered.

"Huh? Oh, I git you. You ain't use ta movin' so fast."

"I most certainly am not."

"Can you tell where we are?" asked Farnsworth.

"I have no idea," said Frafan. "I don't know if I'd be able to recognize my own home if I went by it at this speed."

"We're slowin' down now," observed Fred.

The sound of air rushing past, and the sound of those plump

round legs on rough sand beneath, was indeed slowing. Puzzled looks were exchanged. Frafan jumped from the top of Fred's cage and hid under the brown sacks just as the van rolled to a complete stop.

Something hard slammed against something hard. He heard steps of The Many Colored Ones on the gravel outside. The jaws of the van opened. From his hiding place Frafan saw the small One jump nimbly inside and grab Farnsworth's cage with a front paw. He slid it along the floor until the large One could reach it. Together They lifted the raccoon and his prison out of the truck and out of sight. Fred and Frafan's eyes met. A moment later the cage came sliding back. Farnsworth was no longer inside! The blue jaws slammed shut, big paws once more scraped along the ground outside, and the van began to move slowly forward.

Frafan raced up Fred's cage. He looked back just in time to see Farnsworth, standing on the far side of a grassy and nearly snowless gully. The woods behind was dense with oak and ash. The little raccoon was standing on his hindlegs, watching the van as it sped away. Frafan raised his paw in farewell. He didn't know if Farnsworth could see him. The gray figure with the ringed tail faded from view around a curve in the path.

"Can ya see the l'il critter?" asked Fred.

"Yes, I saw him."

"He okay?"

"Yes. He seems just fine." Frafan peered down at the dog. "They just let him go, Fred." There was wonder in his voice. "They set him free, right at the beginning of the trees."

"Yeh."

"...And you think They're taking you home?"

Fred grinned. "Can't figure what else They'd do with me. They do some ding-binged funny things, but never saw 'Em eat a dog."

Frafan turned back to the window. The scene had become one of more long barren fields of dirt and snow, patches of trees, some close and some in the far distance. He paid no attention. His mind was a jumble.

Farnsworth was gone, evidently free. Free to go back to his family. And Fred was convinced he was going to be taken home. That left just him. And exactly where was he going? The Many Colored Ones, who obviously controlled the movements of this van, could have no plans for him. They didn't even know he was along. Despite his feeling that it was important for him to be where he was, just what did a wild ride in this thing called a van have to do with the search for Ephran and Kaahli? What were Klestra and Janna doing? Where would they go now that he'd left them without any explanation? Rushing away from his woods at breakneck speed, how would he ever find his way back to the comfortable nest of Jafthuh and Odalee?

The jiggling ride suddenly changed. The ground beneath must have become very smooth. The sound of gravel was gone, replaced by a steady whirring. Frafan got to his paws.

He hesitated a moment and murmured, "Fred, we're there."

"We're where?" asked Fred.

Frafan closed his eyes, lowered his head, and said, "We're in the warren of The Many Colored Ones."

CHAPTER XIX

END OF ONE TRAIL

Janna wept silently for a long while after the smoke- breathing van rumbled away. Klestra was unable to comfort her, which didn't surprise him. He didn't feel much like being comforted himself. Even Ruckaru was at a loss for words. It was not until the pigeons returned, fluttering through their entrance in the roof, did Janna cease her sniffling. She looked up expectantly then, along with the other animals on the floor of the barn.

"Ladies!" cried Ruckaru, "What news?"

The pigeons, out of breath, were unable to speak for a time. Finally Flutterby managed, "They set..."

"...Farnsworth...," gasped Peppercorn.

"...Free." finished Payslee.

"Free?" echoed Ruckaru.

"Yes..."

"Opened his cage..."

"Near edge of the woods."

"That...uh...b...blue thing...didn't eat him?" stuttered Janna.

"The blue van...," said Peppercorn.

"Does not eat...," said Payslee.

"Animals or birds," said Flutterby.

"Oh?" said Janna, more puzzled than embarrassed.

"Did you speak to him?" asked Klestra.

"What of Frafan? And Fred?" squeaked Janna.

"According to the raccoon...the treeclimber and dog...were doing well when he last saw them...in the carrier, ah, van," said Peppercorn, breathing easier now.

"We talked to the raccoon for only a few moments," said Flutterby.

"He had little to tell us, and was anxious to find his family," said Payslee.

"Free!" Ruckaru repeated, as though in a trance.

"Ruckaru," Flutterby said firmly to the rooster, "why do you make an issue of the fact that The Many Colored Ones let the raccoon go?"

"Yes, we've told you we've seen Them allow animals and birds out of their cages in the past," said Peppercorn.

"Do you have trouble believing us?" asked Payslee.

"Of course I believe my beautiful pigeons!" protested Ruckaru. "But you must understand this freeing of Farnsworth is important for two reasons."

When he was certain he had everyone's attention (including the

147

horses, who were peering over the tops of their stalls at him) he explained, "First, if They would forgive a raccoon, who we all know loves to raid their fields of corn, then how much easier to excuse a delicate brightly colored bird of small appetite? Such as myself. Secondly, though I may believe what you say regarding what They have done with caged birds and animals in the past, we all know how fickle these two-legged Animals tend to be. I feel greatly encouraged these particular Many Colored Ones do not seem to have changed their ways. Not as yet, in any case."

"Good thinking!" Klestra said to the beaming pheasant, who preened his wing feathers with his beak. "You see, Janna, Frafan will be fine! Why should these Many Colored Ones harm a treeclimber who, after all, causes Them no trouble at all? Why, we spend nearly all of our time in the deep woods, eating buds and nuts and berries."

Janna felt a bit relieved. She tried not to dwell on the fact that the pheasant's logic was built entirely on the premise that cages were a punishment for eating The Many Colored Ones' corn. That theory was far from proven fact. The whole answer belonged to The Many Colored Ones Themselves.

She sniffed one last time anyway, and smiled at Ruckaru and Klestra with a smile she did not feel as sincerely as she wished she did. "Did you see where they took Fred and Frafan?"

"Alas...," sighed Payslee.

"The blue van travels very swiftly on its smooth path and plump round legs...," said Peppercorn.

"We could not keep up," finished Flutterby sadly.

"No matter," came the unexpected voice of one of the horses, "the brave treeclimber has done the only thing he could do."

"It's true," agreed Klestra. "Frafan followed the only trail left to follow."

"I hope he finds what he seeks," said the horse.

"Why can't we go where he went?" asked Janna. "We can wait here for the van to return and," she shuddered, "...jump into it as he did."

"That may involve a long wait," said Flutterby.

"It does not leave this place often," said Payslee.

"And when it does leave, it does not always follow the same path," said Peppercorn.

"You might find yourself in far different surroundings than your brother," said the horse. "Besides, one seeker should be enough to find the lost. As long as the lost are all in the same place, that is."

Janna sighed and sat on her tail. She gazed at the floor. The tears were gone. Dried up. She did not feel like crying anymore. And why should she? She had done her best. Besides, there was a new duty. She put on the brightest face she could and spoke to Klestra.

"We must go back then," she said. "We must tell my family what's happened here. Frafan and I promised Mayberry we would keep him informed too. We have to tell all of them Frafan carries on the search. It's important they know what we know. It will lessen their worry. It will give them hope."

Klestra frowned. "Well," he said, "since the crows won't come near this place we can't even try to send a message with them."

"What about my wonderful pigeons?" volunteered Ruckaru.

"Yes, we could carry your message," said Peppercorn, "but who would we give it to? A crow will invariably ignore a pigeon."

"And vice versa," said Flutterby. "I doubt if any message we carried to the deep woods would be heeded."

"We don't really belong to either place, the woods or the farm, you know," said Payslee.

"Best we carry our own story anyway," said Janna. "It's a strange story, a confused and twisted one."

"If we're to get any information to the forest before next warm season...and unless we want to remain barn-dwellers for a very long time...we better leave very soon," said Klestra. Then, as an afterthought, "I only hope we can find our way."

"Aha! Now that's where we can be of help," said Flutterby.

"Certainly!" said Payslee.

Everyone turned to Peppercorn, waiting for her to finish the thought, for her to explain how the pigeons would perform one last service for the squirrels. But she said nothing, only sat dumbly, looking at her sisters' faces. She finally broke into an embarrassed grin and shrugged her wings.

"We can guide you back the way you came, to a known landmark," explained Flutterby with an annoyed glance at her spotted sister.

"Of course!" said Payslee.

"Most surely!" recovered Peppercorn.

Klestra's ears stood up. "Do you think you could lead us as far as a place of large stones...on the bank of a stream?" he asked hopefully.

"Rocky Point!" cried Peppercorn.

"We most definitely know how to get to Rocky Point," said Payslee.

"First thing at sunup," said Flutterby.

Broken dreams have sharp edges

Wellnecott
"Never Enough"

CHAPTER XX
A PLACE SET ASIDE

he sights that swept past the moving van left Frafan speechless. Even though they'd talked with Fred about it after the ambush at Rocky Point, he had not realized that such incredible numbers of Many Colored Ones' dens, all in one place, was really possible! From where he sat, they were all his eyes could see. They were built nearly one atop the other, with scarcely room for clean air to blow between.

Not surprisingly, the dens sparkled in a rainbow of colors, and the difference in size was nothing short of astounding. Some rose almost as high as the tallest trees. Others were squat, with nearly flat black roofs. Some had those holes, "windows" he kept reminding himself, covered with the same clear film he was looking through right now, windows so large the inside of the den could be clearly seen. Some dens had a few tiny windows and some none at all. Some were built of slats of colored wood and some of squarish rocks, all the same size and color.

The earth around the van was very nearly smooth. No rolling hills or shady swales gave relief to his eyes or his heart. No cool green grass covered the earth, no prickly gooseberry or thick sumac bushes waved in the gentle breeze. Most disturbing was that there were few trees. The cool sun beat down on a landscape of straight and jagged lines.

More than sight was overwhelmed. His nose confirmed he was far from home. Terrible air filled his nostrils. It reeked of the sweat and excretement of these frightening things, cars and trucks, things which drank the vile thin red water.

Many Colored Ones were everywhere, in every nook and cranny. They varied enormously in height and width and and, of course, their pelts were every conceivable (and many heretofor inconceivable) color. Some pelts fit tight, some hung loose. Some of The Many Colored Ones stood still. Some strode along on their back legs, small forepaws swinging uselessly alongside. He noticed a few pairs holding one Another's front paw. For balance, he wondered? They weaved in and out, around each other, following smooth paths on the earth. They wobbled and tottered and raced in all directions, reminding Frafan of a family of brown ants he once playfully disturbed while they were collecting food.

There were cars and trucks and vans, rolling along on their uniformly plump legs. A few were much like the one he was in. Some were larger, most were smaller. They sped along, barely missing one another, stopping and starting. Every car or truck contained at least one Many Colored One. Now and again, with no warning, one of them would squeal in a most frighteningly loud and harsh manner, apparently

protesting a perceived bit of cheating or stretching of the rules of whatever game or contest they were involved in.

Everything, every single object he lay eyes on — except the dens themselves — were creating mindboggling noises. Clattering, clanging, hooting, screeching, scraping...the most powerful thunder of the warm season would be a whisper in comparison!

Fred could obviously hear the racket, but he seemed bored. He even yawned once or twice, and didn't bother to so much as try and look out the window while Frafan oohed and ahhed. "How ya figure ta find Ephran?" he asked suddenly.

"In this...this place," replied Frafan, swallowing hard. How indeed. "I really don't know. I guess I'll just start somewhere and keep on going. Sooner or later I should hope I find a clue."

"Think he's here?"

"I couldn't say," said Frafan. "It would seem odd that he'd come to such a place if he had a choice."

"But he prob'ly didn't," observed Fred. "Have a choice, that is."

"Probably not," agreed Frafan. "Not if he got here the way we did. I know I'm going to need some help, and Klestra and Janna are a long way back...somewhere.'"

"Wish I could help. Yer gonna feel real outa place 'round these parts."

"I don't doubt that," said Frafan. He took a deep breath and thought of Ephran and Blackie and of the many times he'd watched The Many Colored Ones near home, puttering around their own den. These were the same kind, just more of Them. No need to accept defeat before the battle. "...But I suppose I'm no more out of place here than you are in the woods. Besides, I hope I've learned something about Many Colored Ones. Or at least I hope these Many Colored Ones are like Those who nest near the den of Jafthuh and Odalee. Maybe I'll get some help from those gray treeclimbers you said have their dens here."

As they spoke, the van began to slow down. It turned abruptly into a smooth black trail, bouncing sharply once, and came to a complete stop. The rumbling of its heart fell silent, and Frafan shuddered to see they were parked between two large dens which seemed to lean threateningly over him. They heard, as well as felt, the Many Colored Ones leave the van.

"Fred, what do you suppose They're doing now?" whispered Frafan in a shaky voice.

The dog's eyes had widened and his tongue hung out. His long tail whisked back and forth against the webbing of his cage.

"Home, Frafan!" he said. "This's m'Master's den!"

The Many Colored Ones from the van had walked to the nearby red den and stood there, looking at it expectantly, as though waiting for something to happen. Sure enough, the door opened and a tall One appeared.

"Whut's goin' on, Frafan?" asked Fred.

Frafan described, as best he could, about the den, its color, its shape, and the One who now stood outside it.

"Sounds like Him!" Fred exclaimed, "sounds like m'Master. Listen, Frafan, why don'tcha get out with me? We can start lookin' fer Ephran right from here."

Frafan slowly shook his head. "I don't think so, Fred. Not because I don't think you'd be a great help. You already have been. And not that I don't appreciate the offer. But I feel I should go further with these Many Colored Ones. If Ephran and Kaahli came to this place — in this van — I'm quite sure they didn't get off at your Master's den. If they had, you or those treeclimbers you spoke of would most certainly have known it long ago. No, I have to keep going. Thanks anyway."

"S'pose that's true," said Fred. "But don't count me outa this. I'm gonna keep lookin' too."

Frafan smiled.

"If yer not gettin' out, I think ya better hide," said Fred. "Unless I miss m'guess, They're gonna open this thing up one more time."

Frafan glanced outside. Sure enough, all three Many Colored Ones were moving purposefully toward the back of the van. Frafan leapt from his perch on the cage and scurried to the pile of bags. Just before he pulled his head beneath them he looked up into Fred's big brown eyes.

"Good-bye, Fred. Thanks once more. For everything."

"S'long, Frafan. Good luck. Got a feelin' we ain't done workin' together yet."

The back of the van opened its gaping jaws once more, only now Frafan realized that they weren't jaws at all. Fred's cage was pulled out, into the brown grass and shallow snow. His tail flailed wildly as the cage was opened. He bounded out, free and barking, and galloped off, out of sight, around the corner of the den. The three Many Colored Ones made strange sounds, sounds that rumbled up from their bellies. They slid the empty cage into the van and closed it up again. In a few moments he heard Them reenter their compartment in front. The van began to move.

Well, here he was, riding to who knew where with a couple of empty cages and a pile of soft material called "bags"! Before he had time to consider his decision about remaining aboard, the van came to another stop. Frafan was not expecting this, and very nearly got caught out in the open, atop Fred's cage, as the back swung wide once again. This time the small One crawled inside (on all four legs the Creature looked more reasonable) and picked up one of the bags. Luckily, he chose one off by itself, not the one that had become Frafan's hiding place.

Should he run now? Frafan wondered. Could he get by the small One before It reached out and grabbed him? The van did not move. Where had they stopped? Was it squirrel he smelled? Frafan lay huddled where he was, dust from the bag tickling his nose, indecision numbing his mind. He heard something slide along the floor and come to rest next to his hiding place. Again, a bang, and darkness returned. Frafan tried not to breathe. What had been put into the van with him? Could it possibly be what it smelled like? He waited and waited for any movement, any sound. Curiosity won...and he peeked out.

Next to him was the same old bag, but now bloated. Sure enough, his nose had not lied, sticks of corn hung from its top! Well, at least he had food. But at the moment he was not in the least hungry.

Frafan felt very much alone and was painfully aware of the two empty cages. Maybe he should have made his break when Fred got off. At least, with Fred around, he'd have one friend and some real protection in this alien place. And there were gray squirrels in the trees near Fred's den. Certainly they would help him. But what would they be like — treeclimbers who made their dens in this place of Many Colored Ones'? Might they know of Ephran? They certainly couldn't know of the deep woods or they wouldn't stay here. Or would they?

Panic grew in his chest. The more he thought of it, the less he liked being closed up in here by himself. He crawled to the top of the corn-filled bag without a thought of eating. Even his interest in that brand new world outside dissolved. He had to get out of here. And he would, next chance. He would scamper through the big jaws, or whatever they were, the moment they opened. He didn't know where he would be or what he would do next but he knew he had to get out.

The van wound its way slowly along, turning sharply and stopping frequently. Through the smooth and shiny walls around him the outside world assailed Frafan with sounds. Strange and awesome sounds: Chattering of Many Colored Ones, the terrible and sudden roar of another car or truck, sometimes a honk or a screech. Then, more abruptly than they'd started, the outside noises faded and there was only the whine of the van's legs on a smooth surface. Just as suddenly, that noise changed to the sound of sand and rocks beneath. He scrambled up the mesh of Fred's empty cage and peered out.

There were trees everywhere! A pool of calm unfrozen water! And not a Many Colored One den to be seen!

This time, when the van came to a rolling stop, Frafan was ready. The jaws had barely opened when he flung himself through them, into the brisk air. He flew to the earth, legs churning. He focused on the biggest tree he could see, a little way across the short grass. He ran as fast as his legs would go, into its uppermost branches. Only then did he look back.

The Many Colored Ones, tiny and far below, had not moved. They simply stared up at him. Could They be smiling? The curve of their mouths certainly looked like smiles. They took the bag of corn from the van and dumped it into a little wooden den that looked much like a cage, only with long holes on the sides, big enough to pull sticks of corn through. They stood for a while then, talking quietly, apparently having forgotten all about him. They slowly got back into their van and coaxed it into breath. The van rolled away across a low hill, and out of sight.

Frafan heaved a long sigh. In the peace and near silence, he took a deep breath and shook himself. The air was not as clean as at home, but fresher than in the back of the van.

This was amazing! From the top of the tree he could see, for some reason beyond his knowing, The Many Colored Ones had left a little piece of the woods right here, right in the middle of their warren! The grass had been chewed short (by cows?), though its tips were still visible above the shallow snow. There was a deserted pathway, constructed of the same sort of hard, black material that the van had traveled on, up and over and around hills. He could make out the edge of the pool of water from here. Trees, most young and strong — oak and ash and maple — were scattered everywhere. And, just over a hill in the other direction, not far away (he remembered the conversation with the horses...seeing is believing!) he beheld a Many Colored One seated upon a horse. He watched for a long time but neither slate-colored mount or slate-colored mounted moved a muscle. Frozen, he wondered?

There were all sorts of things to look at and wonder about, but he had little time to do so, for no sooner had the van disappeared than a gray squirrel showed up, moving through the thin snow, in Frafan's direction. Ecstatic at seeing one of his own kind, Frafan was about to call out when another squirrel appeared in the corner of his eye, coming toward him from another direction. And then, yet another.

Instead of shouting a greeting, something told Frafan to hold his tongue. These treeclimbers were acting strangely. It wasn't the fact that they were traveling on the ground — the trees here were too far apart for jumping. What puzzled him was that these squirrels were being downright careless. It was one thing to run along the ground. It was another entirely to act as though they didn't see or care what was around them, on the earth, in the sky, or in the trees. He was quite sure none of them had even noticed him in the high branches of the big tree. They seemed to be intent on a single landmark. He watched and waited until he was certain of it: They were converging on the corn in the cage.

The first of them had almost reached the golden food when Frafan raced down the tree, shouting, "Wait! Don't touch it!"

The gray treeclimber Frafan faced was a large male. He looked both surprised and puzzled.

"It may be a trap," Frafan tried to explain, thinking of Laslum and his temptation by corn.

"A trap?"

"Yes. It might be dangerous to reach a paw in there."

Frafan tried to think quickly. Would these treeclimbers, who lived among The Many Colored Ones, know of their traps and cages? Maybe not. How could he explain that such things could mean the end of freedom? Maybe the loss of breath?

Before Frafan could form more words in his mouth, the big gray sneered at him and said, "Dangerous?" With that, he stuck his front paw into the cage and pulled out a long stick of golden kernels.

Two other squirrels came up to the cage, both grays. They ignored Frafan but kept a close eye on the big squirrel. When he seemed busy, pulling seeds from the stick with his teeth, they quickly dug out smaller sticks and ran off.

Frafan was most anxious to speak to any or all of them. For a while he was amazed into silence by their aloof and unfriendly attitude. Could they be so hungry as to ignore each other and himself, a stranger in their midst? He decided to strike up a conversation with the large male.

"I'd like to introduce myself. I'm called Frafan. I've come a long way, from the deep forest. I'm in desperate need of information and help. I'm searching for my brother and his mate."

Silence.

"I wonder if you might know them..."

More silence. A few disinterested stares.

"...Or of them."

The heavy squirrel finally cocked his head at Frafan and said, "Hey! You chatter too much. Watch the others. They keep their mouths closed except when I talk to them or let them eat. They mind their own business. You'd better learn to do the same."

Frafan's chin dropped. What kind of a greeting was this? Were these really gray squirrels? Or did they just look like gray squirrels?

The big treeclimber went back to his meal, wasting more of it in the surrounding snow than he got into his mouth. Frafan picked up a few of the scattered kernels, pushed them back into his cheeks, and ran to a nearby box elder tree.

He slowly chewed on the sweet corn. It nearly stuck in his throat. What in Brittle Branches had he gotten himself into? Could these really be relatives, brothers and sisters almost, that ignored him...or told him to mind his own business? Were all of them that nested here like this? He looked up. Three more gray treeclimbers were moving through

157

the snow toward the cage of corn. Thank Blue Sky and Green Leaves, somebody here had to be normal!

Frafan left the tree once again. The other squirrels watched the food with one eye and the big gray, who was still working on his stick, with the other. Two of the treeclimbers had stopped short and sat on their tails. Curious thing, thought Frafan. They must be hungry. But they seem to wait for the big fellow. The third squirrel he'd seen approaching caught his attention. It was a female. She ran differently from the rest. More assured...and graceful. Looked to be a good leaper.

He looked at her profile for a moment, then back to the others, still sitting as the big squirrel ate. Why did they just sit and watch this large fellow? Was it...

His eyes jerked back to the female. Something familiar... she turned a bit more toward him, intent on the corn. He saw her face clearly and fully. Air fled from his chest. The cry rose from him like a wail of anguish:

"Kaahli!"

CHAPTER XXI

BROTHERS

Her eyes took him in, pointed ears to shabby tail, with a sort of weary curiosity. There was no sign of recognition. She turned back to the corn. Then, very slowly, the glazed expression left her face. She inhaled quickly, almost a gasp.

"Frafan!" she cried, "Is it really you?"

They embraced and looked deep and hard at one another through bright tears.

"Frafan," she choked, "I can't believe it! How did you know? How did you find this place? Is anyone with you?"

"I am alone, Kaahli. There are many questions. I have at least as many for you as you have for me. But just now there is only one. I can ask or answer no other until I know. Is my brother...is Ephran...here?"

"Of course, dear Frafan, of course he is here with me. Your brother is here." A light came into her eyes and she spoke slowly and softly.

"Yes, he is here. And maybe your coming to him will be enough. Come, I'll take you to him."

"In a moment, Kaahli...," he managed in a tight voice, "in a moment."

He turned his face to the sky and closed his eyes in silent thanks for whatever wind, whatever cloud, whatever sunbeam, set his paw on this path. For friends and for luck. For dreams of wide-open and frightening jaws. He did not bow his head as tears of joy and relief flooded down his cheeks.

Then he wiped his eyes and turned to her with another thought. "Young ones...?" he asked.

"No, Frafan," she said, dropping her eyes. "No young ones. There will be no young ones born in this place."

The other squirrels, having watched this puzzling reunion, turned back to the big gray squirrel and his sloppy eating. Not one of them uttered a word to Frafan or Kaahli. Not one of them seemed the least bit interested in anything but filling their stomachs.

"Oh, Frafan, there is so much to speak of," said Kaahli. "I never dreamed I would see you here. I've nearly quit dreaming of familiar faces. I was beginning to wonder if I'd ever see anyone from the deepwoods again."

"I only wish everyone back there knew what I know now," said Frafan. "There are so many who want to know. So many who wait."

While they talked, a small gray squirrel, smaller even than Frafan, timidly approached the cage of corn. His eye never left the big

159

ill-mannered gray, who continued to spill far more corn in the snow than he ate, but seemed not to care. Watching for his chance, the little gray cautiously reached for a slender stick of corn.

The large treeclimber pounced. With a squeal of surprise and pain, the small one found himself flipped on his back. The large gray stood over him, a frightening half-smile, half-snarl on his face. The smaller squirrel covered his face with his front paws, shivering in fear.

"Say you!" said Frafan, wiping both eyes with his paws, "hold on there a minute." He took a step toward the big squirrel.

"Frafan!" hissed Kaahli in warning.

The bully looked at Frafan as though he were some sort of earthbeetle he'd just as soon crush. "Hey! You got somethin' to say, owlbait?" he sneered.

"Owlbait? Who do you think you're calling owlbait? It looks as though you and I better have a talk about manners."

Frafan spoke bravely but his face felt flushed and his paws were cold. A quick look around revealed that, besides himself, Kaahli, and the little gray who lay on his back in the snow, there were six other treeclimbers standing around the corn cage. Most of them looked as though they were ready to run.

For a moment the smirk left the bully's lips. "Listen, you halfgrown son-of-a-weasel; you're new here and don't got the rules straight yet. So I'm gonna give you a second chance before I turn your tail into nesting material. I'm gonna tell you something and you better remember it: Stay outa my way. Especially when I'm busy with food. The food is mine. Understand? Not yers or theirs..." He nodded at the others. "...Mine. You'll eat when I decide to let you. When I'm done, you can fight fer what's left. Another thing: Never talk to me unless I talk to you first. And watch that smart mouth of yours or I'll close it permanently. Are you gettin' all this or is your brain as small as the rest of you?"

Frafan, confused and angry as he'd ever been, was so flabbergasted that all he could do was blubber. "Well, well...," He was about to carry the discussion right to the tyrant's face, difference in size forgotten. Before he could move his paws, the big gray turned and leaped unto the black path. He called back, "Hey! I'm goin' to my nest. Don't want to be seen hangin' around with lowlifes the likes of you."

While Frafan, mouth still wide open, watched him scamper through the shallow snow, Kaahli helped the small squirrel to his paws. "Are you hurt, Queesor?" she asked.

"No, he didn't hurt me. Didn't hurt me at all," said the little treeclimber as he brushed snow from his bushy tail.

"I'm sorry he did that to you," Kaahli said, looking at Queesor with concern and, Frafan thought, as though she was partly responsible.

161

"Well, my turn, I guess. Have to take my turn."

"Queesor, I'd like you to meet Frafan, second brother of Ephran," said Kaahli.

"Ah, this is why the bully left so quickly then! And with so much corn left for us. The brother of Ephran has come." Queesor's face took on a dubious look for a moment, then he smiled and said, "Though you are as small as I am, you are a most welcome sight, a most welcome sight indeed!"

"Well, thank you very much," said Frafan, still upset with the bully and more than a little puzzled at this small squirrel's words. Why would he be a "welcome sight" in this place? And what did his size have to do with it?

"Frafan has just arrived and has not yet seen his brother," said Kaahli. "Would you like to come to the nest with us?"

"Oh yes! I'd be very pleased to run with you. Very pleased."

"Let's take some corn for Ephran," said Kaahli, and with her teeth picked up a small stick which sported some irregularly scattered kernels. Queesor looked surprised when Frafan picked up as big a stick of corn as he could carry.

The other treeclimbers had paid little attention to Frafan except during the short confrontation with the big squirrel. But he wasn't alone in being snubbed. They pretty much ignored one another too. Oh, there'd be a scowl and a sharp word if two paws reached for the same morsel. "Watch where you're going!" if paths crossed unexpectedly. "Hey, give me that!" if an especially plump stick of corn was just out of reach. Otherwise they went about their business of collecting what the big squirrel had scattered as though they didn't know one another.

Kaahli turned and ran off at a leisurely pace, through the short grass and the thin layer of snow. When she stopped to rest on an open and windswept hillock, Frafan dropped the corncob from his mouth and said, "Who was that ill-mannered large squirrel — and what's his problem?"

Actually, the weird attitude of the squirrels other than the bully was a question bothering Frafan at least as much as the one he asked, but he decided to wait until he was alone with Kaahli and Ephran before he brought that subject up. He wasn't so sure how a native of the place, the little fellow running with he and Kaahli, would react to such questions.

"His name is Wytail," said Kaahli.

"He thinks he is master of all the gray squirrels in this place," said Queesor, "All the gray squirrels."

Kaahli said, "He has little to do with any of us except to give orders and insult...and attack the smaller ones. I tried to say a few words to him when Ephran and I first arrived, but he threatened to bite my ear..."

"And then he said she was pretty," said Queesor, "and said if she didn't behave he'd drag her off to his nest. Yessir, to his nest."

"He what...?" Frafan asked.

"I don't want to speak of it," said Kaahli, with a firm chin. "I just ignore him now."

"He's a disgusting bully," said Frafan. "What right did he have to attack Queesor like that...and to keep you away from the corn?"

"He's bigger than I am. Much bigger," said Queesor softly.

"What kind of an answer is that? What does Ephran think of him? Why hasn't something been done?" Frafan was more and more incredulous.

"Ephran doesn't really know Wytail," said Kaahli, a sadness filling her eyes. "When we first came, Wytail seemed very concerned about Ephran. It seems your brother's name was known — even in this place. But Ephran was weak. His body was barely mended. He paid no attention to Wytail. He slept a great deal. And...well, you'll see."

"I will leave you here," said Queesor. "My nest lies further on. I am pleased to have met you. Yes, very pleased. I would like to talk again. After you spend some time with your brother perhaps. Your sleeping brother. The next time food is brought, maybe. Maybe?..." he said hopefully.

"Of course," said Frafan. "I'll come with you to gather food. Next time we'll talk to some of the others. We'll talk to Wytail too, explain to him that he's one of us. Teach him some manners. Everyone should have an equal chance at the corn."

Queesor looked confused, as though there'd been a misunderstanding. Before he could speak again Kaahli said, "We'll see you soon, Queesor. Frafan is anxious to see his brother. And I'm getting cold."

Frafan winked at Queesor, he hoped with a degree of assurance that he didn't necessarily feel. Queesor stared back, still looking slightly stunned, as though shutting one eye at a time was a most wonderful trick. Frafan picked up his corn and trotted off after Kaahli. He made himself forget about strange-acting gray animals and bullies. He'd had enough of that in Great Woods Warren. He was so anxious to see Ephran — and to hear more about him — he wished Kaahli would run faster or he could ask more questions. But his mouth was full, and she was the one who knew where she was going, so he decided to follow quietly and concentrate on his surroundings. It would serve well to know the lay of the land for planning their escape anyway.

The area of short grass and sparse trees was not as large as he'd first thought. Closely packed dens of Many Colored Ones were clustered nearby. In every direction he looked big wooden or stone dens surrounded this little piece of misplaced woodland. Already a few lights were showing though their clear windows. There were so many strange things; gently curving and smooth paths, wide wooden sticks made into funny shaped structures that were scattered here and there under the trees, a short pile of big stones like part of the wall that hid Redthorn at Rocky Point. So many questions... He would have to explore and ask. What else was hidden on the far side of these rolling hills?

He very nearly ran over Kaahli when she suddenly stopped at a sad-looking tree with few branches. The tree leaned at an angle, not a sharp or determined angle and not a jaunty angle — sort of a droopy angle. Clinging to the scarred trunk were three cages, made of wood, fastened to the tree by some unknown force. At first he thought they were cages, but they lacked doors...or the terrible hard mesh.

In the flat face of each cage-but-not-a-cage was a hole that looked like it had been chewed by a slovenly muskrat who had been in a hurry at the time. And beneath that, like a flattened snout, stuck a little weathered platform of wood.

To his puzzled look Kaahli mumbled, "Home," and started up the trunk. When she came to the place second from the top she turned and waited for Frafan. He scrambled up to her, to the mouth of the little den. The other two dens were empty. She motioned for him to enter.

He poked his head through the hole and dropped the stick of corn inside. It was dark...and his nose gave him another impression; it was musty in here. It wasn't being kept as clean as he would have thought. He crawled in. The walls were flat, scratched and discolored. In corners and along the ceiling he could tell where, in warmer times, insects too had made this their home. The den's roof had warped and a few of the hard shiny twigs used by Many Colored Ones to fasten pieces of wood together could be seen. He knew what it was as soon as he'd seen it, but it would not be easy to get used to the idea of sleeping in a place built by Them.

A male gray squirrel lay in a far corner, curled tightly. Frafan had shed tears of joy to hear his brother's name. Now fresh tears came to his eyes. They were not entirely the water of happiness, however: Ephran looked terrible. He lay asleep, mouth open, fur thinned and unkempt, belly bulging.

Kaahli, who had entered behind him, called gently, "Ephran. There is someone here to see you."

One eye opened slowly. It studied Frafan for an extraordinarily long time. Then a spark flared there. The other eye opened. Ephran raised his head.

"Frafan!" he cried, and struggled to his paws.

They hugged each other in silence. Kaahli stood by, tears running down her cheeks.

Frafan found his voice. "Ephran, I can hardly believe that I have come to the place I sought. I must know everything that happened: How

164

you escaped the Many Colored Ones with the thundersticks, how you and Kaahli came to be here, how soon we can leave, and everything in between."

Ephran gently pushed his brother away.

"Yes, of course," he said, "you would want to know everything. And it would be interesting to hear how you found us, since we left no trail. Interesting tales for both of us, I'm sure, but of little use. Too bad really."

For the second time today, Frafan was shocked wordless. His brother's face was cloaked in pure sadness. The flame that had sparkled in his eye for a single moment was gone. His words were slow, his voice flat.

"Ephran...!" was all Frafan could manage to say. It was a plea.

"I'm very tired, Frafan. I'm tired a great deal. I must sleep more. Kaahli can tell you all about the misadventures that brought us to this place. And you can tell her of yours."

"Too bad? Did you say it's too bad I came here? I must have misunderstood. Those words make no sense..."

Ephran turned away and lay down. When Kaahli touched his shoulder Frafan realized his mouth was still hanging open. "Come," she whispered, her face nearly as sad as Ephran's.

Outside the den she said, "We'll go to the den of Queesor. We can talk there."

"Kaahli!" Frafan cried, "What is the matter with him? That is not Ephran. I don't know that squirrel."

"Not here...," she said, shaking her head, "We can't talk here." She ran down the tree, not looking back at him, and raced off across the thin snow.

He followed her. Maybe it was something in the air here...the way everyone acted so strangely...that big squirrel called Wytail...and now Ephran. She ran to a small tree standing by itself. In the tree was a single den, identical to Ephran and Kaahli's.

"Queesor's," she said, and ran up the tree. She poked her head in the hole, looked back down at Frafan, and said, "He's not at home. Come up. He won't mind if we use his place. I come here often."

Under other circumstances Frafan would have been bursting with questions — and the questions were on the tip of his tongue. Had they tried to leave this place? Did they get here the same way he did? If so, how did they get to the Farm of Cages in the first place? What did she mean, she "came here often?" Oh yes, the questions were there. But the main question, that of Ephran's peculiar behavior, was the very one that left Frafan staggered and speechless.

He hadn't moved his paws, so Kaahli said again, "Come up to the nest, Frafan. Queesor won't mind. Queesor is a friend. Maybe the only friend."

CHAPTER XXII

TALES TALL BUT TRUE

Frafan told his story first, mostly because he had to — he desperately needed to talk, to take his mind off what he'd just seen and heard. First Ephran's appearance, then his words, had taken the legs from under Frafan. He was not in the mood for sitting and listening. He told her everything he could think of — from the crows' visit, to the snowstorm, to the ride in the van. He told of his salvation in Great Woods Warren, about Redthorn and Fred, about finding Klestra and learning what little the red squirrel knew of Ephran's and her own disappearance. Kaahli smiled when she heard timid little Janna had set out on the search with him. She became excited when he mentioned Mayberry, Fred, and Truestar — and very quiet when he told of the big barn, and the cages, and the pigeons.

"Well," said Kaahli after he'd finished, "I must say that you have had a most amazing adventure. One I know Ephran would have loved to be along on himself...at least the Ephran we both remember. I do hope Phetra and Roselimb are safely back in their nest." She closed her eyes for a moment.

"I know you want to learn what happened to your brother and me, to explain both what you haven't seen and what you have, but I hardly know where to begin. Some of what you hear will be hard to accept — like believing in the existence of the faraway lands Marshflower told about, those without snow. Strange," she said with a sigh, "it now seems perfectly reasonable to believe places like that really exist."

"I understand," he said. "Contrary to what we all thought, there is a lot of world outside the deep woods."

"Indeed. Our parents could never picture it. Sit back then, Frafan, if you are ready, and hear where we've been and what we've done."

Just then came a scrambling sound on the bark of the tree and Queesor's head appeared at the entrance of the den.

"Oh! Hello, hello!" he said. "Do I interrupt something?"

"Hello, Queesor," said Kaahli. "I think it's your privilege to interrupt what you please. This is your den. But we are just talking. I am telling Ephran's brother how we came to be here: in this place of few trees and short grass."

"This place is called a park. Remember, I told you. A park. Are you in my nest because Ephran is resting again?" asked Queesor. "Is that why you're in my nest?"

"Yes," said Kaahli slowly, "Ephran is resting. Again."

"Please come in, Queesor," said Frafan. "I suppose you've heard this story before but you're welcome to listen once more."

"I guess I've heard part of it. I guess," said Queesor as he squeezed through the hole, "but I wouldn't mind hearing it again, one more time, if it's all the same with you. I'm still not sure, really sure, that I understood what I heard the first time. Very unusual business. Very unusual."

"Lay down here, next to me," said Frafan, moving closer to the smooth wall. "We'll try to understand it together." He folded his tail around himself, on what was evidently supposed to be a comfortable resting spot in a corner of the den. However, the floor was not comfortable. It was hard and lumpy.

"Start at the beginning, Kaahli," said Frafan.

"Yes. The beginning. The beginning, by all means," added Queesor.

"Very well," said Kaahli, clearing her throat. "It all really begins the day that Cloudchaser was hurt..."

"Cloudchaser," said Frafan. "Isn't that the duck whose young Ephran saved from a hawk?"

"The same."

"If I remember correctly, Klestra told Janna and I that Cloudchaser was hurt badly by the thundersticks and flew off to a evil place called Lomarsh," said Frafan.

"Yes, he was badly hurt. But he did not land in Lomarsh. He was able to fly a long way from The Pond, even though one wing was nearly useless. The tip of it had been broken by a small stone thrown by the thunderstick. Another stone had entered his breast. Despite his wounds, he was able to fly to that den of Many Colored Ones, the one with the big barn and the yellow den..."

Frafan interrupted again. "The Farm of Cages. Did you say that the thundersticks threw small stones?"

"Yes. But that's another story."

"Stones," breathed Queesor, "small stones, she says."

"In any case," Kaahli continued, "Cloudchaser himself had an amazing experience. As I said, instead of falling into Lomarsh as Klestra thought, Cloudchaser glided through the air a very long way, close to the earth, to the very place that you found the animals, the pigeons, and the big noisy thing you call a van. Those Many Colored Ones came upon him then..." She hesitated.

"And they cared for him. Tended his wounds," Frafan finished for her.

Kaahli gasped. "How did you know?"

"The caged raccoon and the pheasant had been hurt and both were being fed and looked after, away from the snow and the cold. It was then I realized They must have cared for Laslum too, after the big sticks and mound of corn fell on him. They put him in a cage for his own good. To keep him safe and protect him from other hunters. How strange."

"How strange indeed," said Kaahli. "It's something Ephran won't talk about. It's one thing he can't understand."

"He can't understand what? That Many Colored Ones would try to help?"

"Yes. That the same creatures that felled the big oak tree, set fire to the woods, took the breath from Cloudchaser's young one, and knocked him from the branches...that Those could possibly do anything good."

"Why strange? What's to understand?" asked Queesor. "They leave food here. They leave food when the air turns cold."

Kaahli smiled gently at him. "That's part of what's so hard to understand, Queesor. It's part of what has Ephran so confused. He feels perhaps this leaving corn for us is simply to fatten us. He does not think it is a good thing."

"It sure tastes good. Real good."

"Please go on with your story, Kaahli," Frafan urged. "Did Cloudchaser recover? Does he come into the story of your being here?"

"Cloudchaser very much comes into the story. When he had time to heal, and when he felt strong enough, he was determined to return to The Pond. There was no assurance he'd find his family there — it was late in the season. But he wanted to see Ephran and I, to tell us he'd recovered...that Those who destroyed hope might give it back. When he returned The Pond was empty and wearing a ring of ice. He hadn't touched the water when he heard the voice of the thundersticks. They were close by and, brave as he is, he had to have been very frightened. But later he told us he realized this time the thunder was not meant for him. It was when he flew off to find out what the sticks pointed at that he saw a lone gray treeclimber jumping from limb to limb. That's when he saw Ephran fall."

"Fell. Ephran fell," said Queesor quietly, wide eyes fixed on Kaahli.

"Yes, he fell. Ephran was hurt badly by the thundersticks that day that seems so long ago..." She hesitated. "And he fell such a long way. From where I and Klestra watched, I thought he was gone forever. While he lay there, under a gooseberry bush, thick red water running from his wounds, Cloudchaser, flying low to the earth, appeared. He could see how badly Ephran was hurt. Red water stained the leaves he lay on, and The Many Colored Ones with their sticks were nearby, searching for Ephran. Ephran, of course, was certain Cloudchaser's breath had been taken away by the thundersticks, so he concluded the two of them must have been reunited in a way fashioned for those who drew air no more..."

"So there they were, under a gooseberry bush, hunters nearby, a wounded squirrel and a mallard..."

"Frafan, please!" she chided him. "I thought it was my turn to talk." Frafan shrugged, a guilty smile on his face.

Kaahli said, "Cloudchaser understood how badly Ephran was hurt, and that he must get him away from The Many Colored Ones, Who were searching around every tree. He eventually convinced Ephran to mount on his back, that he would take him for a ride..."

"You can't mean...a ride in the air?" asked Frafan, mouth wide open. "Oops! There I go again. Sorry."

"Yes, of course. In the air. Ephran always wanted to fly, you see."

"I know that. Klestra told us. And last warm season I often caught Ephran watching swallows swooping gracefully in the air. But wishing you could fly from one tree to another, and accepting an invitation to fly on a duck's back, are two different things entirely!"

"I told you some of this would be difficult to believe," said Kaahli with a little smile.

He could only shake his head.

"Cloudchaser had no idea if he could actually carry a fullgrown gray squirrel on his back," she went on, "but it was the only way he could think of to get him away from danger."

"What a wild idea!" said Frafan. "All that weight...through the sky..."

"Cloudchaser said he had to. There was no other choice. The strength had to be there. And he knew Ephran would not refuse a ride in the sky, especially if it were to find me a new nest. Cloudchaser, you see, had heard me talk about a new nest ever since we returned from the den of Jafthuh and Odalee."

"So Cloudchaser brought Ephran, on his back, to a place he knew he would be helped," Frafan said to Kaahli, to get her started again. "That is an astonishing feat of strength and courage."

"It was an incredible act of unselfish love," said Kaahli in a quiet voice.

Frafan shook his head slowly back and forth. "I must meet this mallard. But what puzzles me is why he didn't tell someone what was happening? Everyone was worried sick. We thought the worst. Now that I think of it, everyone except me still does."

"He tried," said Kaahli. "Each time he returned to The Pond he found the place deserted. Part of the problem was that many of our friends were gone and many already asleep. He saw not even a crow."

"Of course there was no one around," said Frafan, "they were all off searching for Ephran."

"Ah!" said Kaahli. A triumphant look appeared on her face. "So that's why! Ephran was sure it was because everyone was frightened of the thundersticks and had gone to hide."

"No," said Frafan, "no one hid. Rabbits, crows, chipmunks, a red squirrel, everybody and anybody who hadn't flown away or crept into their den to sleep...everyone was looking around Great Hill for Ephran."

"Red squirrel friends, red squirrel friends," mumbled Queesor. "Uncommon. Most uncommon."

"But wait!" Frafan said, turning back to Kaahli, "What did you mean, 'each time' Cloudchaser returned? Do you mean he flew back after rescuing Ephran?"

"Yes, he flew back,' she said.

"But why? And how? He must have been exhausted by carrying Ephran all that way. Oh...Wait..." Frafan leaned toward her. "It was you he came back for. Wasn't it? To show you the way. To have you follow him. Am I right?"

"No, Frafan, I did not follow him. I could not run so fast as Cloudchaser flies. And that day I could not make my legs work at all. No, Cloudchaser came back to get me. To carry me as he carried Ephran."

"He carried both of you?"

"Yes, Frafan, both of us."

"Kaahli," he said, " this does get more and more difficult. I tried to guess what happened from what little Klestra saw."

"Poor Klestra," she said. "I can imagine how confused he must have been."

"How could Ephran hold on to the feathers, hurt as he was? Or you, for that matter?" asked Frafan.

"Cloudchaser says Ephran was asleep most of the time. But his grip never loosened. It was nearly his last grip. As for me, I almost slipped off many times, I'm told. I really don't remember the flight. Ephran at least remembers the first part of it. Cloudchaser said he had to talk to me constantly, to remind me to hold on."

"I must meet this mallard. Where is he?" asked Frafan.

"With Marshflower, I hope," said Kaahli. "He rested and waited in a puddle near The Farm of Cages until he knew Ephran would recover. We talked every day. Then he left to find his family."

"He took you both to the farm. Does he have any idea where you are now?"

"Not as far as I know."

"And you could not send a message from the farm back to the woods, could you?"

"No," said Kaahli. "Crows would not come near. Obviously,

171

you know why."

"Yes," said Frafan, "we met the ferocious silver skyhunter, but we didn't get a chance to see it fly."

"Ferocious skyhunter, you say...," said Queesor loudly, who had nearly dozed off during the talk about ducks. "Ferocious skyhunter? What sort of ferocious skyhunter?"

"The skyhunter turned out to be a plaything of The Many Colored Ones, Queesor," said Frafan. "It was not dangerous at all."

"We did not see it fly either," said Kaahli, "but I heard the pigeons talking and laughing about it. From their descriptions of its snarling and screaming I must say that I could not blame the crows for being frightened."

Frafan got to his paws. "There is only one more question. And I suspect I know the answer to that as well. You came to be in this place, this park, the same way I did, didn't you?"

"Yes," answered Kaahli, "we took the same ride...in the back of the same van. That ride, which I remember very well, was more frightening than the one on Cloudchaser's back."

"Ah yes," sighed Frafan. "Well, that's all behind us now." He looked down at Queesor, who had finally fallen asleep. "I've learned a lot and seen things I never dreamed existed. I have many more questions, but they will have to wait. If we can't get a message to the deep woods, we must leave soon. Everyone is worried. Let's go and wake Ephran. He must be rested by now. We have to make him understand that the time is come to make plans...plans for our trip back to the deep woods."

CHAPTER XXIII

MORE SNOW, LESS COMFORT

xcept for the time of heavy snow and bitter cold, when he and Janna found shelter in Great Woods Warren, the cold season stayed mild. Frafan could not help wonder if it was the exception or the rule. Since this was his very first cold season, he could not know the answer from his own experience. And, since treeclimbers tended to sleep for long periods, especially through the worst times, he knew that the oldtimers' remembrances might very well be inaccurate. Even father admitted that after a few seasons of waking and sleeping, sleeping and waking, one tended to get confused and eventually got one cold season totally mixed up with another.

Regardless, this particular season had to be unusual for those huddled inside the shabby little den. Instead of sleeping away the cold season, as his body told him he should, Frafan was actually closing his eyes less than he did during the warm season. For one thing, the nest was very thin and drafty. Kaahli explained that leaves to pad the floor, so plentiful in the woods, were hard to come by here. The Many Colored Ones had picked them up just as she was about to go out and collect them. Ephran had gazed at her with a knowing look when she said she couldn't understand why They did this...he said it was done to make things a bit more miserable.

More serious than the discomfort of a skimpy nest was the constant struggle and gnawing worry about food. Frafan's first day at the corn cage had been an exception; there had not been as much food since.

No matter how little food they brought through the hole in the den, no matter how much Frafan complained about the bully who limited their supply, no matter how dainty the proportions of corn at mealtime, Ephran would simply say, "It will have to be enough."

At first it was. The amount and variety did seem sufficient. There was occasional grain besides corn. Oats sometimes, and once, a pile of walnuts. Until, as was inevitable in the cramped quarters, Frafan accidently bumped up against Kaahli.

He was astounded. There was nothing to her but fur and ribs! Only then did he remember how often she'd say she'd eat outside today, or she'd gobbled down a few acorns on the way home from the food cage and really didn't care for more. Only then did he understand she was making sure Ephran got enough to eat, even if she didn't. That Ephran would grow fatter and lazier while she starved. Frafan vowed to himself that he would watch her and be certain she ate. He wished he could talk to Ephran about it. He wished he could talk to Ephran about any number of things, like going home.

After he and Kaahli told each other of their adventures that day in Queesor's den, Frafan could not wait to get back to the nest and speak with his brother. Even now, days later, it bothered him greatly to recollect their conversation.

"Ephran," he'd begun, after he and Queesor woke a grouchy Ephran from shallow sleep, "Kaahli and I have been talking. I think we agree the time is come to start planning. As soon as you feel up to it, about the hows and whens of returning home, you know..."

"Not going back," Ephran said sharply, unfocused eyes looking over Frafan's shoulder.

"Not going back?"

"You heard. I'm staying right here."

"Here?"

"What are you, a catbird or something, repeating every word I utter?" asked Ephran, his face somber.

"Why here? What's here?" Frafan persisted.

"Why? Because this is where I'm supposed to be."

"This is where you're supposed to be?"

"You have become a catbird," said Ephran, not looking up, chewing on a soggy bit of corn, yellow juice running down his lip.

"Brother, your words are strange. They make no sense. Why do you say this place is where you are supposed to be?"

Ephran looked up, a pained expression on his face. "Why, little brother, do you think The Many Colored Ones brought us all to this place? Because They love us? Because They think we will all be happy here forever?"

"Well...I...I never thought of it like that. I suppose it is just a place, um, for us to stay while..."

"Since you can't seem to get the point, I'll tell you. They want to be sure we're fed. Nice and fat. They want us to stay in one place. They want to know precisely where we are all the time, every moment."

"Oh, come now! What about the others who've been here since birth, like Queesor. They don't..."

"If it hasn't dawned on you yet, let me finish," said Ephran coldly. "Us being here will make their hunting easier. They know right where to come when They want us."

"Ohh, Ephran!" said Kaahli.

"Interesting theory," said Queesor, managing to look excited and bored at the same time. "Interesting theory."

"Ephran, where did this idea come from? Even if it was true, or maybe especially if it is true, why would you think of staying here?"

"You think the answer is to run? I ran. I ran in the woods. My home. Where I knew the trees and the hills and the ravines. You know what happened. Look around you, youngster. Where are you going to run?"

Frafan found himself breathing hard. "We are not in cages," he said. "And I'm not thinking of where my paws find a grip. I'm thinking of father and mother. What of Janna and Klestra who traveled so far with me — searching for you? What of all your friends near The Pond?"

"What of them?"

"Don't you want to go back and see them? Don't you want to go back into our woods again...among the tall trees, the songs of birds, the days of adventures and play and running?"

"Did I hear you say 'our woods?'"

"Well, as much ours as anyone's...and everyone's."

A sort of sneer appeared on Ephran's face. "You still don't understand, do you? Can't you understand that it is no longer our woods?"

"Please, Ephran. Be reasonable. You must come back with me. You must speak once again with father and mother, with Klestra and Mayberry..."

"You go back. You tell them I'm fine. Tell them I'm satisfied."

"And happy?"

"Happiness has nothing to do with it."

Frafan was finally shocked into silence, shaken to his core. Who was this squirrel who looked like Ephran yet spoke with a stranger's tongue?

Since that flurry of conversation, Ephran had sunk back into a brooding silence, broken only by occasional nods or grunts. He was, for all intents and purposes, closed to them. He was convinced The Many Colored Ones who had tended him and Laslum and Cloudchaser were an anomaly, a few gentle misfits who had almost certainly been driven away from their warren for being so different. Or possibly their good deeds were only to keep birds and animals healthy until they were needed for food. Kaahli explained that Ephran felt The real Many Colored Ones, Those who ruled, were at best thoughtless and at worst downright cruel. It was They felled the oak, set fire to the woods, hunted down Cloudchaser and his son, and finally knocked Ephran from the branches. They had marked him, and very possibly all treeclimbers, for extinction. Even the occasional Ones he'd seen since he and Kaahli had come to this place, strolling along the paths, were almost certainly spies, messengers for the evil Ones. "Keeping count of us," Ephran would say.

Frafan could not agree with any part of this confusing and hopeless frame of mind. As far as he was concerned what Ephran needed, whether he knew it or not, was to go home. Home, to the deep woods, where he could breathe deeply of untainted air, run through leafy branches, watch the first sunbeams burst through sparkling nightfog, have fresh and untainted food provided by the bushes and trees.

On their trips to and from the food cage, where Ephran never went, Frafan would quiz Kaahli. "Why won't he at least talk about leaving, about going home?"

"Maybe he's afraid," said Queesor, running with them, "I'd be afraid. Isn't everyone afraid?"

"No, Ephran is not afraid," said Kaahli, "not for himself, in any case. He is certain, if we tried to leave, we would either be hunted down before we got to the deep woods, in which case he fears for me, not for himself. Or else, if we actually got away, he would only provide a path for Them to follow. He thinks he would lead Them to our families, just as his building his nest on The Pond, and trying to convince birds and animals to nest there, led to disaster."

"He thinks about Them a great deal, doesn't he?"

"All the time."

"What can I do? How can I convince him he sees far more than is there?" asked Frafan.

"I don't know," she replied, "I think I have tried every conceivable argument."

Even though Ephran ate some, and even though Wytail scattered and ruined a great deal of it, Frafan decided he had to try to collect a little extra food whenever he could. It was partly habit, a lesson learned over and over again from Odalee. Besides, he wanted Kaahli to eat more. She wouldn't touch it, however, insisting she was getting enough. He stored the tiny portions in a corner of the den, under a thin covering of leaves, out of sight and out of mind.

Not that there was a great deal extra to be had, but the other squirrels would let it lie where it fell, to be picked up by rather hostile starlings. When Frafan asked Queesor why the squirrels left the food for birds, he answered, "Too much work. Too much work to carry food. Besides, there will be more tomorrow. Tomorrow will bring a fresh supply."

"You can't depend on that, Queesor. You must help me convince the others The Many Colored Ones are not..."

But Queesor would shrug and run off, or change the subject. Frafan decided his first priority had to be to stay well and look after Kaahli. And try to find some way to change Ephran's thinking. So he kept his distance from Wytail. He tried to talk to the other squirrels at the food cage, after Wytail left. A few might listen to him for a moment or two, but none seemed willing to change their habit of eating what Wytail scattered around...and make that do until the next day.

Eventually Frafan found himself nearly isolated. Trying to talk to Ephran was like talking to a tree. Kaahli was so depressed by Ephran's attitude and, Frafan knew, by his own inability to change it, that she had little to say. The other squirrels stayed mostly to themselves and shunned Frafan when he came near. His ideas were too bizarre for them.

Queesor was the only treeclimber who had time for him, and he found himself seeking the little gray out more and more often.

Queesor had been born and raised in this place he called "park," this sanctuary in the midst of Many Colored Ones. He'd never been more than a few treelengths away from the nest where he first drew air and saw light. His parents nested here too, obviously in a different den, and he spoke with them occasionally. But the relationship was cool and distant, as Frafan had noticed it was among all the treeclimbers here. Queesor asked a great many questions about the family of Jafthuh and Odalee.

"They sound wonderful, Frafan," he said, "truly wonderful. When you return, might I go with you? I think I would really very much like to go with you."

"Of course you can, Queesor," replied a totally surprised Frafan. He wondered how Queesor would even begin to manage in the deep woods. "But we best not leave until I convince Ephran he must come too. It would be very difficult to make our way without his sense of direction and...his courage."

Frafan and Queesor spoke of many things. When they spoke of what Queesor had not seen or heard; the high squeal of a hawk overhead, the hooting of an owl on a dark and blustery night, the speed of a fox on the open meadow, these stories made him moan and whimper in fright. Yet, times when Frafan's heart nearly stopped in terror; when a big truck rumbled by — or when one of the gigantic silver skyhunters of The Many Colored Ones howled above — Queesor never so much as blinked.

One overcast day, when the air was warmer than usual, Queesor, Kaahli, and Frafan picked up their small portions of corn. They were late in getting to the food cage and, though Wytail was nowhere in sight, he left plenty of signs that he'd taken what he wanted. Frafan hopped out into the snow and found a few golden kernels, half buried. He shared what he could find with Kaahli and Queesor. Everyone stuck one or two kernels in their cheek for Ephran.

On the way back to the nest Frafan said, "What I don't understand is why I can find so few acorns. There are certainly enough oak here. The trees are small but many seem old enough to bear nuts."

"That's true," said Queesor, "very true. There are acorns. We eat them while we can but The Many Colored Ones keep them cleaned up. Yessir, all cleaned up. They snip the grass short and carry it away, along with most of the acorns. Yep, most of the acorns. Only the smallest escape those long branches with many twigs that They rub across the land to gather acorns and leaves together. Leaves and acorns together."

Frafan frowned. "I don't see how They get so much accomplished. I've seen very few of Them here." Of course he remembered seeing One, now and again, moving slowly down one or another of the smooth black paths. Once he saw One running and, as far as he could tell, nothing was chasing It.

"There are many more of Them, all over the place, when warm air returns. Many more," said Queesor, as he jumped over a small twig in his path.

"These dens we nest in are confusing, too," said Frafan. "Do you suppose they are actually made by Many Colored Ones just for us treeclimbers?"

"No," Queesor said, "I don't think so. I think the wooden dens were originally meant for ducks. Yessir, meant for wood ducks."

That answer clarified nothing for Frafan. Why would Many Colored Ones build dens for ducks any more than They would for squirrels? He decided to move on to another topic. "We should teach the squirrels here to plan. Get the acorns as soon as they hit the ground. Collect and save corn. Pick the leaves to pad their nests before they fall from the trees. Things like that. What do you think, Queesor?" asked Frafan.

"Too much work."

"In the woods," said Kaahli, "we would not survive if we did not plan ahead, if we were not willing to work at it."

"Ah yes," said Queesor, "it sounds terribly boring and dreary. Dreary and boring." He grinned and added, "If you take me along I'm willing to try it though. Yessir, willing to try it."

"We may have to try it without Ephran. What do you think, Kaahli? Would you come with us if Ephran refuses to leave?" asked Frafan.

She shook her head. "I could not. It would crush him totally if I left him."

"I must warn you I cannot stay here. With or without my brother, I have to try to find my way home as soon as I smell the warm season in the air. Even if I must make plans alone."

Queesor stopped at the base of Ephran and Kaahli's tree. "Well, here we are at your nest."

Kaahli ran up the trunk and returned immediately. "Ephran is still asleep. Let's go to Queesor's den and talk."

"See!" said Queesor. "The most clever squirrel I've heard of just sleeps. Ephran sleeps and does not plan."

Fly together . . .
Or fly apart.

        Socles: Faint Glimmers, Chap. VI
        Source: Aloysius P. Boatworthy

CHAPTER XXIV

THE AWAKENING

At one point Kaahli wondered aloud if the cruel air from far away across the big forest had fallen asleep permanently. Her mention of it seemed to awaken the very thing all those who stayed behind feared; the bitter spirit of the cold season. It started as tiny intermittent ice pellets, driven by puffs of chilly air. It built to a frightening, relentless and bitterly cold gale that caused the den in the little tree to shudder. The air, hazy and dense with tiny flakes, moved so strongly that it swept the hilltops bare, and snow accumulated in depressions in the earth and along the sheltered edges of the nearby frozen pond.

Five times in three days Frafan left the den with the idea of getting corn. He went alone, leaving Kaahli curled next to Ephran, her tail over both of them, her slender body shivering more than his. Not once in those five attempts did he reach his goal. For one thing, the air was so cold he didn't feel he could survive for long outside the den, where he was protected from the wind, and where at least a bit of heat was generated from three bodies. Secondly, even if he could have, it would have been useless to run all the way to the food cage. From a rolling knoll, about halfway between their den and the wide and smooth path that passed by the cage, he could easily tell The Many Colored Ones were not paying their usual visits. There were no long tracks in the snow from round legs. There were no golden kernels or redbrown sticks scattered on the white earth.

Only once did he even see another squirrel, it approaching from the far side of the park. Like himself, it sat on its own windswept hill, seeing what he saw, gazing at the empty cage. Their eyes met for a moment and Frafan meant to raise his paw in greeting. But he hesitated, feeling more than seeing the desolation in that look. Before he could move his leg, the other squirrel turned and hurried off in the direction from which it had come.

In the days that followed, he waited and waited, watched and worried, but The Many Colored Ones did not appear. At first his stomach growled and twisted inside him. Then it became numb and quiet. Frafan became truly frightened when he realized he wanted to do nothing but sleep.

As the wind whistled outside the den and their tree grumbled in discomfort, Frafan, Kaahli, and Ephran began to chew on the small pile of corn and few tiny acorns that Frafan had stored under the leaves on the floor. The food's little stopover under the damp leaves of the nest had not improved its texture or flavor. But most was edible. There was only enough to last a few days and they ate without comment or thanks, and

181

tried not to think how cold and hungry their neighbors might be...or to worry how long this cold spell might last. Twice Frafan almost made it to Queesor's tree and, though it wasn't far, it was further than the cage of corn. And the trip, into the bitter wind, was a painful one. When he got close he chattered loudly but it was simply too cold to go on.

"There is no sign of him. No tracks in the snow at the base of his tree," he told Kaahli.

"He must be at the den of his parents, to share the warmth of their bodies," she replied.

"Where is that?" asked Frafan.

"I don't know where their nest is. Queesor rarely speaks of them. They have been at the food cage the same time we were, but he's not introduced me."

Hours grew long. Frafan watched the sun because there was nothing else to do. He could not imagine, for the breath in him, how it could be up there, shining bright as could be, emitting dazzling light but no warmth. Five times, on its long trek through the sky, flanked by shiny cold rings of color at either horizon, he watched.

Finally, on the sixth day, clouds covered the earth and, while they slept, gentle snow fell. Frafan and Kaahli woke to an earth cloaked in fresh whiteness and, on their noses, the warmest air they'd felt for a long time.

"The cold is gone!" Kaahli cried.

Frafan's eyes sparkled. "Ephran!" he said, "Come and see! There is new snow...and a freshness in the air..."

"Humpph," said Ephran, without opening his eyes.

"Let's go find Queesor!" Frafan said. "Maybe he will be in his nest now. He must be as hungry as I am. We can all go to the cage of corn together."

"Yes," agreed Kaahli, "Maybe there will be corn today."

Once more they tried to rouse Ephran, tried to get him to show some enthusiasm for the break in the weather. But he declined their invitation with a grunt and rolled over on his side. Frafan thought he detected a flash in Ephran's dull eyes in the moment they beheld the fresh snow, but it flickered out as quickly as the light of the firefly. Frafan could tell Kaahli was disappointed once again, but she hid it well.

Kaahli and Frafan scampered through the damp snow, avoiding the deeper drifts. There were many patches of brown grass. The snow at the base of Queesor's little tree was undisturbed.

"I guess he hasn't returned from visiting his parents yet," said Frafan with a sigh. "It looks no different than it did when I was here a few days ago."

"You don't suppose he's asleep in there?" asked Kaahli.

"Well," said Frafan, with a surprised look, "I guess that's entirely

Into the High Branches

There was no sound from the den.

possible. Sleeping is, after all, what treeclimbers are supposed to do when the air is very cold."

"Queesor! Come with us to get food!" Kaahli called.

There was no sound from the den.

"Come on, lazy!" shouted Frafan. "You can't sleep in there forever."

A puff of tepid air swirled around the hole in Queesor's wooden den and caused a lonely, sighing sound. Frafan's grin faded. His eyes met Kaahli's.

She ran up the tree ahead of him, hesitated for a moment at the den's entrance, then slid into the nest. Behind her, he peered into the darkness, eyes accustomed to bright sunlight. He couldn't see through or around her so he crawled into the wood shavings and scattered leaves next to her.

Queesor was in his nest all right, alone in a far corner, tail curled around him. He seemed to be fast asleep.

Ephran opened one eye as Kaahli and Frafan arrived back at the den. They were quiet. That, he thought, was unusual. Generally they came bouncing in, all excited and chattering, always about some silly thing or other. He closed his eye again. Frafan curled against the wall away from him and Kaahli lay down, far enough away so that her body did not touch his.

For some reason this made him angry. More angry than when they made a lot of unnecessary racket. He thought about moving roughly against her, but decided not to give her the satisfaction of knowing he wanted to be near her.

As he was about to fall back asleep he felt movement. He opened both eyes. It was Kaahli. At first he thought she must be laughing, because her shoulders were shaking...ever so little. He would have to speak to her. If they didn't irritate him in one way, they found another. What had they seen outside? What was so funny? Or had he snored without realizing it? Then he heard a low sob.

With less effort than he thought might be needed he roused himself. "Kaahli! What is the matter?"

She did not turn to him. She did not answer.

"Kaahli, why do you shed tears?"

She managed a single word. "Queesor..."

"What about Queesor?"

She sobbed the harder.

Now fully awake Ephran demanded, in a voice loud enough and with enough authority so that it surprised even him, "Frafan, why does Kaahli weep?"

"For Queesor," Frafan said to the wall.

"I ask again...What of Queesor?"

"He breathes no more. He is cold and stiff as the branches of this tree."

Ephran looked as though something had bitten him. "No breath...?"

Kaahli continued crying. Frafan did not turn around.

"Why?" said Ephran, "How? What happened?"

Frafan turned to his brother, his eyes dry and hard as rock. "You really can't imagine, can you?"

"The Many Colored Ones..."

"They are part of the answer. But They did not catch and harm him, if that's what you're thinking."

"No thundersticks?" Ephran seemed genuinely confused.

"There's been no sound of thundersticks," said Frafan coldly. "Even you in your trance could hardly have missed the great noise of thundersticks."

"Food," he said quietly.

"Good! Very good! Queesor came to depend on The Many Colored Ones to feed him. Just like everyone else in this place. They brought food to the cage for such a long time that he expected it. Then They fooled him. They didn't show up with their corn. I wonder how many other treeclimbers lie in these trees, stiff and unmoving."

"How terrible," mumbled Ephran.

"Yes. How terrible. Too late to apologize now."

"Apologize?"

"Yes. Apologize."

"Who?"

"You."

"Me...Apologize? Why should I apologize?"

"Why indeed? It was a farce from the outset." Frafan's tone was cold. "Why should the squirrel that they all looked up to feel any twinge? He never existed anyway. There could be no such thing as a treeclimber that might dare take on a hawk. Or open a cage. Or befriend a fox. Or fly with a duck. That would be one very special squirrel indeed. A very wise and brave squirrel. He or she would certainly not lay, holed up in a rotting den, ignoring the troubled world outside, refusing counsel and help for those who needed help the most..."

"Oh, Frafan," Ephran said, shaking his head, "you don't realize how right you are. It was a farce. It is a farce. The Many Colored Ones have made it a farce."

"Many Colored Ones...Many Colored Ones. That's all I hear about is Many Colored Ones. It sounds as though you think They can do anything. Tell me, do you think They created the woods, The Pond, Great Hill...?"

"They made this place....," said Ephran grimly, "those huge dens so close by, the endless black paths, thundersticks..."

"I ask again: Do you think They created the woods?" demanded Frafan.

After a long pause Ephran quietly answered, "No. But They control it. They can level the trees. They can bring fire to consume it. They can point their thundersticks at whatever They want to destroy."

"Yes," said Frafan, "They can. Maybe They can destroy the woods, but They haven't. They can also allow a family of treeclimbers to eat all the corn they can carry from a corncrib. And They can take a badly hurt mallard, or gray squirrel, or pheasant...and make them to run or fly again."

"Ah, so They can. But which of Those rule? Which of The Many Colored Ones are the egg-eaters? I don't know. The Ones in this nearby warren have not shown the length of their claws."

Kaahli, whose tears had stopped when the discussion between the brothers started, sat up. "Ephran," she said, "you once convinced me fire did not care to attack our families. You said it only went where the wind pushed it. Is it not possible that Many Colored Ones are like that, that They do not, most of Them anyway, wish us well or ill?"

"I don't know."

"She's just asking if it's possible, Ephran. Possible that there may be good Many Colored Ones and bad Many Colored Ones, but that most of Them are just indifferent. That They don't mean us harm."

"Maybe."

"Then there must be hope. If only those who are brave and intelligent enough come forth to share with others, then there is hope. If a treeclimber who has proven himself worthy of trust might consider trying to help and teach his kind, there is hope."

"You expect too much. You speak high-sounding words to a coward," said Ephran.

Frafan seemed not to hear his brother. "If such a great squirrel existed in their midst," he continued, "wouldn't he be here for a reason?"

"That's enough now, Frafan," said Ephran.

"...Might he help them make their life a bit easier, instead of making things for those around him more difficult?"

"Frafan..." Ephran's eyes narrowed but Frafan ignored him.

"He could have taught them to save a little extra for bad times. They might have listened to him. He could have driven off the tyrant who scatters and wastes the very food they need to survive. He could have suggested they gather acorns as soon as they fall, or before they fall..."

"Stop this Frafan. Right now!"

"Did he do any of these things? Did he offer some of his strength and knowledge? No. What, exactly, did he do? Why, he lay in

186

a pool of self-pity and despair, as though everything The Many Colored Ones did, their very creation of this place, was directed against him and him alone. Selfish?...so selfish that he couldn't even see that he was eating himself into a ball of fat with his mate's share of corn, while she starved..."

Ephran flew across the den and landed atop Frafan before Frafan could begin to defend himself — if he had planned to. Frafan, however, did not raise his paw. He had time only to roll over unto his back and to meet his brother's eyes...with a look of sadness and disappointment so deep and strong it might as well have been the blow of a powerful and gigantic claw.

The anger and fight left Ephran like a puff of air.

Kaahli had risen to her paws. She seemed too exhausted to say anything. She only sighed when he asked, "Is it true, Kaahli? Does your stomach growl in hunger while I lie in my own pain and grow fat?"

He took his paws from Frafan's chest.

"You think I've failed everyone, don't you? Especially you."

"I have not been adrift," said Frafan. "I have no need of a hero. I am only a searcher. And I don't recognize what I've found."

"Kaahli...!" He groaned. There was no support in her eyes.

Ephran slowly returned to his place and lay down. He felt dizzy. His chest hurt. Why were they treating him like this? What did they expect of him? Couldn't Frafan see that the treeclimbers in this place were hopeless? Would they have paid any attention if he'd told them to carry extra corn to their dens? A few, maybe. Queesor? Probably. Would any of them have backed him in a showdown with Wytail? Who could say? Most importantly, was this park really an animal food farm for The Many Colored Ones? Did They control everything? Could They keep him here if he didn't want to stay? And did he really feel he was the "honored" guest? There was no evidence. Frafan was right. There had not been the roar of a thunderstick the entire time he and Kaahli had been here...and no one, especially The Many Colored Ones, had paid him the slightest heed.

It was fear then. Fear and the loss of hope. He should recognize it. He'd been near it before. Oh, dear Odalee...wise Rennigan...and brave Cloudchaser. What might each of you say to me now?

In the quiet he peered through the small entrance at the infinitely blue sky and the beam of light which was born there. His thoughts went back to another time, to another place far away, to another squirrel, one far younger than the one who lay here now. That young squirrel was filled with questions, and enthusiasm, and ambition. One whose eyes looked upon a similar scene, who did not know how much he had yet to learn. Had this one, the one laying here now, finished learning?

A fleck of dust, or maybe a tiny splinter of wood bark floated aimlessly for a moment. It seemed to hesitate at the far side of the light. It turned slowly, searching for him. Suddenly, it flew directly at him, as though powered by a strong wind.

The impression that he would be struck again, as he was that snowy day on the high limb, was so strong that he flinched and grunted. But nothing touched him — and the fleck disappeared as it left its cone of light.

He closed his eyes but sleep was far away. His heart beat in his ears. Safe? Were they safe here? Did he want to stay here? Until when? Forever? Did he really not care if he ever saw his beloved Pond again?

Ephran stood up. Frafan's back was turned but Kaahli's dark eyes were fixed on him.

"Kaahli...Frafan," he said. "Time is come. Time to wake up. I beg your forgiveness. I can only hope there is a Great Hill of forgiveness in your hearts."

Frafan rolled over slowly, frowning. Kaahli's brow lifted, as though she'd just bitten into a nut and tasted something that surprised her, something other than the musty taste of a walnut.

"I mean it," he said. "I was wrong. I had the chance to be a friend, to teach and to help. I, of all creatures, should know what friends are for. I know how luck is made. I needed Klestra to show me once, Cloudchaser to declare it. This time it takes my brother. I am sorry."

"Ephran..." Kaahli rose to her paws.

"No need to say anything now," said Ephran. "I can't blame you for not knowing whether it's me that's talking or that other squirrel, the one who's been laying here, sick inside, for these many days. I'll have to prove myself all over." He sighed. "It's The Many Colored Ones, you know. I'm still not sure if They plan to claim the entire woods. I still don't know why They brought us and keep us here — or why the others are here."

"But," said Frafan, "the point is, are these Many Colored Ones, these Creatures you don't understand, going to keep you from being the Ephran I used to know?"

"I have to be the Ephran you knew, my brother. At least as important is that I am the Ephran I know I can be." He took a deep breath. "The Many Colored Ones don't belong in the woods, Frafan. This is their place, right here. Why do They bother us in our place? And we don't belong here. Neither do the other treeclimbers who have dens here. They have no idea what they are missing."

"Well, brother, are we going to tell them where things might be better?" asked Frafan with a toothy grin.

Or shall we keep it our secret?" asked Kaahli. The words came out between smiling lips, but she was not entirely sure sharing was a thing the treeclimbers in this place would understand.

CHAPTER XXV

INTRUDERS AND INVITATIONS

efore doing anything else, Ephran insisted on visiting Queesor's tree. He ran up the little ash and sat silently in the entrance for a while. No tears stained his cheeks. His face was set — and as cold as Queesor's body.

Finally he turned and said, "Let's find Wytail...and the rest of our cousins." His voice was flat.

Frafan nodded but Kaahli's body tensed. "Ephran, are you sure you're up to this?" she asked.

"I'm sure." He met her gaze. "Unless he met the same fate as Queesor, Wytail will be at the place you go to gather corn. I've heard you say he's always the first one to the food. I want to be there when The Many Colored Ones arrive...and before Wytail does."

On the way to the cage of corn, Ephran asked Frafan to tell again all he'd told Kaahli. And so Frafan recounted his adventures, about Mayberry and Fred, Klestra and Janna. He decided to leave out the part about Phetra and Roselimb. Ephran listened closely to every word. They came to a small hill that overlooked the path and they climbed a maple tree. A few other squirrels were out and about. Some sat quietly in the sun, on windblown grassy areas. A few moved around, aimlessly it seemed. But all were watching — and waiting. The food cage could be seen from the maple, partly buried in snow.

"Are there as many here as before?" asked Ephran.

"I can't say for certain," said Kaahli. "They come and go, you understand. I don't think so though."

Ephran's lips formed a tight line.

They sat in silence, Kaahli shivering now and then. Finally, a growling sound approached. A truck was moving down the black trail, wading through little drifts, smoke and puffs of snow curling behind.

Frafan's eyes left the truck and swept across the hilltop on the other side of the path, the direction from which Wytail always arrived. If he had survived the bitter cold he would show up soon. With those big ears of his he would hear the truck coming. He would not let anyone get to the food before he did...especially this time, when it had been so long between meals.

Sure enough, a larger and heavier squirrel, one who moved considerably faster and with more assurance than the others, appeared on the far hill.

"Wytail did not starve," announced Frafan.

Just as the food truck came to a stop, Wytail chattered loudly. The squirrels on both sides of the path knew the meaning of that signal. They stood stock still. He had announced his presence and given the command they stand aside, starving or not. All the squirrels, save one, obeyed.

Ephran ran down the tree and jumped to the earth. The Many Colored Ones were busy brushing snow off the cage with long forelegs, and dumping corn from brown sacks into it. Kaahli and Frafan followed Ephran.

"Ephran," said Kaahli, her voice thick with worry, "Wytail is a very large squirrel. Food or no food, he seems to be in good condition. He will be angry if we eat before he does."

"I expect he will," said Ephran.

"Do you think it wise to provoke him?"

"By helping ourselves to his food, do you mean?"

Kaahli did not reply for a moment. Then she said, "I understand what you say. But your body is not strong. It has not been used. Now that I have my mate back, I want to keep him."

"I know I would do poorly in a fight with a determined enemy. I doubt Wytail is in a whole lot better shape than I am. It doesn't sound like he has to work very hard for his food. Or for anything else, for that matter. Besides, the mate you want would not let this bullying continue," he said.

"Wytail is downright mean," said Frafan, who had caught up to his brother. "I've never met a squirrel like him. I think he is dangerous."

"So I've heard. He is not the only dangerous one here."

They went slowly, waiting until The Many Colored Ones threw the empty bags back into the truck, crawled into the muttering thing Themselves, and sputtered away. Nevertheless, they arrived at the cage first, primarily because Wytail had taken time to stop and bedevil an elderly gray treeclimber. The other squirrels watched silently as he chased the animal in circles, laughing and taunting all the while. When the older squirrel became so winded that he lay down in the snow to catch his breath, Wytail sat beside him, taunting and flicking his tail in the pitiful creature's face. His cocky grin faded when he looked up and saw Ephran at the food cage.

"Hey, you! Get away from that corn!" he shouted.

Ephran said not a word, acting as though he heard nothing but the breeze in the branches. He picked up a plump stick of bright yellow corn and turned it round and round in his paws, as though inspecting it for rot. Or for bugs. Then, apparently satisfied with its appearance, he tore off one of the seeds and began to chew contentedly, gazing off into the big blue sky.

Wytail looked as though he might have a fit. He sputtered and hissed.

Trying to act calmer than he felt, Frafan hopped up to the food. Imitating his brother, he snatched a stick of corn and proceeded to nibble on it. Wytail sputtered the louder. Then Kaahli moved next to Ephran, found some scattered kernels, and began to pop them into her mouth. All three acted as though they were the only squirrels in the world. They ignored Wytail. Nearby — but well away from the food box — the other treeclimbers stood flabbergasted.

Overcoming his amazement at last, a deep growl rose from Wytail's throat. He charged across the frozen earth, aiming his body directly at Ephran. Ephran dropped what he'd been eating and, teeth bared, faced Wytail's charge.

"Ooohh, Ephran!..." said Wytail, as he sideslipped to a stop. "Silver Stars! Hey! Didn't recognize you at first... ah...you don't get down here...t'the food...very much."

"Not surprising you wouldn't recognize me, Wytail. I was pretending I was someone else," said Ephran.

"Yeh? Oh..."

"Anything else you wanted to say?" asked Ephran.

"Why...eh...hey, yah! Did want to say something..."

"Well..."

"Yeh, sure. Hey, what I wanted ta tell you was that I been sort of keepin' track of the food here. Even before you showed up. I make sure things are divided square, you see? Kinda oversee this corn stuff. These others..." He glanced at the squirrels around him, eight of them now, excluding Ephran, Frafan, and Kaahli. Frafan thought the big gray looked and acted nervous, even as he gave Ephran a wink he supposed was meant to tell Ephran they were friends, accomplices maybe, that he was part of Wytail's scheme. The other squirrels stood watching and listening, wide-eyed and silent.

"...These others make a mess of things if they're not, uh, sorta kept in line. Hey! Know what I mean? They waste stuff. Too lazy to know how to use it. But, hey! Since you're up and around again we can share duty here! Okay? Hey, listen...I think we can safely say this here food is yours and mine. You know? Whadaya say we eat first here and later..."

Wytail reached for a stick of corn. "...then we can talk about..." Quicker than the eye could wink, Ephran's foreleg flicked out and batted the stick from Wytail's paw.

The silence became immense. Frafan could feel it crushing him. The only sound was far-off mingled groans and hoots and screeches coming from the warren of The Many Colored Ones.

"Hey! What...what are you..."

"Today you eat last, Wytail. You can judge distribution and waste among the others while you're alert. That's much easier on an empty stomach than it is while you're stuffing your face," said Ephran.

At that moment, and before Wytail could attack, if that's what he intended to do, the onlooking squirrels scattered in all directions. Some scampered up nearby trees while some ran as fast as they could across the snow-covered earth.

At first Frafan thought they were running from the prospect of a fight, that they were afraid they might be caught in the scuffle. But, within an eyeblink of hearing Them, he saw Them: Four Many Colored Ones fairly burst over a nearby rise in the ground, uttering loud and harsh sounds, bearing down on the food cage as though They had every intention of overrunning it.

Wytail turned toward Them, paw still hanging in midair where Ephran's slap had left it. Kaahli's mouth had fallen open in surprise. Frafan didn't take time to think. He ran.

Kaahli was at his side and Wytail just behind him. Where was Ephran? With great effort Frafan overcame the voice inside that insisted he run...and keep on running. He turned back. Wytail swerved to miss him.

Ephran had not moved. He stood on his hindlegs, among scattered sticks of corn, teeth and claws at the ready.

Two of The Many Colored Ones were blue. One was brown. They were about the same size as the smaller of the Two who'd brought Frafan here in the van. Not fully grown, Frafan thought. Absolutely huge anyway. One smaller than the Others, with a yellow pelt, was sitting on its tail, behind the brown One, on what appeared to be a bright splash of color, a thing riding smoothly and lightly on the snow.

Bedazzled and frightened as he was, it took a bit before Frafan realized that the oblong colored things behind each of the larger Ones; blobs of green, red, and black, blobs that looked like the hollowed-out objects Fred had eaten out of, only much larger, were actually being pulled along by a slender vine attached to the forepaw of each of the larger Ones. Frafan understood immediately; these funny contraptions were to slide over the snow in! The small Yellow One was being pulled along behind the Others. Another curious invention, another ingenious plaything, but no time to wonder...

"Ephran!" Frafan chattered, "Come! Quickly!"

Ephran gave no hint he heard.

From the corner of his eye, Frafan saw Wytail peeking from the backside of a slender elm and Kaahli at the base of a larger tree, an agonized expression on her face, the attention of both riveted on Ephran. The other squirrels watched from wherever they'd happened to stop when they felt they were far enough away. They stared out from branches, from frozen earth, from treetrunks ...one female from a prickly bush she'd climbed in panic.

The Many Colored Ones stopped just short of Ephran, on the snowpacked black path. They dropped the vines They'd been holding,

Into the High Branches

"Go! Move on!"
he chattered"

193

freeing their forepaws.

"Ephran!" Kaahli groaned.

One of the Blue Ones chattered in the direction of The Brown One, then took a step toward Ephran. Ephran did not move. The Brown One made a noise as did the tiny Yellow One. Were They trying to talk to Ephran? One picked up a stick of corn, but did not put it to Its mouth. It swung its front leg back, as though to throw the food at Ephran. The Yellow One said something loudly. The One with the stick made a funny sound back, but lowered its leg and dropped the cornstick. The second Blue One took another step toward Ephran and held out Its paws.

With every fiber of his mind and body, Ephran wanted to run. His legs ached to take him to his brother, to his dear mate, away from this looming danger, these huge and unpredictable Creatures. A voice inside screamed. The scar left by the tiny stones burned like blue fire. There would be no way to count the beats of his heart.

But he stood his ground. He had to. Just as he had to jump on the hawk's back, as he had to follow Kaahli into Maltrick's den, as he had to direct the hunters' attention to himself that day at the base of Great Hill.

"Go! Move on! Go to where You belong, wherever that is," he chattered. "I don't know what You want here but we squirrels have matters of our own to settle."

Ephran's loud demand stunned Frafan. What was he doing? Did he really believe the Creatures could understand him? Even if They could, did he think They would obey?

The closest One took a step backward. Then another. They made a few quiet sounds among Themselves. The Yellow One raised its forepaw to Ephran and waved. Then the three Large Ones turned away, picked up the vines They'd dropped, and ran down the path. The colored blobs slid quietly along, the little Yellow One bouncing along behind. The Yellow One looked back once, yellow hair blowing over its eyes. Then They disappeared over another hill. Their sounds became fainter and fainter, and finally those disappeared too.

The place was totally quiet for a few minutes. One of the squirrels shouted, "He did it! He frightened Them off! We can eat!" As though released by a springy branch, the treeclimbers raced back to Ephran.

If it surprised Ephran that they ignored him (it did not surprise Frafan), he didn't show it. After all, they were near starvation. The squirrels attacked the corn amid happy squealing and chattering. They laughed and scolded and ate until they could eat no more. For once there was more than enough. There were two reasons for that, of course, but those eating their fill would have thought of only one.

Wytail slowly descended the elm. He walked back toward the

corn and lay down on the packed snow. Eyes closed, a passerby might think he was sleeping.

Finally, when the others had finished, Ephran said, "Come on, Wytail. Let's eat. There's more left here than we can possibly handle."

The large squirrel lifted his head, got to his paws and, for a few heartbeats, Frafan wondered if now, at last, Wytail would attack Ephran.

Without a word to one another, or to anyone else, Wytail and Ephran set to eating their fill of corn. They chewed in silence. Later on, when they spoke of this day, no one could remember Wytail's manners being so good.

Instead of running off for their dens, as they usually did, the squirrels stayed nearby, finding ways to look busy. Frafan suspected that, despite their basically disinterested attitude, they could not really believe this Wytail-Ephran business was settled. They wanted to see how it all ended. He could understand that. Something more was bound to happen. Besides, they would have to wonder about a squirrel who would make Many Colored Ones run off. It would seem only natural they would want to get to know Ephran better. But then, in Frafan's experience, these were not natural treeclimbers.

After he finished a final kernel of corn, Wytail licked his paws once, brushed his whiskers carefully and, without a word, turned and loped off, up a snowcrusted hill. Frafan caught himself exhaling a big sigh.

The other squirrels looked at one another, a few shrugged, and they began to disperse.

"Friends!" Ephran shouted. "May I have your attention for a few minutes? ...Before you go back to your dens." With a quick run and leap, Ephran landed atop the food cage.

The squirrels stopped and turned back, more out of surprise and curiosity than anything.

"I am called Ephran. I'm a relative newcomer and stranger here. I understand some of you know of me and my mate, Kaahli. This other gray is my second brother, Frafan, who arrived here recently from our home in the deep woods, traveling a long way in his search for Kaahli and me."

Frafan nodded and smiled at them. Puzzled looks were all he got in return. It occurred to Frafan that Ephran did not really know his audience. His isolation from everything around him had been nearly complete. Some of the listeners might know Ephran's name but, despite the courage they'd just witnessed, he very much doubted very many of these squirrels cared who Ephran and Kaahli were. He was certain none of them cared who he was.

Undaunted, Ephran continued. "As some of you know, I was brought here after Many Colored Ones wounded me with a thunderstick...and Others healed me. I did not — and do not — understand why They tried to destroy me and then gave my breath back. I do not understand why They brought me to this place you call park. Once I thought it was because it is like one big cage, a place to keep me — to keep all of us, like cows — until They decide what to do with us. My brother and my mate insist that idea is wrong. Maybe it is. I was once certain that far more of Them wished evil than good, but I'm no longer certain of that either..." Ephran paused and looked intently at his audience.

"I don't think any of that is important. What's important is that none of us really belongs here."

Ephran waited. A few of his listeners glanced at each other with questioning eyes, as though Ephran spoke in a tongue they could not understand. Most of them continued to stare with expressions ranging from bemusement to downright puzzlement.

He was about to continue when a shaky voice wheezed; "Hold on there a moment, youngster!"

The speaker was the old male, the same one that Wytail had teased and taunted. All eyes turned to him.

"My name is Steadfast," he announced. "I have breathed air more seasons than you and Wytail together. As a matter of fact, I was born here, in a den next to the very one you now nest in. I scampered and played and grew up in this grassy park. I have always called it home. Though we are gratified — 'amazed' would be closer to the right word — at your audacity in facing down both Wytail and these Others, so that we might eat, I think you can understand why I question what right you have to determine that we don't, in your words, 'belong' here."

"Steadfast, I am honored to meet you," said Ephran, "and I am happy to hear the voice of one who has survived so many seasons. I wonder how many others here can match memories with you."

The older squirrel squinted at Ephran. "Whether you are without fear or sense, Ephran, I cannot tell. In any case, it does not become you to tease your elders. You know as well as I that the seasons of a treeclimber are limited. I am the exception here, not the rule."

"Good Steadfast, I do not tease my elders. My only point is how many times one sees the leaves fall depends on many things," said Ephran. "One of the most important is where one chooses to make his or her nest."

"Ephran," said Steadfast, "I have not nested in the deep woods as you have, but my parents did. They came to this place by choice. They were not brought here. They found the woods a frightening and inhospitable place. 'Bitter as acorns' was one of their favorite sayings."

"There are many kinds of nuts, and they are wonderfully different," objected Frafan, who stood near his brother at the base of the

196

cage of corn. He had been watching Wytail run slowly off, not the direction he usually went, and had heard only the part about bitter acorns. "Besides, there are fresh green buds much of the warm season..."

"'Fresh green buds'!" sneered a skinny male squirrel. "Yuk! We eat them only when there is nothing else."

There was a snicker from the crowd.

"I don't think we meant to get off on the subject of food. There are many tastes..." said Kaahli quietly.

"Why not? Food is the most important thing of all," said a younger female. "Where do you get your food in the deep woods?"

"Of course food is important. I don't know that I'd agree it's the most important of all. In any case, we save it," said Kaahli, "we eat buds at the beginning of the warm season. We collect and bury nuts for the cold..."

"'Collect and bury'?" repeated an older female, a befuddled look on her face.

"What is so wrong about this place?" came a new voice, before Kaahli could explain about putting food away in a safe and secret place.

"It's not so much what's wrong with it," replied Frafan, looking over to Ephran. "It's what just isn't right. The kind of nest you stay in here for one thing. They are not true squirrel nests. Ah...the air, for another," replied Frafan.

"The air?"

"Yes. The air. It smells, always, of the playthings of The Many Colored Ones."

"How does the air smell in the deep woods?"

"Like flowers, when the warm season returns," said Frafan, spreading his paws wide, "sweetness of blossoms, fresh rain on the forest floor, sun in long grass. Clean and crisp when snow covers the earth. And not just smells...sounds too," he added, speaking faster and faster in spite of himself. "Our air is not filled with the squeal and snarl of monsters fighting for passage on hard black paths. We awake to the warble of the wren, the sassy chatter of a bluejay, or the wondrous song of the cardinal. Here, in this place, during most of the day I could not hear the gurgle of water even if there was a stream nearby."

"The sky is bright blue there," said Kaahli, her face lit with excitement, "except, of course, when there are clouds, come to give the earth a drink. The stars and moon shine so brightly..."

"You make the deep woods sound so peaceful and happy," said Steadfast, "but besides not tasting corn, my parents did not taste peace in the deep woods. What of hunters?"

"Yes," came another voice, "how about hunters?"

"There are hunters in the woods," nodded Ephran, "of all kinds. The risk is real. But if danger comes, it is among your trees, where you know the hiding places and the hunter doesn't. In the woods you are not dependent on the very creatures who represent the greatest danger. If a squirrel is reasonably careful, he or she can guard against danger. That becomes hard to do if the danger is constantly there. One lets their guard down if the hawk nests in the next tree."

"Squirrels can learn to manage with food and hunters, you know," said Frafan. "One has to learn and plan ahead. One has to be willing to work a bit for the advantages."

"Work?" repeated the female. "Why work?"

"You don't seem to have the secret of planning ahead when it comes to thundersticks," shouted a younger male.

"It all sounds like a great deal of trouble," observed Steadfast with a small smile, "just to nest with hunters."

Frafan felt himself growing warm. These squirrels were not only disinterested, they were downright impolite. None of them, except perhaps for Steadfast, had any understanding or appreciation of what Ephran had just done for them. He could tell Kaahli was getting frustrated too, but Ephran seemed very cool and confident. He was almost smiling.

"You don't understand," Ephran said, "and I don't really blame you. What we're trying to tell you is that it is different and better in the woods. Time does not weigh heavily. There are always things to see. Things to do. Trees...trees like you wouldn't believe...tree after tree to climb and close enough to one another to jump about in. You build your own nest — the way you want it built. You eat when you want. You do not depend on someone or something to bring your next meal."

They peered at him, waiting, he knew, for something they could understand. He felt that he didn't know how to say it. He tried to think of Rennigan.

"Corn is indeed sweeter than acorns or green buds," said Ephran, "no doubt about it. Foxes and hawks are more plentiful in the deep woods than they are here. That's a given. Short grass is easier to run in than long, if running on the ground is what you like. What none of you can see is what you've not seen, which is not surprising. But listen to my brother, Frafan. He knows more about The Many Colored Ones than I do, and more of the woods than you. He has traveled the path Kaahli and I traveled to get here — only his eyes were open while mine were closed. Frafan...," he turned to his brother, "after all the places you've been, would you choose to stay here or return to the woods?"

"No question, I will not stay here."

"Why not? My ears hear a weak case for the deep woods. One I cannot appreciate," piped up a female squirrel who had been listening intently to the debate.

"Nevertheless, we are going back," said Ephran, "as soon as the

198

cold season loosens its grip. I only asked for your attention to invite anyone who wishes to go with us."

"Too dangerous," said Steadfast again, and a number of them shook their heads in agreement.

"Dangerous? Yes, I suppose it seems that way," said Ephran. "Maybe none of us can avoid danger. But there is a certain predictability and order in the woods, maybe a predictability of unpredictability, if that makes any sense. Anyway, I know what to expect of foxes and hawks. I know when the warm season comes the walnut and oak will produce my food. I know every morning where the sun will rise and set and, with my wits and will, I have some control over whether or not I see it. And from which tree."

The squirrels fell silent.

"Steadfast speaks of peace. I ask you, at what price? It appears to me the price has been giving up your freedom, your courage, your willingness to sacrifice, and, worst of all, your caring for one another. A friend of mine might ask you if you have any chance of making your own luck. Look into your hearts and tell me if you control what happens to you here...how well it works to depend totally on Them and to make no preparation for the future. If you still aren't sure after looking there, then I invite you to look into the den of Queesor."

A voice came from the back of the group. "I looked."

Ephran met the gaze of Wytail who, unnoticed until now, had returned to the group of squirrels. He'd evidently been standing there for some time.

"Hey...I'm comin' with you," he said.

CHAPTER XXVI

FIRST ONES HOME

Will you be all right now?" asked Payslee.

"Can you find your way?" asked Flutterby.

"...Wherever you're going," added Peppercorn.

"Don't worry about us," answered Klestra. "Why, you've led us right to Rocky Creek! Any old red squirrel would know its way from here."

Flutterby asked, "Its way where?"

"Why, back to The Pond, I suppose," said Klestra, glancing at Janna. "I would like to take what news we have and share it with Mayberry and the families of Ephran and Kaahli. But I'm afraid I don't have Ephran and Frafan's talent for finding my way around in the woods. I depend largely on what I remember from the last time I was at a place. I might follow the path a little further the second time I visit, but I make sure I can always see something I recognize. Do you think you could find the den of Jafthuh and Odalee, Janna?"

Janna scratched her neck and said, "No, I'm pretty sure I'd have us lost in no time. We've been lucky. And we had Frafan. As father said at the outset, this is no time for travel, not unless there is a very good reason."

As though to support her thought, a big cloud with ragged edges spit a few snowflakes as it passed over the trees. Peppercorn glanced up at the cloud. "Light from the sky will not be with us much longer," she said.

"Days are short now," agreed Payslee.

"Best that we all go to where we're going while we can still find the path," said Flutterby.

"Oh, my dear pigeons, we are so grateful for all your help," said Janna.

"And even more for the hope you've given us," said Klestra.

"Hope?" the pigeons said in unison.

"Yes, hope. Hope that my friend and his mate still breath air and scamper among sturdy limbs...somewhere. Hope that Frafan will stay well. And hope that he will be able to find them."

"We were happy to do what we could. We bid you good-bye now," said Flutterby.

"Best of all things," said Payslee.

"May the acorns on your tree grow big as apples," said Peppercorn.

"And may smooth air lift your wings," answered Klestra.

The pigeons fluttered into the darkening sky and swung gracefully off in the direction from which they'd come.

"Do you think...we'll ever...," Janna stammered.

"See them again?" said Klestra. "I don't know. I suspect they might visit Rocky Point more next warm season than they have in the past. So perhaps we will."

"Do you think Ruckaru will be freed?"

"Ha!" cried Klestra. "The colorful rascal will be just fine if he doesn't lose his head when They open his cage — and fly smack into the side of a tree. Would you like to go to The Pond now?"

"Yes, I would. It would be good to rest for a time in the den of Ephran and Kaahli."

She followed Klestra silently through the branches near the earth. Her thoughts turned to Corncrib farm and her family. Should she have tried to find her way home? Had Phetra and Roselimb made it back after the terrible snowstorm? Jafthuh's and Odalee's minds must be filled with worry and dark thoughts every waking moment. To try to find them would be a foolhardy thing to do though. Might the crows help? Could they carry anything but a simple message? Was any message she had to give worth carrying anyway? To make any sense it would be complex, and contain precious little comfort. The rest of this cold season would almost certainly find her safe from the cold wind — but Ephran and Kaahli were still missing. And now, so was Frafan. Mother would hardly be reassured, despite the fact Klestra felt...somehow encouraged. Actually, she felt more at peace now than she had for a long while...

"Hello there!"

Janna, lost in her thoughts, was startled by Klestra's greeting, though it was not meant for her. She hadn't noticed the male cottontail beneath them, huddled against a greywhite stump covered with frozen moss.

The rabbit lifted his head, a surprised look on his face. "Hello to you," the buck said. "You're Klestra, aren't you?"

"Yes, I am. And, if I remember correctly, your name is Brightleaf. You live in Bubbling Brook Warren." He turned to Janna. "I met Brightleaf the day The Many Colored Ones came. He was one of those who searched for Ephran. Brightleaf, this is the sister of Ephran. She is called Janna."

"Delighted," said Brightleaf. "I still find myself looking for your brother, you know...in an especially thick clump of bushes, or behind a large oak root."

"I thank you for your help and concern," said Janna, "but there's no need to search around here any longer."

"Oh? Why is that?"

"Because he and Kaahli are gone, far away, carried off we think, by..."

"Perhaps moved to another part of the forest," Klestra hastily interrupted, "to spend the cold season recovering from his wounds. We cannot be sure, however."

"Ah! Really!" said Brightleaf. "The possibility exists they did escape then. This is the first piece of encouraging news we've had. I must carry it to Bubbling Brook Warren. Many long ears will be happy to hear those words."

Janna wanted to tell more, but quickly realized why Klestra had interrupted. How would this deepwoods rabbit begin to understand cages, barns, or trucks? The whole idea of Ephran and Kaahli being carried off by a van would sound like crazy talk. No, the whole story would raise too many questions, make it too hard to believe.

"Do you think you might get word to Mayberry?" she asked Brightleaf.

"Mayberry, eh?" the rabbit repeated thoughtfully. "I know him. I doubt any of us from Bubbling Brook will travel so far as Great Woods Warren while snow covers the earth...or any of his warren will visit us. If, by chance, there is an opportunity, what word would you have Mayberry hear?"

Janna turned to Klestra. "What should we have Brightleaf say?"

The red squirrel thought for a moment. "Tell Mayberry that Janna and Klestra have returned to The Pond after seeking Ephran and Kaahli. Tell him we were able to follow their path for a long distance and there is strong reason to believe they both still breathe. Tell him Ephran's brother yet searches...and that we hope he has found the answer."

The cottontail nodded soberly. "If possible, the message will be given." He shivered. "It grows colder. I must get back to the warren. I bid you farewell."

Janna and Klestra said good-bye and watched Brightleaf lope off, across the thin layer of snow. Janna felt the bite of the wind. It was indeed getting colder.

"Klestra," she said, "I'll say again I'd be grateful for a quick acorn and then to curl in the leaves of the den of Ephran and Kaahli."

"We're almost there. I'm anxious to close my eyes in my own den too. Now that the trees are bare you will be able to see Ephran and Kaahli's nest from mine. So you can leave me at my tree and not get lost."

"Maybe staying in a strange den in a strange part of the woods will satisfy mother and father for my Alone Time," said Janna with a tight smile. "Which seems rather ridiculous now. I think I've probably gone through more adventure and danger than most treeclimbers could dream of going through in a whole season by themselves."

"I'm your witness," said Klestra.

As they moved on, tree to tree, Janna asked, "Is there any way we can get word to my parents about what's happened?"

"Crows would be the only chance, but they're both independent and undependable. This season is hard on them too, you know. Food is not easy to come by for any of us. They have little time to run errands. Besides, they might say they would carry a message, perhaps really meaning what they say, and then forget to do it anyway."

"The rabbit...?"

"You heard Brightleaf. Rabbits don't travel far from home. Unless we can find a few weird traveling ones...like some squirrels — who shall remain nameless."

As they turned a bend in Rocky Creek, and the frozen Pond came into view, a voice from a branch above them said, "H'lo there!"

"Ohh! You startled me," said Janna, looking up at an old fox squirrel who gazed back at her...with one eye.

"Ain't seen you 'round here before," he said.

"I haven't been here much," said Janna.

"Ahem!" said Klestra. "My den is nearby. May I ask who we're talking to?"

"Ah! A red fella," the squirrel said, turning his eye on Klestra. "Name's Rennigan."

"Rennigan!" They both gasped.

"Mean sumpthin' to ya?"

"Ephran's friend...the one who took care of him just before the warm season..." Klestra said.

"Yep. That's me. Figured ya must know Ephran. Red and gray t'gether like this."

"I'm so pleased to meet you, sir," said Janna. "I'm Ephran's sister, Janna. This is his good friend, Klestra. We've heard so much about you."

"Good ta meet ya. Hope whut ya heard 'bout old Rennigan weren't all bad."

"I should say not," said Klestra. "It's surprising and sad that I should get to meet the favorite character of Ephran's stories now."

"Somethin' wrong with now?" asked Rennigan.

"He's gone, you know. Both he and his mate, Kaahli. Disappeared. We think they went to a place of Many Colored Ones. A place of large dens, and cages. We just returned from there. We can't be sure they were there at all and, if they were, they've been taken from that place too. Actually, we have no idea where they are now. Ephran's brother, Frafan, carries on the search."

"Gone eh?" said Rennigan, "That's what I was 'fraid of. Came ta see 'em a little while back, when I heard there wuz trouble here by The

"Keep to the
High branches!"

Pond. Weren't in their nest. Knew where it is, ya know. Been keepin' one eye on thet Ephran, off and on when I'm in this here part of the woods, ever since he left me. Hoped maybe he'n his mate wuz just off jumpin'. Whut happened?"

Once again Klestra related events of the day of the first snow, the day the thundersticks spoke so loudly.

"First snow. Thundersticks," said Rennigan thoughtfully, scratching his backside.

"Does it mean something to you, Mr. Rennigan," asked Janna.

"Figure it does. Did ya know how they left here? I mean, how they got from here to wherever ya just come back from?"

"No. We have no idea how they got from here to the barn of cages," said Klestra. "That's the one bug in the walnut. That's why we can't be sure Frafan might be on the wrong path entirely."

"I heard them thundersticks thet day, thet day of first snow...," said Rennigan.

"You were here then!" exclaimed Klestra, "near The Pond!"

"Not so near," said Rennigan, "ya kin hear them sticks a long ways from where they bark, ya know. No, I was up in a tree some distance from here. But I saw a duck."

"A duck?"

"Yep. Big mallard duck."

"Where did you see a duck?" asked Klestra.

"Where else do ya see a duck? In th'sky, a course. At the time I thought t'wuz a passin' strange duck, up there in th'snow. Then I thought mebbe it was me was strange...seeing things, ya know? Shoulda come over ta their nest... Real strange, anaway, as I said."

"What was strange?" asked Janna who, without realizing it, had moved closer and closer to Rennigan.

"The ding thing had two tails, that's whut was strange."

"What...?"

"Yep. Ya heard right. Two tails. One feathered and one furry."

"I don't understand," said Janna, shaking her head slowly.

Klestra's face lit up. "I do! Anyway, I think I do. I found a bright green feather in a gooseberry bush. And Ruckaru said there had a been a big mallard in a cage in the barn." He took a deep breath. "Rennigan, is it possible? I would have sworn Cloudchaser fell into Lomarsh. But I couldn't be sure...it was such a long way from here..." He shook his head in wonderment. "Could he have flown away and healed his wounds? Could he have come back and carried two squirrels, one at a time of course, to safety on his back? Big and strong as he might be, could Cloudchaser have taken his friends away from the danger here?"

"Well," said Rennigan, "at th'time, I figured if I weren't

206

dreamin' then I was seein' the only gray treeclimber I know that'd ride a duck's back. Matter a fact, I was sure enough who woulda' had ta be that I hollered at 'im."

"You called to Ephran?" said Janna.

"Yep. Don't know why. Dumb thing t'do, I s'pose. If t'wuz really him, he was far above all the trees. But if t'wuz him I wanted him t'know that we wished 'im well."

"What did you shout?" asked Klestra.

"Couldn't think of much. Just told 'im what his mammy told 'im — keep to the high branches."

* * * * *

Book three of the Deep Woods Trilogy,

TO FIND A WAY HOME

will be available soon.

P.M. Malone
  Looking for friends in the high branches.

Terry Lewison
  With faithful companion, Whisper.